"MAGDALENA, YOU MUST GO UP THERE."

"That's what you think, dear." I turned and headed for the front door. At least that was my intention. And while I do not, for a moment, ascribe any special powers to the demented Diana, I found myself inexplicably turning again and heading for the stairs.

"Why me?" I wailed as my feet carried me up two treacherous flights. The Miller stairs, while not as impossibly steep as mine, were an obstacle course of precariously stacked junk and slippery surfaces.

"Don't worry, Magdalena," coaxed Diana. "Like I said, in my second dream you survive."

"What if your dreams mean nothing?"

"Don't be ridiculous. And besides I'm right behind you."

Those were the last words I heard before the lights went out in my head.

PLAY IT AGAIN, SPAM®

A PENNSYLVANIA DUTCH MYSTERY WITH RECIPES

Tamar Myers

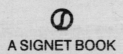

A SIGNET BOOK

SIGNET
Published by the Penguin Group
Penguin Putnam Inc., 375 Hudson Street,
New York, New York 10014, U.S.A.
Penguin Books Ltd, 27 Wrights Lane,
London W8 5TZ, England
Penguin Books Australia Ltd, Ringwood,
Victoria, Australia
Penguin Books Canada Ltd, 10 Alcorn Avenue,
Toronto, Ontario, Canada M4V 3B2
Penguin Books (N.Z.) Ltd, 182–190 Wairau Road,
Auckland 10, New Zealand

Penguin Books Ltd, Registered Offices:
Harmondsworth, Middlesex, England

First published by Signet, an imprint of Dutton NAL,
a member of Penguin Putnam Inc.

First Printing, April, 1999
10 9 8 7 6 5 4 3 2 1

PUBLISHER'S NOTE
This is a work of fiction. Names, characters, places, and incidents either are the
product of the author's imagination or are used fictitiously, and any resemblance to
actual persons, living or dead, events, or locales is entirely coincidental.

This book is dedicated
in loving memory of my *baba,* Tshiala.

One

Three months to the day after my husband left me, I landed facedown in a cow patty. I am told that there was absolutely no connection between the two events. The fact that they both left the same taste in my mouth is supposedly coincidental.

At any rate, tornadoes are rare in central Pennsylvania, and the jury is still out on whether or not the windstorm that flattened my barn and demolished my house was indeed a twister. But I know what I saw. I was up in the north pasture collecting my two Holstein cows for their evening milking when I saw the dark funnel racing down Hertzler Road, and then suddenly turn and head right at my two-hundred-year-old farmstead. I made a beeline for the nearest ditch, but it was halfway between me and the approaching storm, and the storm was faster. I never made it. One minute I was running like the wind—into the wind—and the next I was out like the light on a squashed firefly.

When I woke up, I was intimately acquainted with bovine waste, my barn was as flat as my A-cup chest, and my house, in which I'd been born some forty-six years earlier, was a pile of kindling. I myself was a good twenty yards away from where I last remembered being.

Mercifully, the two Holsteins had been spared. Bessie and Matilda had been kind enough to wander over and keep me company until I regained consciousness, and in fact, Bessie was gently nuzzling my face with her large, moist lips—either that, or she was snacking on my hair which, quite frankly, was in need of a trim.

It took four and a half months to rebuild the house and barn, but a whole lot longer to rebuild my life. My once-thriving bed-and-breakfast business in Hernia, Pennsylvania, was kaput. Sure, I'd restored the inn, but it was unlikely I was ever going to restore that certain caliber of clientele. You see, ever since the rave review in *The New York Times,* I'd played hostess to the rich and famous. Folks with complicated lives paid big bucks to live simply for a few days. As a matter of fact, when the tornado hit I had a two-year waiting list, but of course I'd had to postpone or cancel everyone on the list. In the meantime that fickle flock had discovered the joys of Montana and Wyoming. Dude ranches were back in vogue—Amish were definitely not. I briefly considered renaming the PennDutch Inn The Big Sky, which would have been a big lie, because from November to March you can't even see the sky because of the clouds.

When the phone rang early that warm spring morning, I wasn't sleeping, but I was deep in the slough of despondence. I must have let it ring ten times before answering.

"PennDutch Inn," I said sourly.

"Fantastic! I didn't think there could be more than one Hernia, Pennsylvania, and I bet there's only one PennDutch Inn, right?"

"Get to your point, dear."

"Well, I'd like to reserve your four best rooms, if I may."

"April Fool's was three weeks ago, buster."

My caller chuckled. "My name is Bob Hart and I'm calling from Tulsa, Oklahoma. I want to make some reservations."

I glanced at my bedside clock. The little hand was on the seven, and the big hand was two dust motes to the right of the twelve.

"It must be awfully early in Oklahoma."

"Well, you know what they say about the early bird getting the worm and all that."

"This is a high-class operation, Mr. Hart. Worms will not be on the menu."

"Good comeback, ma'am."

"I do my best." Frankly, my tart tongue had been lolling about listlessly in my mouth for some time. Depression is the arch enemy of rapier wit, after all.

"So, do you have four rooms available?"

"For which dates?" I flipped the empty pages of a notebook I keep by the phone.

"Next week. My wife and I will be—"

"Next week?"

"Perhaps I could speak with the owner," Bob had the cheek to say.

"I *am* the owner, dear. I'm just checking my calendar. This is a very popular establishment, you know."

"Oh, indeed I do. I read all about your place in *People* magazine. Last year, wasn't it? They called it a 'gem,' I believe. '*The* place to kick back and relax.'"

"Oh?" I sat up. My inn had been featured in so many articles I'd long ago lost count—but the *People* magazine spread, that I remembered. My personal phone had

3

rung off the hook for a week after that, with half of Hollywood and the cream of Washington clamoring to get on my waiting list. Not that it did any good now. Those fickle friends of fortune were off frolicking in greener and higher pastures. No doubt some of them were dancing with wolves.

"Yes, ma'am. That was some picture they ran too."

"You may call me Miss Yoder, if you wish," I said generously. Thank the Good Lord news of my inn's demise had not been the subject of a follow-up spread. "So you remember that picture?"

"Miss Yoder, how could I forget that picture? You were the tall, good-looking woman standing next to Barbra Streisand, weren't you?"

"She lets me call her Babs," I said, perking up considerably. "But I still have to call him James."

"How about it, Miss Yoder? You think you can squeeze us in?"

"Four rooms you said?" My new PennDutch has six guest rooms, all of them as empty as my heart the day my Pooky Bear told me he had another wife stashed up in Minnesota.

"Yes, ma'am. There'll be four couples. Do these rooms have private baths?"

I snorted. "Heads of state have stayed at my inn, dear. Of course they have private baths. The question is, can you afford my rates?"

"What are your rates?"

I named the figure that was equal to the gross national product of your average third-world nation. It was, in fact, half of what I used to charge the rich and famous.

"That will be fine," Bob said without a second's hesitation. "Please make the reservation under my name,

Robert E. Hart. My wife and I will be arriving Sunday
night from Tulsa. Our flight lands in Pittsburgh, where
we plan to rent a car. The other three couples will be
flying in Monday morning."

"Tulsa too?" I asked. Alliteration has always been my
forte.

"No, ma'am. Jimmy and his wife—they're the Hills—
are from Arkansas. Frank and Marjorie Frost are from
Missouri, but they live in Anchorage now. So guess
where Scott and Dixie Montgomery are from."

"Alabama'?"

Bob hooted with delight. "No, Minnesota."

I forced a polite chuckle. "Well, I'm sure you will find
our little Amish and Mennonite community very interesting. We're not overrun by tourists like those folks
over in Lancaster."

"Yeah, the wives are really looking forward to that.
Sandy—that's my wife—wants to buy some Amish quilts.
But for us men, it's more of a reunion. We haven't seen
each other in almost fifty years."

"Fraternity brothers?" I asked in alarm. The only creatures allowed to swing from my chandeliers were spiders.

"We're army buddies, ma'am. Retired officers. We
were all members of the 43rd tank brigade in WWII."

"Oh." Perhaps I should explain that I am a Mennonite
woman, born and bred. My grandparents were Amish.
Both sects are strict pacifists, and have been so for hundreds of years. My deceased mother would roll over in
her grave if she knew I was allowing a group of former
warriors to sleep under her roof.

"Miss Yoder, I sense some hesitation. I mean, if there's
a problem—perhaps you could recommend another inn
in the area."

On the other hand, it wasn't Mama's roof anymore, was it? And they were *retired* from the military. I prayed for a sign from above, and instantly was hit with an inspiration.

"I have a special plan called A.L.P.O.—it stands for Amish Lifestyle Plan Option. For an extra twenty dollars a day per room I allow guests to do their own housekeeping. It makes them feel more like a part of the community."

"That sounds like fun."

"It *does*?"

"A little work never hurt anyone. Helps to keep the old ticker in shape, you know."

I breathed a sigh of relief. "Will that be Visa or Master-Card, dear?"

"I got them both right here, little lady. One in each hand. How about you choose?"

"The one in your left hand." At the rate he was paying, he deserved to be humored.

"That would be Visa. Say, little lady, I'd like to reserve a conference room as well."

"Will an old-fashioned parlor do instead?" It was a *new* old-fashioned parlor, of course. The tornado saw to that.

"Uh, how much extra would that be?"

"Fifty dollars a day, dear. Believe me, that's a steal."

"Does it have a fireplace?"

"A real fireplace with genuine logs. None of those fake logs with a gas flame. In fact, I'll even let you chop wood for me, and I won't charge you a penny more."

"Ah, a real log-burning fireplace. Well, in that case, you have a deal. You know, Miss Yoder, you're a woman after my own heart. *Hart*—get it?"

I forced a polite chuckle. Of course I got it. What I

didn't get was why four couples from west of the Mississippi would converge on Hernia, Pennsylvania. That was a long way to come just for quilts. Why not hold the mini-reunion some place more central like St. Louis? If I'd taken the time to ponder that question a little longer, I would have spared myself a whole lot of trouble—trouble that almost cost me my life. Alas, one of my guests was not to be so lucky.

TWO

I barely had time to replace the receiver in its cradle when the phone rang again.

"A deal is a deal," I snapped. "The A.L.P.O. plan stays."

"I beg your pardon?" a woman said in cultivated tones.

"Mrs. Hart?"

"Excuse me, I must have a wrong number. I'm trying to reach the PennDutch Inn."

"You've reached it, dear. How may I help you?"

"My name is Samantha Burk, and I'm calling to reserve a room for next week."

"Just a minute, dear, while I check to see if there's an opening." Trust me, that is not the same thing as lying. I did check—the fact that I already knew the answer is irrelevant. "Well, you're in luck, dear. I do happen to have a room available. Will it be just you?"

"No. My husband, Dr. John Burk, will be with me. We would like to arrive Sunday evening if it is at all possible."

"That would be fine. It's always good to have a doctor at the inn. Saves on the extra expense of house calls." I chuckled pleasantly.

"Oh, no, John's not a medical doctor. John has a Ph.D.

He's a retired professor of history. He taught at Duquesne University for twenty-five years."

"Oh, so you're Pittsburghers?"

"Yes. I mean, we live in Oakmont, just outside the city."

"Close enough, dear. There's a wonderful bookstore there—Mystery Lovers Bookshop. Do you know it?"

"I practically live there. Mary Alice Gorman and Richard Goldman are two of my best friends." Samantha enunciated every word.

"Are you a teacher, dear?"

She laughed pleasantly. "No, I'm afraid not—but I get that question all the time. I'm a retired musician. We have to be precise in our work."

"What sort of musician?" I asked warily. I have had many pleasant encounters with the musically gifted, but it's obvious that some of the newer rock groups failed to learn manners at their mamas' knees. Take, for instance, Defeated Moles and Stink Cabbage. And now that you've got them, keep them far away from me. And as far as I am concerned, they aren't even musicians.

"I am a concert pianist," she said. "Actually, I should say *former* concert pianist. I give only two performances a year now—it's arthritis, you know. It's getting harder and harder to span an octave. Say, you wouldn't happen to have a piano at the inn, would you? I try to practice four hours every day despite the pain."

"Mix a tablespoon of pectin with a glass of red grape juice. Drink two of those a day, and it should help with the pain. There is no charge for this advice," I said generously. "Now as to the piano—I don't own one, but there's a perfectly good piano just down the road at

9

Beechy Grove Mennonite Church. I'm a member, so you can just say I sent you."

"Is it a Steinway?"

"I'm not sure about that. I do know there's a henway in one of the Sunday school rooms."

She bit. "What's a henway?"

"Oh, about three pounds."

Much to her credit, the good woman laughed out loud. This was almost too good to be true. Guests who possess a sense of humor *and* are cultivated and refined are as scarce as a henway's teeth. And her husband was a historian no less! Perhaps I should have solicited customers from Pittsburgh years ago. I mean, who needs the glamour of Hollywood and the power of Washington when there is culture to be found in one's own backyard?

"I look forward to meeting you," I said cheerily. I hadn't felt that good in weeks.

"I look forward to meeting you as well. Oh"—her voice was suddenly an octave higher—"will there be other people staying at the inn?"

"Of course there'll be other guests, but we'll find plenty of time to chat. Be a dear, will you, and bring me a copy of Selma Eichler's latest mystery, *Murder Can Singe Your Old Flame*. In fact, pick out several other mysteries at random. Just make sure they're new releases, so I won't have read them. Better yet, get Mary Alice to help you. She knows my taste."

"I'd be happy to. Now"— she paused to delicately clear her throat—"you said there will be other guests there this week. What *sort* of people will they be?"

"What?" I jiggled my pinkie in my ear to clear out the wax. Perhaps I'd heard wrong. Prejudice seldom rears its ugly head at my inn, but when it does, it always comes as a complete surprise. Rest assured, I always send it packing.

"You know, *our* sort."

"And what sort would that be? Because for your information, I just happen to be a lesbian African-American woman with a Spanish surname who practices the Jewish faith—oh, did I happen to mention I was physically *and* mentally challenged?"

"No, what I—"

"And fat!"

"I mean older people. Mature adults."

"Oh?"

"My husband is a very nervous man, you see, and some of these young people today—well, to put it bluntly, we prefer an older crowd."

"Is that it? No need to worry, dear, not unless your husband is bothered by the sound of clacking dentures. They're all World War II veterans and their wives."

"Well—"

"I hope you understand that silence doesn't come cheap," I said, presenting her with the last potential obstacle.

"I'm sure that won't be a problem Ms.—?"

"Yoder," I said, and then gave her a figure even higher than the one I'd quoted the veterans.

"That sounds fine. Do you take credit cards?"

"Yes. Oh, did I mention the Amish Lifestyle Option plan? For a mere fifty dollars extra you get to play Amish and clean your own room. Do your own laundry as well."

"How charming! Put us down for that too."

I took her credit card number, and then bid her adieu before I could yield to temptation. There's a charming little stone bridge in Hernia that has theoretically changed hands several times in recent years. Rumors abound that I may have something to do with this.

I couldn't contain myself; I just had to tell Freni. Five—no, make that ten—paying guests, and all within the space of ten minutes. And Freni said no one in their right mind would pay that kind of money to stay in a reconstructed inn!

Freni Hostetler is my cousin. We are not first cousins, but we share eight sets of ancestors seven generations back. By my reckoning that makes us closer than first cousins—possibly even half sisters—although Freni is thirty years older than I, a contemporary of my parents. The truth is my people are so intermarried that not only am I my own cousin, but I constitute a full-fledged family reunion. Throw in a sandwich, and I'm a family picnic.

I slipped on a blue long-sleeved dress that comes well below the knee, stockings, and a pair of sensible shoes. My undergarments are none of your business. My toilette consisted of using the device of the same name—I do not waste my money on makeup—and gathering my shoulder-length hair into a nice, conservative bun, over which I pinned a white organza prayer cap. The thermometer on my windowsill registered in the mid-fifties so I decided against a sweater. The two-mile hike to Freni's house traverses a rather steep hill, and I eschew sweating. Perhaps that's why I was never very good in—well, never mind. A brisk walk would keep me warm enough.

The path between my house and Freni's is the same path our common ancestor, Jacob Hochstetler, was forced to follow after he was taken captive by the Delaware Indians in 1750. Of course at that time it was already an old hunting path, and it was woods the whole way. The woods have now shrunk to a mere ribbon that crowns the crest of the hill, the remainder being corn fields. Still it is a joy to walk along this path, listen to birdsong, and above all, escape the telephone.

Freni doesn't have to worry about distancing herself from a phone. As an Amish woman she doesn't own a telephone. Her house doesn't have electricity. When Freni and her husband, Mose—also a cousin of sorts—travel, they hitch their horse, Sadie, to a buggy. The most complicated piece of machinery Freni owns is her sewing machine with its foot-powered treadle, upon which she sews herself garments even more conservative than the ones I wear.

By the time I reached the Hostetler house, the day had warmed considerably, and I was just beginning to break into that dreaded sweat. Several more days of this weather and the tulip buds would open. I fervently hoped that Freni had a nice pitcher of lemonade waiting in her gasoline-powered refrigerator.

I knocked several times on the unpainted kitchen door, but there was no answer. I turned the knob, and the door opened. Freni was standing by the kitchen sink, her broad back to me.

"Freni," I called loudly. I once made the unfortunate mistake of surprising my cousin, who is a mite hard of hearing, and got a broom in my face. And this from a pacifist!

My cousin turned. "Ach, Magdalena, come in."

"Freni Hostetler, whatever are you doing?" In her right arm she cradled three five-pound bags of flour. In her left arm, precariously balanced between her ample bosom and stubby little hand were three pint-sized mason jars filled with water.

"What do you think I'm doing? I'm practicing, of course!"

"Practicing what? Did you get a job in a bakery?"

She glared at me through wire-rimmed glasses. "The babies! I'm pretending to feed the babies. Barbara's not going to have enough milk for triplets, you know. Ach, I don't think she'll even have enough for one. She's even flatter than you, Magdalena. Why, that woman is as flat as Kansas."

"How would you know? Have you ever been to Kansas?"

"No, but Barbara told me."

Barbara Kauffman Hostetler is Freni's formerly despised, but now tolerated daughter-in-law. For twenty years Barbara, who hails from Kansas, has been unworthy of Freni's son Jonathan. Then something came unstuck in Barbara's plumbing and the woman bloomed. There were three buds at last count, and blossom time was four months away.

"Wouldn't it be safer to feed just one of the babies at a time?"

Freni muttered something in Pennsylvania Dutch that sounded like "What would *you* know about feeding babies, you who is forever doomed to be as barren as the Gobi Desert?" Fortunately my grasp of the dialect is minimal, and I chose to interpret it as something else entirely.

"Thank you," I said. "I've always like this shade of blue on me."

Dark eyes rolled behind thick lenses. "So, would you like to hold little Freni?"

"That's a bag of flour, dear. In fact, they're all three bags of flour. Now, do you want to hear my good news or not?"

"Yah," Freni said, "slap me."

"That's 'hit' me, dear, and slang doesn't become you. Anyway, you wouldn't believe what happened! I just got two calls, and now the inn is booked solid for next week—well, five rooms at any rate. You know what this means, don't you?"

Freni shrugged, and the mason jars clanked ominously.

"I need you back at work."

My kinswoman is the only cook the PennDutch Inn has ever had. Her meals are really quite tasty, despite the fact she relies heavily on the three favorite Amish food groups—sugar, starch, and grease.

Freni frowned. "I quit, remember?"

"Freni, you've quit more times than Cher's had surgery. Besides, think of the brand-new buggies my bucks can buy your babies."

She sighed, which meant I had made my first breach in her defenses.

"Please, pretty please," I begged. "It'll make the time go by faster until they're born."

"Movie stars?" Freni asked with studied casualness.

"Maybe," I said just as casually.

"Mel?"

"Mel who?" I knew exactly who she meant, but I was afraid now to tell her the truth.

"Mel Gibson! The one with the skirt."

As a *plain person,* one who is supposed to live in the world, but not be *of* it, Freni is ostensibly unaware that star-worship exists. In real life, because she is my cook—well, most of the time—the woman sees more stars than an astronomer. She dotes on Denzel Washington and fawns over Ben Affleck, but Mel is the apple of her eye. I'm sure Freni would give her life for the man—maybe even one of her unborn triplet grandchildren.

I swallowed hard. "So, maybe it's not movie stars this time."

"Ach, not *him*! I'm seventy-eight years old, Magdalena. I'm too old to be chased around the Inn again. And all those Secret Service men just looking the other way!"

"You're seventy-five, dear." Freni is the only woman I know who pads her age—perhaps in a misguided attempt to gain respect. "And it's not him, anyway. It's a reunion of World War II vets."

There was the sound of breaking glass and splashing water, followed by the thud of five pounds of flour on a wooden floor. Freni and I stared mutely at the remains of one of her faux grandchildren and its breakfast. She was the first to find her voice.

"*Ach du leiber!* Now see what you've done?"

"I think we have the beginnings of a giant pie crust, dear."

"That"—she pointed to the floor, thereby putting the remaining two faux babies in jeopardy—"is my little Mose."

"Mose shmoze," I said, my patience wearing thin. "I need you back at work."

Freni shook her head. "For shame, Magdalena, and you call yourself a pacifist. Your mama would roll over in her grave if she knew there were soldiers sleeping in her house."

"Leave Mama out of this," I snapped. "Besides, it's not her house now. It's been totally rebuilt, so it's all mine. And anyway, they're not soldiers now—they're old men." I graciously refrained from adding "like you."

"Tch, tch, tch."

"Don't you tch, tch me, dear. Someone had to fight the Nazis. If these brave men hadn't, those little grandbabies of yours would be goose-stepping around Hernia shouting 'Seig Heil'."

"Ach," Freni squawked, and another faux baby hit the floor. She fumbled with the two mason jars for a few seconds but it was a lost cause.

"Oops. Looks like you could use a little more practice, dear."

"Out!" Freni screamed. "Get out of my house this minute."

"So you'll come back to work? Because they're not all going to be vets, you see. Their wives are coming too, and then there is the concert pianist from Pittsburgh and her historian husband. They—"

"Yah, yah," Freni said, pushing me with one hand, her other stubby arm gripping the last bag of flour. "I'll come, if you go."

I was out of there like an atheist from a revival meeting. Like the atheist, I should have stayed long enough to see the error of my ways.

Three

I used to get up with the chickens. Literally. I don't mean to say that I slept in the hen house, or they in my bed, but we got up at the same time. Before the late, great disaster—which I still say was a tornado—I owned a flock of fifty-three laying hens and one irascible rooster. The cock was named Chaunticleer and his favorite wife—also my favorite hen—I called Pertelote. To my knowledge they were the only literary fowl in Bedford County, and very near and dear to my heart.

Then along came that horrible storm and my flock went flying, never to be seen again. Undoubtedly some were eaten by foxes and raccoons, but I have a sneaking suspicion a few managed to sail over the border into Maryland and ultimately ended up on the dinner tables of folks living there. Most of my hens were past their laying days and far too old to be consumed by humans, but those Marylanders, I've heard, will eat anything that Comes flying down the pike.

At any rate, I was up and dressed by five-thirty, and had just sat down at the kitchen table with my first cup of coffee and the *Bedford Times,* when someone rapped sharply on the door. It was a good thing I was no longer holding the cup, because I jumped so high I got altitude sickness. Okay, so maybe that's a slight exaggeration, but I was really spooked, and it took me a while to find my voice.

"Who is it?" I finally rasped.

"It's me." The speaker was obviously a male and his voice vaguely familiar.

"Be more specific, dear. The last time I checked there were almost eight billion 'me's in the world. Which one would you be?"

"It's Samuel Berkey."

That narrowed it down, but not as much as you might think. Berkey is a common Mennonite and Amish name, and Samuel is as ubiquitous as maple trees in Vermont. I knew eight men by that name in Bedford County, and six over in Somerset.

"It's Samuel Berkey the Bishop's son-in-law."

"That narrows it down to two, dear."

"Samuel Berkey with the straggly beard."

"Ah, that Samuel Berkey. *Strubbly* Sam." I strode to the door and flung it open. "Why didn't you say so to begin with?"

Samuel blinked. He is an Amish man, perhaps in his early seventies, and he dresses in typical garb for this region: black pants, white shirt, black vest, and black coat. His shirt and coat fasten with hooks and eyes rather than worldly buttons. His pants are held up by suspenders. He wears a straw hat on weekdays, and on Sundays a wide-brimmed, black felt hat. Since he is a married man—well, a widower now—he wears a beard, and it is this feature that immediately distinguishes him from the other men in his generation. Sam's beard is sparse to the point of looking messy. *Strubbly*, we call it in Pennsylvania-Dutch.

"Come in Strubbly Sam," I said not unkindly. In a culture where so many share the same name, nicknames are not derisive, they are necessary.

Sam stepped in, and his glance swept the expanse of my kitchen. No doubt he was allowing himself the luxury of gazing upon modern electric-powered appliances he could never use, much less own. I'm sure had his wife Amanda been alive, he would have memorized every detail to recount that night at the dinner table.

"Here, for you," Sam said, and handed me a wire basket, practically spilling over with eggs.

"Thank you." I took the gift with mixed feelings. I knew Strubbly Sam by sight and reputation, but these were the first words we had ever exchanged. Sure, I saw him at the feed store from time to time, and sometimes at Cousin Sam's Corner Market, but we definitely did not move in the same circles. I was a Mennonite *woman,* after all, and he an Amish *man.* For a fleeting moment I flattered myself with the notion that Samuel Berkey had come to pay court. But because he was an *Amish* man, and I a *Mennonite* woman, this was highly unlikely. He was also old enough to be my father. Still, I tried to picture myself in a stiff black apron and a black bonnet, perched on the front seat of a buggy built for two. When the buggy turned down the drive of a farmhouse that lacked central heat and air conditioning, the fantasy faded.

But an egg is an egg, and I had an inn about to fill up with guests. I transferred the eggs from the wire basket to a large blue crock. Alas, several of the eggs were in less than pristine condition.

"You should have washed the eggs," I said gently.

"Yah, that's what my Amanda would say."

I pointed to a chair, but he shook his head.

"So, Strubbly Sam, to what do I owe this honor?"

"Honor?"

"This visit—these eggs. Something on your mind?"

"Yah, Big Magdalena—"

"*Big* Magdalena? I may be five foot ten, but I'm skinny as a mop handle!"

"Ach"—he turned a lovely shade of salmon under his wispy whiskers—"there are things besides height and weight to consider." I would have liked to think he was referring to my bosoms, but since I have a concave chest, there wasn't enough evidence there to hang my hat on. Besides, his pale blue eyes were focused quite clearly on my probing proboscis.

"Why, I never! It is an honest Yoder nose. Just consider yourself lucky, buster, because you Berkeys have a little Yoder blood too."

Strubbly Sam seemed startled. Then I remembered that he was not originally from around these parts, but from one of those far-flung Amish communities, like Nebraska or Paraguay. According to what Mama told me, Strubbly Sam had been on his way to Lancaster to visit some distant relatives, and when it was almost dark, sought accommodations with an Amish family for the night. The family he picked just happened to be the bishop, who just happened to have three of the most beautiful daughters ever to descend from Eve. Strubbly Sam never made it to Lancaster, and never returned to Paraguay, or Nebraska, or wherever he was from. Perhaps those foreign Berkeys lacked Yoder blood.

"Okay, so maybe there aren't Yoders where you come from, but you've seen plenty enough here to know that my nose is not unique."

"Ach, it isn't just me who speaks of Big Magdalena."

"*What?* You mean the entire community gossips about my shnoz?"

He removed his hat, revealing strubbly hair. "But there are six Magdalena Yoders in Bedford County, and nine in Somerset. It is only a name, Big Magdalena."

"Don't call me that!" I snapped.

He twirled the straw hat on his left index finger. "You are angry with me now, yah?"

I remembered the eggs. "Merely miffed, dear. So, Strubbly Sam, what is it you have on your mind?"

He gazed at my new bread-maker, a machine Freni refuses to use. "You are having guests, yah?"

"That's what an inn is all about, dear. But I hate to disappoint you if you think you're going to get a glimpse of Hollywood. For one thing, no one has arrived yet, and for another, this is not a Hollywood crowd."

"Soldiers, yah?"

"Why, that gossipy little Freni! And they're not soldiers—they're veterans."

"But veterans of a war, yah. Is that such a good idea?"

"Not you too!" I wailed.

"Big Magdalena—"

I glared at him.

"Ach, Magdalena, our people are committed to peace."

"Quite true, dear, but these are elderly men converging to reminisce. They're not going to be waging war on the countryside."

"Yah, but—"

I held up a quieting hand. "And if they do, you can take refuge in my basement."

Strubbly Sam smiled sadly. "What does Lustige Freni have to say about this?"

"*Merry* Freni? Boy, do you have a wrong number!"

He frowned, obviously confused.

"That woman is as merry as a mule with a burr under its saddle," I said kindly.

"So she's against it, yah?"

"Is that what you think? Well, she's coming in to work today," I said smugly. "Why don't you ask her yourself?"

The threat of a chance encounter with Merry Freni sent Strubbly Sam speedily on his way. In fact he left so quickly he left behind his wire basket.

Samantha Burk and her husband, John, were the first guests to arrive. I was amazed at how tiny Samantha was—even her hair was short. I couldn't imagine how such tiny hands, barely larger than cat paws, could span an octave under any circumstances. But I was downright taken aback by her striking resemblance to an acquaintance of mine.

"Say, you wouldn't happen to be related to Abigail Timberlake?" I asked as I wrote down their license plate number.

"I beg your pardon?"

"Feisty little southern gal, owns an antique store called the Den of Antiquity?"

"Never heard of her."

"Hmm. You're the spitting image of Abby—well, except that you have almond-shaped eyes and are a good ten years older."

Samantha smiled. "The 'almond' eyes, as you so nicely put it, are the result of one too many facelifts."

I clamped a hand over my mouth, lest my other foot try to get in as well. I should have known better, of course. I've seen movie stars whose eyelids close automatically whenever they open their mouths. The Good Lord only gave us so much skin to play around with, for heaven's sake.

"Oh, that's all right," Samantha said quickly. "I'm not at all embarrassed by the subject. I had a face lift so I could look younger for my public. Many people don't realize it, but concert pianists are celebrities. We have fans. We have images to uphold."

I must say that I had never thought about concert pianists being celebrities. No doubt she was right, however; the mountain of luggage her husband had piled next to the front desk confirmed her celebrity status. I made a mental note to be nicer to Vladimer next time he called asking to reserve a room.

A car door slammed outside. Then another. Then the sound of raised voices, possibly even an argument.

"It seems like the next batch of guests has arrived," I said brightly.

"Please, miss," John Burk said, reaching for the as yet unproffered key. "Could we hurry this along a bit?"

Those were the first words the man had said. I was beginning to think his was a forced retirement from the history department at Duquesne. Mute professors have got to be a liability.

I stared at him. He was taller than me, and I'm five-ten. He was a good fifty pounds overweight, something I cannot be accused of being, and had scarcely any hair. Trust me, I have plenty of that, and in all the right places. But there was something ominous about him, something I can only describe metaphorically. John Burk looked like he walked around with a little rain cloud, not much larger than a powder puff, suspended above his head.

"What a charming accent," I finally said. "Are you originally from Minnesota?"

For a split second he looked like a deer caught in the headlights of a car. "You have an excellent ear, Miss Yoder. I was indeed born in Minnesota."

"Minneapolis?"

"New Bedford—a tiny little town on the Canadian border. I'm sure you've never heard of it. Anyway, I consider myself a Pennsylvanian now."

"Welcome to Pennsylvania, dear."

He grimaced. "I've lived here for fifty years. No doubt that's longer than you have."

I wrinkled my considerable nose. "No doubt, dear."

"Miss Yoder, is there any way to hurry this along? I have a migraine headache and would really like to lie down."

"Hold your horses," I said sweetly, "your credit card company has me on hold."

The diminutive Samantha put a comforting hand on her husband's arm. "You go on up to the room, dear. I'll finish up down here."

He gave her a quick kiss that seemed stiff and unnatural, and snatched the key from my hand.

"Well, I never!"

He strode off without as much as a grunt of apology.

"Third room on the right," I yelled at his back, "and be careful going up those impossibly steep stairs. I'm not liable if you take a tumble."

Actually, I probably am. I don't know what possessed me to have the same wickedly steep stairs rebuilt in my new inn—although I did have them carpeted to make them less slippery. A woman had fallen to her death on the old stairs, for crying out loud. Perhaps it was nostalgia—not for the corpse, mind you—but for life as it used to be. Before the inn blew down, *before* I married Aaron Miller, who was already married, thereby consigning myself to the rank of unwitting adulteress.

"What an evil man," I muttered.

"Please excuse him," Samantha said earnestly. "John is really a friendly, outgoing man. It's just that these headaches can be so debilitating."

"Just the same—"

"I brought those books you asked for," she said smoothly.

"You did?"

"They're in one of these bags. I'll get them for you the second I unpack."

"Great!"

The Burk credit card cleared. I jotted down the confirmation number and handed her the slip to sign.

"Anyway, I was speaking of my ex-husband, dear. Well, in a sense he was my husband—I mean, we were never *legally* married, but—" I caught myself. "What are we going to do about all this luggage?"

She dashed off her signature. "Send it up with the bellhop."

"I *am* the bellhop," I wailed.

"Oh, that's most unfortunate. Well, I suppose you could leave it there, until John feels better. Except for this"— she pointed to a large suitcase— "and that." She pointed to a matching train case. "And of course, these three."

"Well, I'll take the big one up for you," I said generously. "I'm sure you can manage the others in several trips."

She shook her tiny head. "I really am sorry, Miss Yoder, but I can't help you. It's my fingers, you see. I can't risk injuring them. You understand, don't you?"

I shook my massive head and muttered something unintelligible.

"Thanks, that's so kind of you," she chirped and flew up the impossibly steep stairs in a manner quite unbefitting a woman of her years.

I was returning from my last luggage run, panting, when the second couple finally came through the door. Since I'd taken my time lugging those genuine, full-cowhide suitcases upstairs, I couldn't imagine what had been keeping this duo in the parking lot. As soon as the missus opened her mug I knew.

"So, what's the big deal? Couples fight all the time."

I took one look at the woman and hated her instantly. I know, that's not the Christian thing to do, but mine was a visceral reaction. The good Lord understands, I'm sure. Her frizzy blonde hair, her long pointed nose, her blue-gray eyes and lanky frame, added up to a sum that made me shiver with disgust. My sister Susannah feels the same way about lima beans.

The man, a veritable giant, winced. "Please, Sandy, not in front of her."

"Why not? She ain't going to hear nothing she ain't heard before."

I stiffened, forcing myself to think of greenbacks. Alas, it was hard to concentrate. The truth be known, I have plenty of money squirreled away, perhaps enough to last me the rest of my life. What I lacked was a sense of purpose, and since it was clear I was never going to have any grandbabies of my own to hold, reopening my business had seemed the right way to go. Only now I wasn't so sure.

"Welcome to the PennDutch Inn," I said in a fake German accent. It is what I do for all my guests, even the obnoxious ones.

"Howdy, Ma'am," the man said. He was too embarrassed to even make eye contact. "Name's Bob Hart. We spoke on the phone."

"Ah, yes. Bob and Sandy from Tulsa. Did you have a nice trip?"

"Ha!" she barked. "That's a laugh! You ever eat sausage cooked in a microwave?"

"Excuse me?"

"Airplane food is the pits, and them ain't mountains," she said, waving her beak over her shoulder.

I smiled a fake American smile. "Yes, they are, dear. They're the Allegheny Mountains."

"That may be their name, but they ain't mountains. I know, cause I seen the real things in Colorado."

I prayed for a Christian tongue, despite my heathen heart. "So, you must be anxious to check in after a long trip like that."

"Yes, ma'am," Bob said quickly.

"Maybe you are," she sniffed, "but I ain't so sure."

"Sandy, *please*."

"*He* said we were gong to an Ayemish bed and breakfast. Only this don't look no different than a regular bed and breakfast." She thrust her needle nose over the counter, parking it inches from my face. "You Ayemish?"

"The word is 'Amish,' dear. And no, I'm not. I'm Mennonite. But this is a bed and breakfast."

Frizzy withdrew her proboscis and turned to her husband. "You see, she ain't even Ayemish. She's just a Manynite."

"My cook's Amish. She wears a bonnet and everything."

Sandy rolled her eyes. "Big deal. They have one of those at the Dutch Kettle restaurant back home. I was expecting to stay with a real Ayemish family—take buggy rides and everything. I sure don't want to spend good money to stay in a dump."

I gasped.

"Okay, so maybe that's a strong word, but this ain't the Taj Mahal."

"Thank heavens for that," I said. "The Taj Mahal is a tomb. Now, if you'll be so kind, the door is that way!"

Sandy gaped at me.

"Please," Bob said, pushing her gently aside. "Please give me a moment to explain."

I tapped one of my size eleven shoes on the hardwood floor. "Your moment passed the minute she walked through that door."

"Come on, Bob." Sandy tugged furtively on her husband's arm. "We don't need to put up with this crap."

Actually, she used a much worse word, which I won't repeat. I glared at her, which was like glaring into a frizzy sun, so I glared at her husband. Bob, quite frankly, was easy on the eyes. Not only was he tall, but he had a square jaw, a strong chin, and hair the color of polished sterling. His only imperfection were his eyebrows, which were still black and threatening to grow out of bounds.

"You go on ahead, dear," Bob said calmly but firmly to his wife. "I'll be there in a minute."

Much to my surprise, Sandy did what she was told. The second my heavy oak door closed behind her, Bob turned to me.

"She doesn't mean what she says, ma'am. She's bipolar."

"That's no excuse, dear. Some of my best friends are bicoastal, and they don't act like that. Besides, I thought you live in Oklahoma." I wasn't going to volunteer the information, but flitting back and forth between the arctic and Antarctica would make me crabby too.

He smiled. "We do live in Oklahoma. Bipolar means she suffers from manic-depression. You know, two mood extremes."

"Oh."

"You see, instead of feeling giddy during their manic phase, some folks feel intensely irritable. Sandy falls into the irritable category."

"No kidding."

"Her condition is not an excuse for her behavior, but I hope it's an explanation."

"Is she on medication?"

"Yes, and believe it or not it helps tremendously. Usually she's much more even keeled. I think this particular onset was brought on by the stress of the trip."

"How long do you think this episode will last?" Boy, was that a mistake. I should have just told him to haul his gangly wife back inside so I could clasp her lovingly to my scrawny bosom.

"It could end any minute. And she's really very nice when you get the chance to know her. In fact, she's kind of like you."

"She is not," I wailed. "My verbs agree with their subjects!"

"Ma'am?"

"Oh, all right. You can stay, but keep her away from me until she evens out."

"It's a deal, ma'am."

Sunday is supposed to be a day of rest, and I was finally doing just that—sitting in the parlor, dozing, when my sister Susannah swirled into the room. Alas, my sister marches to the beat of her own drum, and it's a rhythm unique to her. The woman eschews conventional clothing and dresses in yards and yards of diaphanous material that she drapes about herself in various methods, depending on how hard the wind is blowing. She is the only woman I know who carries a live dog—a minuscule, mangy mutt named Shnookums—around in her bra. Susannah never wears proper shoes—only sandals—even in the dead of winter, and if her feet sometimes get cold, her face never does. Only one other woman in the world wears as much makeup as does Susannah, and that is our assistant police chief, Zelda Root. Both Zelda and Susannah claim to have given Tammy Faye lessons in the art of makeup application, and both admit that they failed miserably in their efforts. Compared to Susannah, Tammy Faye sports that freshly scrubbed look.

"There you are!" Susannah cried, as her outfit drifted into the room behind her. "I've been looking all over for you, Mags."

I opened one eye. I hadn't seen my sister in almost three weeks. During that time I hadn't been more than ten miles from the inn.

"Oh, Mags, you're just not going to believe it. I've got the most exciting news to tell you!"

I opened the other eye. "You've decided not to join that ashram in India you were raving about the last time I saw you?"

"That ashram was in West Virginia, not India. And besides, they wouldn't take dogs."

"Remind me to send them a small donation."

"Oh, Mags, you're just impossible! I'm going to marry Melvin, that's what."

"Mel Gibson is happily married, and even if he wasn't, Freni gets first dibs."

Susannah rolled her eyes. It is her only talent, but I must say, she is unparalleled at it. Perhaps it is just an optical illusion, but it appears to me that she can roll them upwards a complete three hundred and sixty degrees, so that the irises reappear above her lower lids. I know this sounds impossible, but just you wait until you've said something really stupid to her.

"Not *that* Melvin—Melvin Stoltzfus."

"Sure, anything you say." As the young folks these days say, I was not about to go there. Melvin is my nemesis. The man looks like a praying mantis, which I'm sure he can't help, but he has that insect's heart and brain as well. Even that would be of no concern to me, *except* for the fact that Melvin is Hernia's chief of police. Unfortunately, my inn has had its share of corpses and—oh, well, enough said. It is my Christian duty to keep a charitable tongue in my head at all times.

Susannah tapped a size-eleven sandal on my hardwood floor. "Is that all you're going to say?"

I shrugged.

"Come on, I know you're dying to say something, so just spit it out."

"You've been engaged to Melvin more times than Elizabeth Taylor's been married," I said kindly. "Why should I take this threat seriously?"

"This isn't a threat, Mags. I've done some serious thinking, and I've come to the conclusion maybe it's time I grew up."

"You know, of course, that once you're married . . ."

There was no need to finish the sentence. My sister knew exactly what I meant. It pains me to say this, but Susannah is a slut. There really is no other word for it. The woman's bedroom door has seen more male traffic than the turnstile at the state fair. I don't mean this literally, of course, because I won't permit hanky-panky on my premises. But where there's a will, there's a way, and Susannah has had her way in every cheap motel this side of the Mississippi.

Please understand that this character defect of hers is not shared by yours truly. Until my ill-fated marriage to Aaron Miller, the only sex I'd ever had was that one time I absentmindedly sat on the washing machine during spin cycle. In retrospect—and I'm sure it's a sin to even say this—I'd have been much better off having a full-blown affair with my Maytag. At any rate, I'm not sure whether Susannah's aberrant behavior is genetic or the result of poor parenting. Could it be neither? I mean, Mama was a virgin when I was born (Papa probably was too), and both parents made it infinitely clear that sex before marriage was wrong. Still, somehow Susannah's apple not only managed to fall far from the tree, it rolled out of the orchard altogether.

Susannah was nodding vigorously. "I know what

you're thinking. But Melvin and I have talked this over, and we both think we can be faithful."

"Melvin?" It had never, even for a second, occurred to me that Melvin Stoltzfus had the option of being unfaithful. Not only is he cosmetically challenged, for crying out loud, but he has the intelligence of a fence post. He once mailed his favorite aunt in Scranton a gallon of ice cream—by *U.P.S.*! And did I mention the time he was kicked in the head because he tried to milk a bull?

"Oh, Mags, he's everything I ever wanted in a man."

"But he's not even human!" I wailed, and then clamped my hand over my mouth before I could say something unkind.

"So, Mags, will you give me away?"

"Will I *what*?"

"You know, give me away like Papa would, if he were still alive."

Frankly, I was touched. Moved almost to the verge of tears. Susannah had been only twenty when Papa died, killed instantly along with Mama in a tunnel, when the car they were driving was sandwiched by a milk tanker and a truck carrying state-of-the-art running shoes. Since then I have been both father and mother to Susannah. I have also bailed her out of jail more times than Robert Downey, Jr.'s, lawyers have had to spring for him. Because I've had to act as parent, principal, and guidance counselor, we have not always seen eye to rolling eye.

"When is the wedding?"

"Wednesday morning at ten."

"This Wednesday?"

"Melvin got us this special rate to Aruba and—"

"But that's impossible, dear. I could never get a wedding put together that soon. I mean, I've got paying guests coming from all over and—well, I suppose I could do something in the barn."

"The barn!"

"That's where I was married," I reminded her needlessly.

Susannah laughed. "Don't worry, Mags. It's all been settled. Melvin's mama is throwing the wedding. I just want you to give me away."

My mouth must have opened and closed repeatedly, like a baby bird begging to be fed.

"You understand, don't you, Mags? Melvin is an only child. This is her only chance to put on a wedding."

"What about me?" I wailed.

Susannah smiled. "You had your own wedding, remember? The one in the barn?"

"But—but—but—" I was sputtering like a grease fire in a rainstorm.

Susannah lunged forward and enveloped me in fifteen feet of filmy fabric. To put it plainly, she hugged me. Neither of us is genetically programmed for such an intimate, nonsexual gesture, and I was stunned. Then, quite inexplicably, four centuries of inbred reserve dropped from me like a discarded mantle and I returned her hug. Perhaps I squeezed too hard. I certainly, and quite stupidly, forgot about the dinky dog lurking in the nether regions of her underpinnings.

The beast howled pitifully.

I staggered backward several steps, but not before the maniacal mutt had managed to mangle my mammary with his malodorous mandibles. Okay, maybe I overstated the extent of my injuries, but I'm telling you—it hurt every bit as much as that time I innocently poked my proboscis in Susannah's electric pencil sharper.

It was a tossup as to which of us howled the loudest, Shnookums or me.

Four

Fortunately no stitches were needed. By the next morning I was feeling fit as a fiddle and ready to take on the world. I was even prepared to swallow my pride and call Elvina Stoltzfus, Melvin's seventy-five-year-old mother, and offer my services. In fact, I was just reaching for the phone when the doorbell rang.

I peeked through the sheers in the door window and espied the cutest little couple, each with a stubby arm around the other. Short, plump, heavier on their bottoms, they were a pair of pears. Since they had a pile of suitcases with them on the porch, I assumed they were guests. I patted my bun to make sure it was in place, fluffed up the bodice of my deflated dress, and flung open the door.

"*Gut Marriye,*" I said cheerfully, and then immediately regretted it. One should never be *too* friendly with guests, after all. I mean, why else is Paris so popular?

"Hey, there! I'm Jimmy Hill," the male pear said, extending his left hand, "and this is my wife Doris."

I pressed the pudgy, proffered palms—although a couple of nods would have sufficed me. "*Velcommen to zee PennDeutsch.*"

"Ooh, I just love the way you talk!" Doris squealed. No doubt the tightness of her jeans, into which she must have been poured, contributed to her unusually high voice.

"Thank you, dear," I said, dropping the fake accent, which is frankly a lot of trouble. "Now come on inside, before every fly in Hernia does the same."

The elderly pears moved in tandem, as if joined at the hip. But even though my front door is six inches wider than the standard, they could not enter as a pair. They laughed as they tried to squeeze their respective bulks simultaneously through that generous frame. I, on the other hand, was genuinely concerned. What if they got stuck? I wasn't about to take a crowbar to my brand-new doorjamb. They would have to remain stuck until one or both lost enough weight to make a difference. If Winnie the Pooh could do it, so could they.

"Why not let go of each other and come through one at a time like normal human beings?" I asked sensibly.

"Today's our golden wedding anniversary," Jimmy said.

I must have showed them the whites of my peepers.

"It's bad luck to cross a threshold separately," Doris screeched. "Jimmy would carry me over like he did when we got back from our honeymoon, but he has a hernia."

"I wonder why," I muttered.

"He was helping a neighbor stack stones." At least that's what I think she said, before her voice went soaring off the register. She might have said "hack bones."

Jimmy grinned. "Doc says I shouldn't do any lifting for a while. We figured an embrace was almost as good as my carrying her. Although as you can see, we've been having a little trouble."

"Then just hold hands," I snapped. "That's what the flies are doing."

Of course they ignored me. But after a few more minutes of groaning and jostling—during which flies from as far away as Pittsburgh showed up—they discovered it was possible to squeeze their tubby bodies through the door if they moved sideways. Since I wasn't about to let Philadelphia flies in as well, I volunteered to get their luggage.

"Ooh, this is charming," Doris squeaked, as I struggled in with an overstuffed American Tourister.

"Just perfect for a second honeymoon, isn't it, love bug?" Jimmy was, of course, talking to his wife.

Doris giggled, and her eyes all but disappeared.

"Do you have heart-shaped beds?" Jimmy asked.

"Vibrating ones?" Doris giggled again.

"This isn't Sodom and Gomorrah," I hissed. "You're going to have to try the Poconos for that."

Jimmy shamelessly kissed his wife on the lips. "A king-size bed will do just fine, won't it, sugarplum?"

I shuddered. "You break it, you buy it."

"Been there, done that," he said gaily.

It was time to lay down the law. "I'll have no disturbing the other guests—myself included. And no unseemly displays of affection now that you're inside."

They nodded, giggled, and smooched again. I was going to have to reinstate a screening process. Clearly there was such a thing as being too happily married. And at their age, yet!

Thank heavens the couple from Minnesota were pleasantly sedate, like proper senior citizens. Although they both insisted on shaking hands, they did so quickly, and their palms were dry. They even carried in their own luggage. What's more, they were one of the most attractive couples I'd seen in years. Sure, they had gray hair and a few wrinkles—they were in their sixties, after all—but they were the kind of couple you might expect to see in a Geritol commercial.

"What a beautiful state Pennsylvania is," Scott Montgomery said with just a hint of Scandinavian lilt.

"Thank you. I'm sure Minnesota is beautiful too."

"And this really is a charming inn."

I beamed. "Thank you again."

"Here, we brought you a present." Dixie Montgomery reached into an oversized stitched leather handbag and withdrew a beautifully wrapped present.

I kept my hands to my sides. "Oh, my, you shouldn't have."

Dixie smiled down at me. At six-foot plus, she was even taller than I. She also had much whiter teeth.

"It's just a little something to bring the flavor of Minnesota to you."

"I mean, you *really* shouldn't have." The last time a guest gifted me, she tried to stiff me as well. The seven-carat "diamond" ring that harlot starlet gave me may very well have once been the bottom of a coke bottle. Fool that I was, I told her she could owe me the money for her bodacious bill. Of course I never saw a penny of it. Since then I've been wary of Greeks bearing gifts. Minnesotans too.

"Go ahead, take it," Scott directed. He was tall, broad shouldered, and the picture of mature health. To resist a directive from him would be contrary to nature—well, mine at least.

I took the present reluctantly. "You're still paying in full, you know."

Scott's teeth were as white as his wife's. "Of course. Now open it."

I shook it. Nothing rattled. Nothing yelped. They were both good signs.

"Bet you can't guess what it is."

"Yes, make her guess," Dixie said.

I sighed. I hadn't the foggiest idea, and I hate guessing games. Aaron tried to make me play one on our wedding night, and I was nearly traumatized for life. Who knew that something so little . . .

"A tin of SPAM® luncheon meat," I said off the top of my head.

Their handsome faces fell. "How did you know?"

"I didn't—you mean it *is*?"

Noble heads nodded.

I ripped off the silk bow, and the heavy, embossed paper. "It *is* SPAM®!"

Dixie looked particularly crestfallen. "You've had it before?"

"When I was a child. I love the stuff, but I haven't eaten it in years. Thank you very much."

"We're particularly fond of it in Minnesota," Scott said. "There must be ten thousand ways to fix it. Go ahead, Dixie, tell her some of our favorites."

"That's ten thousand lakes, dear," Dixie said gently. "There are a million ways to fix SPAM®."

I was still wary. "I'm sure there are dear, but do you always give tins of food to your hotel hostess?"

Dixie blushed. "Well, you see, Scott is on a low-fat diet, and this is SPAM® Lite."

"So?"

"So, I heard that Amish and Mennonite cooking is—uh—how should I say this—uh—"

"Spit it out, dear."

"Heavy."

She had heard right. We are a people of the soil, farmers by tradition, and have developed the highly caloric cuisine needed to fuel intense physical labor.

"You could have asked for a low-fat diet," I snapped. "You didn't need to beat around the bush." Although frankly, as long as Freni wielded the ladle, they would be lucky to get the occasional overcooked vegetable.

"Sorry about this," Scott said. "It was my idea."

"I'll give this to the cook, dears," I said graciously. It was time to move on. "Say, there's another guest staying here who hails from the land of ten thousand lakes. Maybe you know him."

Yeah, right—like I know everyone in Pennsylvania. Still, it was possible for two acquaintances to meet unexpectedly in another state, especially if they were both from Minnesota. I mean, with that much water, how many people could there be?

"Oh?" Apparently Scott Montgomery didn't think it was such a silly comment.

"His name is John Burk. He's from a little town in western Minnesota on the Canadian border called New Bedford."

Scott shook his head.

"About your age, a bit taller than me, and almost bald?"

"I mean I've never heard of the town. I'm from Noyes, and you can't get any closer to the Canadian border than that."

"Well, that's what he said. I remember, because we have a Bedford in Pennsylvania. In fact, you probably saw the signs for it on the turnpike."

"We did," Doris said. She yawned, and then quite unexpectedly stretched. Her fingers almost touched my nine-foot ceilings. "Excuse me. We had to get up real early to catch our flight. Is the room made up now?"

"Indeed it is. But your group leader—I mean, Bob Hart—did explain that you will be on the A.L.P.O. plan, didn't he?"

Two gorgeous sets of teeth presented themselves for my inspection. "He did indeed," Scott said. "Dixie and I think it will be fun."

"Loads," Dixie said, and yawned again.

I thanked them again for the SPAM® Lite.

I would have opened the SPAM® Lite right there in the lobby, sliced off a piece with my letter opener, and had myself a nice midmorning snack had not the frost been on the pumpkin—well, in a manner of speaking. Allow me to explain.

You see, I have a pumpkin-shaped doormat that was a Christmas present from Susannah. I don't do kitsch, and I would have thrown the pumpkin rug out, along with the ceramic geese with the bows tied around their necks, had they not been the very first Christmas presents my sister ever gave me. And also the last. At any rate, I was just fitting that cute little key over the metal tab when I heard a loud thump against the front door and felt the ground shake. Having just recently survived a tornado, and in the not-too-distant past a fiery outhouse, an earthquake seemed like the next logical calamity. It was getting to be more than I could bear.

"Oh Lord, take me now!" I begged.

Alas, no welcoming angel appeared, but a second thud rattled the panes in the lobby window.

"Not the *other* place," I wailed. "Yes, I stole Granny Yoder's scented soap, but it was just a sliver, and I was five years old. And what happened that time I sat on the washing machine during spin cycle was purely an accident. But I'm sorry for both of these things!"

The building shuddered and shimmied a third time, causing the coach-style lamp above my head to swing like a metronome.

"I said I was sorry! I'll donate a dozen bars of lavender soap to the Mennonite Home for the Aged. I can't get rid of my washing machine, Lord, but I'll throw away most of my vacuum attachments."

Mercifully my prayer was answered. The inn settled back on its foundation and all was well with the world. I breathed a quick prayer of thanksgiving.

But before I could even say amen I heard a distinct moan coming from the front porch. No doubt it was the devil himself come to get me.

"All right, you can have the washing machine!" I wailed.

There was one final thud. "Oh, shoot!" my supernatural visitor said.

I cocked my head. The devil I learned about in church, and the one I taught about in Sunday school, was most likely to use stronger language.

"Who's there?" I called.

"It's me, Marjorie Frost."

First I locked the door, and then I peered timorously through the peephole. It looked like the cargo hold of an airplane had dropped its load of baggage on my walk and porch, but I didn't see any living creatures. Certainly not the Prince of Darkness.

I unlocked the door, and using my shoulder as a defensive brace, cautiously opened it a few inches. That's when I saw Marjorie Frost, sprawled across the pumpkin rug, like a newborn colt who had yet to find its legs.

She looked up at me, grinned foolishly, and got awkwardly to her feet. "Sorry about that. I've always been a klutz. My husband says I'd be better off with just one leg—then I wouldn't accidentally trip myself." She held out a hand. "My name's Marjorie Frost."

"Just a minute, dear." I looked up at the sky, where one wispy cloud was floating overhead. "This wasn't an earthquake, so what I said before doesn't count! But just so you know I meant what I said, I'll look for soap on sale in Wednesday's paper."

"Is there someone on the roof?" Marjorie had a pleasant, eager-sounding voice.

"In a matter of speaking. I'm Magdalena Yoder, but if it's all the same to you, dear, I'd rather not shake hands. It's the most effective way there is to pass colds along, you know."

She looked confused, but thankfully did not insist on pressing the flesh.

"If you're looking to book a room, dear, I'm afraid you're out of luck. We're full up."

"Oh, but I'm sure we have reservations. We're here for the reunion of World War II tank drivers."

I examined her more closely. She was of only medium

height, but big boned, and with long legs. She reminded me of a foal I'd seen just the day before. Both had chestnut brown hair, but Marjorie's was shoulder length, and her hazel eyes peered earnestly out from a face as soft and smooth as gardenia petals. Despite what she had just said, the girl couldn't have been a day over eighteen. I had bunions older than she.

"Then you must be the Frosts' granddaughter. They're the last couple to show up, but nothing was said to me about you. I'm afraid you're going to have to bunk with them on a cot, and/or find a room in town. And by that, I mean Bedford. Back up by the turnpike."

Marjorie bit her lower lip. "I was afraid this was going to happen. I told Frank—well, never mind. The truth is, Miss Yoder, I'm not Frank's granddaughter; I'm his wife."

"Get out of town! How old is your husband?"

She winced. "Seventy-six, but he's in very good shape."

"How old are you, dear?"

"Thirty-two."

"In a pig's eye," I said kindly.

She glanced down and studied Susannah's pumpkin. "Okay, so I'm twenty-four. But I'm mature for my age, and Frank has always been young at heart."

"Is he rich?"

Her head jerked up. "I beg your pardon?"

"Of course he is. What a silly question for me to ask."

"Miss Yoder—"

I held up a quieting hand. "I have yet to see a girl your age attached to a *poor* man in his dotage."

She gasped. "Frank is hardly in his dotage!"

"Don't feel embarrassed, dear, I've seen it a hundred times. It happens the other way around, too. You may not read about it much in the papers, but take it from me, Cher has had her share of boy-toys." I smiled brightly and waved at the jumble of suitcases. "Are all these yours?"

"Oh, yes. Well, there's a few more small things in the car. But we won't need them until later."

I scanned the small parking lot. There was my red BMW, and three other cars. Since neither Susannah nor Freni drives a car, that left one vehicle unaccounted for—presuming the couple hadn't been so foolish as to hire a cab to bring them out from Pittsburgh.

"Where is your car, dear?"

She colored. "Uh—er—we forgot something. Frank had to run back into town."

"To a pharmacy?"

Her color deepened.

"Just remember, you break it, you pay for it, dear." I've had two bedsteads broken by amorous couples, and one downed chandelier.

She studied the pumpkin again.

"Well, come on in, dear," I said. "If we stand out here any longer you'll turn twenty-five." I chuckled pleasantly.

"Is there a bellhop?" she asked tentatively.

While I might be willing to schlep a few bags up my impossibly steep stairs, I was not about to move a mountain of baggage—no, make that a mountain *range* of luggage. It may have been just the shadow of the passing cloud, but I'm positive I saw a Sherpa wearing an oxygen tank disappear over the rim of one of the higher piles. I mean, why should I risk my back when the coowner of all these suitcases was younger than my hairnet?

"You get to be the bellhop," I said cheerily, "and it will only cost you fifty dollars extra."

The hazel eyes blinked.

"Oh, don't worry, I'm sure Daddy Warbucks will pay for everything."

Okay, so that was mean of me. I had no reason to pick on her, other than jealousy. Would that I had married a rich man when I was young and of breeding age!

Just so you know, I paid mightily for my callousness. The nicks and scratches on my floor, doors, and walls cost hundreds of dollars to repair. A troop of chimpanzees could have done a better job of schlepping bags upstairs, and at least *they* wouldn't have gotten lipstick on the stairs carpet.

"Ach!" Freni clapped her hands together. "This SPAM® Lite luncheon meat is wonderful! Are you sure the English invented it?"

To Freni, anyone not currently of the faith—and sometimes, depending on her mood, that includes me—is "English." It doesn't matter if you were born in an igloo, or happen to be a tribal chieftain in Botswana. If you're not a practicing Amish person, you're "English." I only barely qualify as "non-English" because I have four hundred years of Amish and Amish-Mennonite forbears, and am still a practicing Mennonite. But even in Freni's eyes, I'm definitely fancy. I drive a car, after all, use electricity, and once during a shameful period of rebellion wore clear lipstick.

"Yeah, I'm sure that SPAM® Lite is an English invention. But hey, Freni, thanks for coming in today. I really appreciate it, what with a full house and Susannah getting married on top of it all."

Freni's dark eyes blinked behind her thick lenses. "Susannah is getting married?"

"Didn't she tell you?"

Freni shook her head. "Who to this time?"

Despite the fact that my sister has threatened marriage on numerous occasions, she has actually been married only once. The man was a Presbyterian, which is just about as "fancy" and "English" as you can get around here. Predictably, the marriage ended in divorce—not because of the Presbyterian's progressive ways, but because Susannah was too fancy for *him*. At any rate, divorce is not an option to the Amish, and as for remarriage—well, Susannah might as well apply to have her name legally changed to the Whore of Babylon.

I looked away from Freni. "She's marrying Melvin Stoltzfus."

"Ach!" Freni threw herself on to the nearest kitchen chair. "Elvina's son?"

"I'm afraid that's the one."

"Does Elvina know this?" Although no longer Amish, but a mere Mennonite, Elvina is Freni's best friend. They grew up together—"shared the same cradle," so they claim.

I nodded, still not daring to look.

"When is this so-called wedding?"

"Wednesday morning at ten."

"Where?"

I turned slowly and squinted at Freni through my fingers. If she was in for a coronary, someone needed to know.

"At Elvina's."

"Ach du Leiber!"

That was it. Freni didn't clasp her chest, lapse into unconsciousness, or even foam at the mouth. She sat as still as Lot's wife might have sat, had she not been standing at the moment of salinization.

I lowered my hands and took a timorous step toward her. "Freni? Are you all right?"

Her shoulders shook under the capelike flanges of her apron. Since I believed that neither of us was genetically capable of weeping in public, it took me a moment to figure out that this was indeed what she was doing. I looked away again, lest *I* be turned into a pillar of salt.

"Freni, dear, Susannah's soul is not your responsibility. Mama and Papa left her in my care."

Much to my horror she turned a tear-streaked face in my direction. "Ach, it isn't her soul! That's between her and God."

I jiggled a pinkie in my left ear to make sure I was hearing right. Either that wax problem was back, or the magazines I saw at the supermarket were right—creatures from outer space did exist. But I had yet to read of an extraterrestrial posing as an elderly Amish woman.

"Run that by me again, dear," I said calmly.

"I said that Susannah's soul is not my business."

"Quick, name all fifty states, and give me their capitals!"

"Ach, you're talking nonsense, Magdalena, and me with my pain!"

"What pain is that, dear? Your bunions acting up again?"

"The pain in my heart," Freni wailed. "Susannah didn't invite me!"

I jiggled pinkies in both ears. "You *want* to go?"

"I've known Susannah since the day she was born! I knew your mother since the day she was born! Of course I want to be there."

"Who were the fifth and sixth presidents of the United States?"

"Ach, Magdalena, more games at a time like this?"

"Either you name them, buster, or I'm kicking you all the way back to your home planet." Okay, so that remark set generations of pacifist ancestors spinning in their graves, but how would they feel about a Martian in Amish drag?

Freni's eyes grew round behind her specs. "Thomas Jefferson and James Madison, in that order. Are you satisfied now?"

I had to take her word for it. Between John Adams and Dwight D. Eisenhower, my presidential file is blank. Yes, I know Lincoln and a couple of Roosevelts were somewhere between those two—and a Truman, I think, but I can't name anyone sequentially. And I went to college, whereas Freni only graduated from the eighth grade.

"Okay, you pass." I wiped my pinkie tips on my skirt. "Look dear, I'm sure Susannah is planning to invite you. I only found out about it yesterday."

Freni removed her glasses and wiped her eyes with a corner of her apron. Funny, but without her glasses she looked ten years older. No doubt the thick lenses hid her wrinkles.

"And Elvina," she sniffed. "That hurts me too. Why didn't she tell me? We're supposed to be best friends."

"Maybe she was afraid to."

"Afraid?"

"More like embarrassed. I mean on account of it's Susannah's second wedding, and Melvin is—well—"

"An ox short of a plow team?"

I stared at her. She seemed to be staring, only half-seeing, back at me. We burst into laughter simultaneously. We didn't laugh for very long, of course, seeing as how we are both wary of intimacy.

"So what do you think of this group of English?" I asked when it was time for us to stop laughing. "They're not like that Hollywood crowd, are they?"

"Yah, not the same." Freni sighed. No doubt she was thinking of Mel Gibson. She had never been to a movie, never even watched television, so she had no idea her precious Mel has been a killer on screen.

Leaving well enough alone seems like a waste of potential to me. "Did you know that in the movie *Braveheart* your precious Mel hacked people to death with a sword?"

"So did Moses and Joshua," Freni said, without batting an eye.

I can stop and turn on a dime, if that means I get to pick it up. "Exactly, dear. So the fact that our guests may have blown a few German tanks into oblivion is no big deal, right?"

"Ach!" She looked like Miss Muffet when she realized that not only was a there a spider beside her, but there had *been* one in her whey as well.

"Give me a break, Freni. It's hard to imagine these gray-haired men as killers, isn't it?"

She nodded reluctantly. "Yah, they're just old, like

me. But they're very strange, Magdalena. Maybe they're spies."

"Spies?"

"Did you know they locked themselves in the parlor this morning?"

"I gave them permission to use it, Freni. It's their conference room."

"But they wouldn't even come out for lunch. I had to leave a tray outside the door!"

Confidentially, that hiked my hackles as well. I'd had to run into Bedford to do some banking and had grabbed a bite there. But normally I eat with my guests, and the meals are at fixed times.

"They'll come out for dinner," I growled. "And they'll be there on time, or they'll do without."

Freni smiled approvingly. Our ancestors are Swiss, after all. We eat on time, we sleep on time, we even go to the bathroom on time. It was the good Lord who invented schedules when He created the world in six days, and it is our Christian duty to follow his example.

"You go, girl," she said, demonstrating that I had hosted one too many Hollywood guests. "But I need you to do me a favor, Magdalena."

I frowned. "I will *not* talk Barbara into giving her triplets up for adoption. You're too old to be their mother. I thought I made that perfectly clear the last time you brought it up."

My kinswoman colored. "Ach, not that! I just need you to run to the market for me. I decided to serve this SPAM® luncheon meat for dinner."

"But I just came back from town," I wailed. "Why didn't you tell me earlier?"

"I hadn't tasted it then, that's why. So, what do you want—fried calves liver or SPAM® Jambalaya?"

That was a no-brainer, as Susannah is fond of saying. I high-tailed it off to Hernia in search of SPAM®.

Five

SPAM® Jambalaya

♦

1 (12-ounce) can SPAM® Lite luncheon meat, cubed
1 cup chopped onion
2/3 cup chopped green bell pepper
½ cup chopped celery
2 cloves garlic, minced
1 (14½-ounce) can tomatoes, cut up
1 (10¾-ounce) can lower-sodium chicken broth
½ teaspoon dried leaf thyme
6 to 8 drops hot pepper sauce
1 bay leaf
1 cup long-grain rice
2 tablespoons chopped parsley

In large nonstick skillet or 3-quart nonstick saucepan, saute SPAM®, onion, green pepper, celery, and garlic until vegetables are tender. Add tomatoes, chicken broth, thyme, hot pepper sauce, and bay leaf. Bring to a boil; stir in rice. Cover. Reduce heat and simmer 20 minutes or until rice is tender. Discard bay leaf. Sprinkle with parsley. Serves 6.

NUTRITIONAL INFORMATION PER SERVING:
Calories 261; Protein 13g; Carbohydrate 32g; Fat 8g, Cholesterol 45mg; Sodium 850mg.

Six

Before high-tailing it into town I did the polite thing and checked on my guests in the parlor. Okay, so I didn't knock, but what's the big deal? It is my inn, after all.

"You gentlemen need anything?" I asked graciously.

Four elderly men stared at me, their expressions every bit as frozen as the figures on Mt. Rushmore.

"You know, pencils, paper, breath mints"—I looked pointedly at Scott Montgomery—"low-fat snacks."

The men said nothing.

I smiled. "Well, how about some gun powder? Maybe a few sticks of dynamite?"

Bob Hart stood slowly. "Beg your pardon, ma'am?"

"For your conspiracy."

"Excuse me?"

"Well, aren't you trying to overthrow the government? I mean, this isn't your average army reunion. You've got to admit that. Even I know that you're supposed to be singing war songs and swapping stories of courage under fire. But it's quiet as a tomb in here." Then I noticed that the shades were pulled. "And dark as a tomb, too. Well, I can easily fix that."

Scott stood, which put him shoulder to head with Bob. "Thanks, Miss Yoder, but we like it like this."

"No problem, really."

I started toward the nearest window, but Bob, moving with surprising adroitness, blocked my way.

"With all due respect, ma'am. This *is* the way we like it."

"Nonsense. You'll strain your eyes."

"Ma'am, you said we could have complete privacy."

"Oh, all right," I wailed, "but if you pass out secret decoder rings, I want one!"

"We've got you on the list, ma'am."

"And a secret spy name too."

"Yes, ma'am," Bob said. "We'll keep that in mind." He didn't seem to be kidding.

It was time to get my tail out of there and into town.

Yoder's Corner Market is the only place in Hernia one can buy comestibles intended for the human palate—which is not to say that all the food sold there is palatable. Sam Yoder has been known to sell iceberg lettuce so old a well-aimed head could sink the *Titanic*. And his prices are sky high. Normally I eschew the place and do my shopping in Bedford. But there are those isolated occasions when I prefer to drive two miles instead of twelve, and to be perfectly frank, feel a need to catch up on local news. Don't get me wrong, it is a sin to gossip, but as a pillar of the community, it is my duty to keep informed. How else am I supposed to pass an informed judgment, never mind set a better example?

Samuel Nevin Yoder is my father's first cousin once removed, but he never gives me any sort of discount. In fact, he won't even honor my coupons. That's because

Sam likes me, you see. Ever since we were in third grade together, and I purposely pinched his pinkie with my three-ring binder, Sam has had a thing for me. The day after I damaged his digit Sam smeared peanut butter in my braids. I retaliated by kissing him, and we have been at war ever since. Sam's biggest victory was when he married Dorothy Gillman from New York State. She was a Methodist, for crying out loud, and Sam twisted that knife he'd plunged when he converted to her faith. I would like to think my ill-fated marriage to Aaron paid him back in spades, but on the eve of my wedding Sam sent me a bottle of alcohol-free Champagne. When my Pooky Bear ditched me in favor of his legal spouse in Minnesota, Sam asked that I return the bottle. Alas, those are hardly the actions of a man still pining for my love.

But back to my mission. I was in luck. Sam had eight tins of regular SPAM® luncheon meat and seven of SPAM® Lite, all neatly stacked next to the albacore tuna. I put fifteen cans in my basket, and then had a change of heart and returned two of the regular cans. I mean, why deprive others of the joy of SPAM®?

I watched carefully as Sam rang up the SPAM®. The man has been known to overcharge me. Perhaps I was looking especially fine that morning, or Sam had had a squabble with Dorothy, because not only did he charge me the correct price, he slipped a York peppermint pattie and a bag of Reese's Pieces into my grocery bag along with the meat. I pretended not to notice.

"So what's new?" I asked breezily. Our little war does not prevent the exchange of information, and Sam likes to dish the dis as much as folks like hearing it.

"Drusilla Stucky had a bunion removed last week."

"That's old news, dear. She asked us to pray for her in church Sunday. The way she carried on, you would have thought she'd stepped on a land mine. Those Stuckys have always been sissies, if you ask me."

"My mother was a Stucky."

I gulped. "Yes, but only on her father's side. Anything else?"

"Harriet Blough's nail fungus finally cleared up. Apparently she'd been soaking her toes in some sort of herbal tea. The new growth is pink and as shiny as tiddlywinks."

"That's nice, dear." I meant it. Harriet took her shoes and socks off once at a church picnic and three people threw up, myself included. "Any news that is not foot related?"

Sam scratched his head. It is not nearly as handsome a head as Aaron's, but it sports a passable amount of hair, and the infamous Yoder nose has been tamed in this instance by the Schrock blood.

"Peter Schwartzentruber passed a kidney stone last night."

"Well, at least we're moving on up!"

"Tobias Gindlesperger bought electric milkers for his Holsteins."

"You don't say!" The truth is, I already knew that the Gindlespergers, an Amish family, had run an electric line out to their barn. According to Freni, the Gindlespergers were on the threshold of leaving the Amish community and joining us Mennonites. Apparently that threshold had just been crossed.

"Now it's your turn."

"What?"

Sam winked. "Don't you have any news for me?"

I thought hard. As a Methodist, Sam lives almost entirely in the world, and as a consequence watches a good many movies. He even owns a large-screen TV. Back in the days when I played Hostess to Hollywood, Sam had displayed a strong interest in the personal habits of celebrities. Brands of deodorants used on famous underarms seemed to hold a particular fascination for him.

"There's nobody famous out at the inn," I wailed. "Just a bunch of World War II veterans and their wives."

Sam wrinkled his nose, which, although tamed, was still considerable. "Military. And you call yourself a pacifist."

"They're old men now! And besides, they're not all vets. There's a retired history professor and his wife."

Sam had the audacity to reach into my shopping bag and withdraw the Reese's Pieces.

"Susannah's getting married," I said quickly before he could get my pattie.

"I know."

"What? Who told you?"

Before Sam could answer, two Amish women wheeled their shopping buggies to the checkout counter. They may have been wearing bonnets, but you can be sure their ears were straining against the stiff black fabric. I stepped adroitly aside with my tins of SPAM® and remaining candy.

As soon as the door whooshed shut behind them I was on Sam like white on rice. I mean that metaphorically, of course. I did not, as he once claimed, have him by the throat.

I plunked the bag of SPAM® on the counter. "Who told you?"

"Melvin himself."

"What? When?"

"You should have heard him, Magdalena. He was in here, not an hour ago, crowing like a cock with a flock of hens all to himself. Said the 'to-do' was going to be at his mama's on account you were too stingy to spring for it."

"Why, that miserable mantis! Just wait until I get my mitts on his carapace."

"I hope you don't mind that he invited me and Dorothy. After all, I'm giving him a twenty per cent discount on the soda pop they'll be serving at the party."

"*Party!* What party?"

"The one Zelda is throwing them tomorrow night. Of course Zelda doesn't make that much money, so Melvin's pitching in."

"Nobody told me about a party!"

"Well, I just assumed—I mean, Susannah is your sister."

I burst into tears.

Sam stared. I don't believe I as much as shed a tear the time he smeared the peanut butter in my hair—even though when I got home Mama spanked me with a hairbrush for wasting food. At any rate, there didn't seem to be anyone else in the market—or if there was, they were hiding in the dry goods aisle—so while Sam looked on, I let it all out. I bawled, I wailed, I gnashed my teeth. I complained bitterly about the inequities of life, the fickleness of fortune, and the burden of loving a sister as thankless as Susannah. When I was quite through I wiped my eyes on my sleeve, blew my nose on the hanky I keep in my bra, and squared my shoulders.

"Well, dear, I'll see you at the wedding."

"You mean the party, don't you?"

"*I* haven't been invited, remember?"

"Magdalena, please don't take this out on Susannah. The whole thing was Melvin's idea, after all."

I reached for my shopping bag, but he was quicker and snatched it away. "I'll tell you some real gossip if you promise to take it easy on your sister."

"No deal."

"It's really juicy."

"Martha Lichty lose her dentures in the outhouse again?"

He laughed. "Better than that. So, you promise?"

I nodded reluctantly, my fingers crossed behind my back. I hate having to lie, but it is foolish to trade one's word for something sight unseen. Besides, taking things out on Susannah is a skill I've honed through the years, and it has always been in her best interest. And anyway, doesn't the Bible warn us not to hide our talents?

"This better be good," I growled.

Sam leaned over the counter and cupped his free hand to his mouth. "Lodema Schrock dyes her hair."

I gasped. "She does not!"

Lodema Schrock is my pastor's wife. She is a one-woman vigilante team obsessed with monitoring the morals of her husband's flock. Rumor has it that she studied at the feet of the Ayatollah. I know for a fact that Lodema eyeballs our hem lengths, inspects our nails for polish, and lifts telltale lipstick stains from coffee cups in the social hall at church. Reliable witnesses tell me that the woman peeks into bedroom windows and rummages through our rubbish. When one of us is found wanting—and there is always a "victim of the week"—Lodema appears on the unfortunate person's porch with Bible in hand and a lengthy lecture in mind.

I must hasten to add that Reverend Schrock does not condone his wife's behavior, although, alas, he is powerless to stop her. The poor man doesn't even know who her victims are in advance. To his credit, however, he has organized the Mennonite Women's Sewing Circle into what he calls "the Lodema alert." As soon as she leaves the parsonage on her righteous warpath, he calls one of us, and we in turn spread the word. Anyone with anything to hide does so, and by a series of phone calls, we are usually able to track her well enough to predict her final destination. The real sinner then high-tails it out of town for the day.

Sam was nodding vigorously.

"She *really* dyes her hair?"

"She comes in here religiously—no pun intended—and buys Lady Marion hair color, formula number twelve. Peach Bark, it's called."

"Thank you, Lord!" I said, my hands clasped together, my eyes tightly closed. One should always give thanks, should one not?

Sam laughed. "Magdalena, what are you going to do with this information?"

I opened my eyes. "File it, dear. One never knows how and when it might come in very useful."

"Glad to be of service. Now, are you going to take it easy on Susannah?"

"As easy as threading a needle in the dark, dear." I snatched the precious bag of luncheon meat out of Sam's hand, and was out the door and in my car in the time it takes a cat to yawn. I may be tall and gangly, but I sure can run.

"Ach, there you are!"

"Please, Freni, not now." I thrust the heavy bag at her.

"But she's been crying, that one."

"It's just pre-wedding jitters, dear." Although frankly, Susannah had nothing to be jittery about—if you know what I mean. I, on the other hand, was terrified on my wedding night. I was even more terrified the morning after, when I suddenly realized *it* was not just a one-time thing.

"Ach, not Susannah! The little one from Pittsburgh."

I shook my head to clear it of sane thoughts. "You mean Samantha Burk?"

"Yah, that's the one."

As if on cue the diminutive pianist pushed through the swinging door from the dining room. Then again, as small as she was, she may have been pushing on it for some time.

"Miss Yoder, you're back!"

"Either that, or I have a twin sister who is a ventriloquist."

Freni gave me a warning frown and then scuttled over to the stove where a pot was merrily boiling over.

"Sorry, dear. Sometimes my tongue gets in the way of my brain. What can I do for you?"

"I need to talk to you."

I motioned Samantha to a high wooden stool, while I took a ladderback chair. When we were eye to eye for the first time I could see that Freni was right; the woman had been weeping.

"I'm all ears, dear."

Samantha looked down at petite, but exquisite hands. "John is missing."

"Have you checked the barn, dear? A lot of guests find my cows fascinating."

She shook her head. "Our car is gone."

"There you have it, dear. He's gone for a ride in the country."

"Miss Yoder, I'm afraid you don't understand. We had a fight."

I glanced over at Freni, who was quietly stirring the air above the bubbling pot. If her ears got any bigger, she could loan them to Prince Charles.

"All married couples have their little tiffs, dear," I said, finally able to speak from experience. "I'm sure he'll be back before supper."

She shook her head again, this time more vigorously. "John has a hot temper, but he cools off quickly. We were arguing about—well, it was something trivial—and he stormed out with the car keys. He does that a lot, you know. But he always comes back ten or twenty minutes later and apologizes."

"So how long has he been gone this time?"

She glanced at her watch. "Almost an hour and a half."

"Count your blessings, dear." I clamped a hand over my mouth, and counted to ten before removing it. "What I mean is, the people around here are very friendly, and everyone knows who I am. If he's lost, he just has to mention my name, or the inn, and folks will point the way back."

"John never gets lost."

"Honey, men are born lost. They don't know which

way is up without stopping to ask for directions—which, of course, they refuse to do. That's why God gave them each an arrow that points to the ground."

She smiled weakly. "John seldom even makes it out of the drive when he storms off like that. Usually he just sits there and pounds on the steering wheel until he's got it cleared out of his system."

There was no need to ask her what the *it* was that needed clearing out. It was hot air, of course, a curious byproduct of the male thought process. Aaron was forever clearing out his system, too, only he blamed it on beans.

"Would you like me to drive around and look for him? You could come with me, of course."

"That would be very nice, but shouldn't we call the police first?"

I rolled my eyes discreetly behind partially closed lids. "You'll have to wait forty-eight hours to file a missing-person report, unless you have evidence to support foul play. Besides, he probably just stopped to pick you some wildflowers."

"Ach," Freni muttered, "it's too early for anything but dandelions."

I glared at my kinswoman. "There are lilacs blooming down by Slave Creek. I saw them myself just a few minutes ago."

"Did you see a blue Saturn in the area?"

"No. Sorry." Frankly, since I bought my red BMW last year, I haven't noticed any other cars. "The Devil's carriage," as Freni calls it, was Aaron's idea—his only good idea, outside of jacking up my room prices again.

Samantha quickly wiped away an escaping tear. "I'd

like to ride with you, Miss Yoder. Can we get started right away?"

"As soon as I make a necessary pit stop, dear."

Being the true Yoder that I am, we were out on the road in thirty seconds flat.

Seven

I tried to distract Samantha with a running commentary on the community.

"That's Sam and Amanda Berkey's farm. Well, she's dead now. Her father was the Amish bishop in his day—the land used to be his. There's an old grist mill back in the woods that supplied all of Bedford County in the early 1800s."

"Really?" She sounded every bit as interested as Susannah does when I recount the Sunday sermon for her.

"Now over there on your right is what remains of the Mishler farm. The Mishler brothers both outlived their wives, retired to the family homestead, and then began selling bits and pieces off, a few acres at a time. Both men are just as sweet as shoo-fly pie, but you'll want to stay well away during hunting season. They're blind as bats, you see, but they insist on hunting. They shoot at anything that moves—or moos." I chuckled pleasantly.

"You don't say."

"See that bit of pink roof through the trees?"

She nodded absently.

"That's the Williams' house. They bought a couple of acres from the Mishler brothers a couple of years back. Dinky and Flora Williams are urban refugees from Philadelphia. They're both nudists, if you can believe that. Of course they're English—I mean, they're not related to me in any way.

"And that's Irma Yoder's house over there. She's a Mennonite widow woman, one hundred and two, believe it or not, and she lives by herself. But she's far from helpless, I assure you. Physically she's as strong as an ox, and has a tongue that can cut cheese."

"How interesting."

"Just up ahead there, on the left, is Hernia's newest subdivision. Norah and Ed Hall live there. They're English, too. Methodist, I think. Norah thinks she's better than the rest of us because her daughter Sherri got picked to be in a margarine commercial. I haven't seen it—because I don't watch television—but from what I hear, little Sherri is dressed up to look like a tub of low-fat spread. Supposedly Norah got real upset when she learned the country wasn't even going to see her daughter's face on TV." I glanced over my shoulder, and not seeing my guardian angel, continued. "The truth is, little Sherri is not all that little and looks pretty much the same, in or out of her margarine tub costume."

"Uh-huh."

"You've seen the commercial?"

"Miss Yoder, please. How far is it to the river?"

"Slave Creek, and it's only another half a mile."

We rode in silence until we got to the creek, which really isn't much to look at, aside from its charming stone bridge. On the south side of the road was a single lilac bush planted in honor of Gloria Schuyler, Hernia's first female mayor. Gloria has since left our fair town to seek her fortune in Pittsburgh. Last I heard she was living up to her potential, working in a ceramics factory that specialized in salt and pepper shakers. At any rate, just as I said, there were several clusters of scented blooms on the spindly shrub. There was, however, no blue Saturn.

"Maybe we just missed him." Samantha's tone barely bordered on the accusatory. She was a classy lady, after all.

"Maybe, but this is the only road from my place to here. We didn't pass a blue Saturn, did we?"

She sighed. "No. I'm just worried, that's all. Like I said before, this isn't like him."

"People change."

"What do you mean by that?"

"Well, uh—take me, for instance. I used to be really opinionated and headstrong. Some folks even called me grumpy, hard to get along with. But all that's changed in the last year, thanks to my bogus marriage and subsequent breakup. Since then I've been a far more compassionate person."

She cocked her tiny head, indicating interest, so I obligingly pulled alongside the lilac and turned off the engine.

"I married a very handsome, charming man who just happened to be a bigamist."

"Oh, my!"

I smiled bravely. "Barely a month after our marriage he sprang the bad news on me. He did it over the phone, no less. At any rate, I thought my heart would break—maybe it did. Maybe when the two halves grew back together, a new Magdalena was formed."

"Miss Yoder, do you mind if I smoke? I know you have a no-smoking rule at the inn, and I usually don't smoke anyway, but I find that when I'm really upset . . ." She fumbled in her purse.

"Light up and die, toots."

"I know smoking causes cancer, but like I said, I very seldom do it."

"I didn't mean the cigarettes would kill you, dear. *No* one smokes in this car, not even my sister Susannah."

She stopped fumbling. "Very well, I can do without. But I want you to know, Miss Yoder, that my husband is not cheating on me. And John is definitely not a bigamist."

I suppressed a sigh of pity. "Appearances can be deceiving, dear. I don't mean to scare you, but there is a potential bigamist lurking in every woman's bush."

"John has no interest in other women."

"You mean—?"

"He has no interest in sex, period. I don't know why I'm telling you this, but John lost interest as soon as we were married. Not just in sex, but in me as a person. I'm not even sure that he loves me anymore."

I restrained myself from asking if John had an available twin brother. It would be nice if a man loved me, of course, but the horizontal mambo, as Susannah so crudely calls it, is strictly for the birds.

"How long have you been married?"

"Forty-nine years."

"Wow. Any children?"

She smiled. "No children. I met John at a New Year's Eve party, and we were married on Valentine's Day. He was already teaching at Duquesne, and I was headed for New York to do an engagement at Carnegie Hall. We've been busy ever since with our own lives—children never even were considered. Not in the beginning. Then my

72

arthritis started acting up, and John was forced to retire and—well, it's now that we regret not having a family. People like us sort of deserve the lives we've built for ourselves, don't we?"

My face stung. I am not childless by choice. I would love to have married and had a child—a house full of children, for that matter—but that just wasn't in God's plan. I couldn't very well have a child outside the bounds of holy matrimony, now could I? And until very recently—here in Hernia, at least—if a single woman adopted a child, she'd have the morals police down on her faster than a hen on a June bug. Boy, would Lodema Schrock ever love to get her meddling mitts on a woman that foolish!

"I would have loved to have been a mother," I croaked.

"Oh, Miss Yoder, I didn't mean you. Honest, I didn't."

She seemed so genuinely distressed at my distress, that I decided to forgive her. Of course she needed to be taught a mild lesson first.

"That's all right, dear. Now tell me something. If you and John are trapped in this loveless, sexless marriage— well, why don't you just get a divorce? Not that I approve of divorce, you understand. But it does seem to be the thing to do these days."

It was my turn to feel like a worm. The poor dear looked as pitiful as Susannah did the day I told her Santa Claus didn't really exist. Trust me, due to that one slip of my tongue, last Christmas was downright miserable.

"But I can't divorce John! If I did, I'd be all alone."

"Don't you have other family?"

"I'm an only child, and my parents are dead."

"Cousins?" I asked hopefully. Surely everyone has a

cousin somewhere, don't they? Of course with me being my own cousin, it's something I'd never thought about.

She shook her head. "Everyone's dead now."

"Friends?"

"My concert schedule kept me on the road too much. You see, Miss Yoder, that's why I *need* John. That's why I must find him." She fumbled in her purse again, saw my stern look, and thought better of it. "And John needs me too."

I nodded, although between you and me, I was beginning to doubt that men needed anything that couldn't be bought at Walmart. "I'm sure he does, dear."

"You don't believe me, do you? Well, it's true. I'm all that John has as well. His family is gone too, and he's always found it hard to make friends."

"Even at work? In the history department?"

"Even there. He's never had what you might call a zingy personality. But he was more fun to be with when he was young."

I said nothing. The scars on my tongue prove it.

"Really, he was. He made me laugh sometimes."

"If you say so, dear."

She said nothing for several minutes.

"Well," I said at last, "we could drive around some more—maybe head over toward Bedford. Maybe he's at Walmart."

"Let's go back to the inn," she said quietly. "I'll wait for him there."

I put my sanity on the line and called my sister's fiancé, Melvin Stoltzfus. I used my private line, which can only be accessed from my bedroom.

"Hernia police," a cheery voice said. It clearly did not belong to Melvin.

My sigh of relief rustled the leaves in downtown Pittsburgh. "Zelda, dear, this is Magdalena. I need some help locating the whereabouts of one of my guests."

"Have you lost someone again, Magdalena?"

"No, and I didn't *lose* my fifth-grade Sunday-school class. They put sleeping pills in my coffee and sneaked out through the window. And it's not my fault—I told Reverend Schrock to put bars on it!"

"Oh. Well, who is missing this time?"

"A guest of mine. Dr. John Burk. Actually, he's not a *real* doctor—he's a fud."

"What did you say?"

"He's a Ph.D., dear."

"Oh. Well, how long has this fud been missing?"

"Uh—well, only a couple of hours, but his wife is really worried. Isn't there anything you can do to help?"

"Magdalena, you know I'd like to help, but Melvin has his rules."

"Yes, but he's not on duty today, is he?"

"Actually, he is. He just ran over to Sam's to buy some band aids. He got a nasty paper cut."

"Making airplanes again?"

"Judge not, Magdalena. Isn't that what the Bible says?"

I sighed. It is so hard to be charitable when the word is filled with idiots.

"Zelda, I'm not asking that you issue an all-points bulletin or contact the F.B.I. I just want you to help me keep an eye out for this Burk fellow."

It was Zelda's turn to sigh. A self-confessed agnostic, she is a much better Christian than I.

"Okay. Give me a brief description."

"Six feet, maybe two hundred and fifty pounds, mostly bald, and has a cumulus cloud crowning his cranium."

"What?"

"Never mind dear. Just put down that he always looks troubled."

"Gotcha. Now I can't promise—just a minute." She put me on hold for the entire length of "Muskrat Love" by Captain and Tenille. Just when I was about to confess my sins and plead to be removed from hell, she got back on the line. "Sorry, they were stuck again."

"Those crippled bats you wear?"

"They're not crippled bats, Magdalena, they're eyelashes. These are the new Tammy Faye Ultralites. They're not supposed to stick like that. Now, where was Mr. Burk last seen?"

"The PennDutch. He stormed off after a tiff with his wife and drove off in a new blue Saturn."

"Oh, my."

"Zelda, what is it?"

"Are you sitting down, Magdalena?"

"Yes." Actually, I was lying comfortably on my bed, my feet propped on a pile of pillows.

"Do you think he might have run off with Susannah?"

"*What?* You haven't been using that bourbon-based eyeliner again, have you?"

"That was blush, and the *color* was called bourbon. Look, Magdalena, I'm trying to be helpful."

"Then what's this stuff about Susannah running off with a geriatric Pittsburgher, for crying out loud? She's marrying Melvin the day after tomorrow!"

I heard the receiver on the other end thud against Zelda's desk, strike something else, and then land on the floor with a loud crack. Only then did I remember that Zelda was hopelessly, and inexplicably, in love with her boss.

"Zelda, I'm sorry! Zelda, can you hear me?"

The noxious song about amorous rodents must have been on tape, because I got to hear it three more times. By the time Zelda picked up, I was resigned to an eternity of torment.

"What did you say about my Melvin and Susannah?"

"I'm sorry, dear, I thought you knew. I mean, you work with the man, for pete's sake. But don't feel bad, dear—I found out just yesterday afternoon."

She was panting like an overweight jogger. "This is for real, Magdalena, isn't it?"

"I'm afraid so, dear. The knot is to be tied Wednesday morning at his mother's farm. So you really didn't have a clue, huh? Because Sam said you were throwing them a big party tomorrow night."

"I'm throwing *Melvin* a party. It's his birthday."

I glanced at the square on my calendar in which I'd drawn a tiny pitchfork. "So it is. Tell me, whose idea was this party, his or yours?"

"I can't help it, Magdalena. He says he still loves me."

"He's incapable of loving himself, dear. Besides, you know this marriage won't last."

"Because Susannah's a slut?" she asked hopefully.

I let that pass. The truth is the truth, after all.

"Now what's this about Susannah and Dr. Burk?"

She sighed—although come to think of it, it may have been a whimper. "I don't know anything about your Dr.

Burk, but I saw Susannah in a blue Saturn just a couple of hours ago."

"You did? Where?"

"Headed north to Bedford on Highway 96."

"Was she alone?"

"From what I could see. Then again, she *is* Susannah."

"Just what is that supposed to mean?"

"Face it, Magdalena, your sister does things in cars Henry Ford never dreamed of. Just last month I caught her up on Stucky Ridge parked in one of those new VW bugs."

"So? She borrowed it from a friend."

"So, when I tapped on the window out tumbled the entire Hernia High baseball team and—"

"Okay, I get the picture. Let me rephrase my question. Was Susannah driving the blue Saturn?"

"It *appeared* so."

"Just wait until I get my hands on her scrawny neck," I hissed. "Maybe there won't be a wedding after all."

"She might still be in Bedford," Zelda said, suddenly cheery again. "You know how your sister loves to shop."

"Walmart, here I come!"

"In the meantime—as soon as Melvin gets back from Sam's—I'll do a little patrolling and see if I can spot your English doctor. He is English, isn't he?"

"Yes, and so are you!" I wailed in exasperation. Although Zelda and I stem from the same stock, no Amish person in the world was going to claim familial ties with an agnostic who applied her makeup with a putty knife.

"Magdalena, can I ask you one favor?"

"Ask, and then I'm out of here."

"Well—uh—it's just that—you see—"

"Spit it out, dear."

Before Zelda could master her mouth there was a loud rap on my door and I was forced to hang up.

Eight

"C ome in!"

"I can't, Magdalena, it's locked." The rapping was louder, more insistent.

"Hold your horses," I hollered.

"You better hurry, Magdalena. This is important."

I unlocked the door and stared down into Freni's disapproving face. "Yes, what is it?"

"For shame, Magdalena, and in the middle of the day yet!"

"*What?* I was on the phone for crying out loud!"

"Ach, youthanisms," Freni muttered. "Your mama would roll over in her grave."

I sighed patiently. Mama has rolled over in her grave so many times the Bedford County Power Department has considered replacing their generator with her coffin.

"Freni, what do you want?"

"Susannah is on the other line."

"Why didn't you say so?"

I practically leapfrogged over Freni and snatched up the receiver that was lying face-up on the lobby desk. "Susannah!"

"Well, it's about time!"

"Susannah, are you all right?"

"Of course I'm all right, silly, but what about you? What took so long? Catch you on the throne, or did Freni stop along the way to pull her hose up?"

I have exceptionally keen hearing, but even a Cabbage Patch Doll could hear the woman screaming in the background. "Susannah, *where* are you?"

"I'm at The Material Girl out on Business Route 220, just past where it intersects with regular 220."

"The what?"

"It's a fabric store, silly. It's right next door to Naughty Ed's Haircuts and More. Actually, I'm at Naughty Ed's, because the lady at The Material Girl wouldn't let me use her phone."

"Why aren't you at Walmart?" I snapped.

"Don't be such a goof-ball, Magdalena. I'm buying my wedding dress."

"Then why aren't you at The Marriage-Go-Round up by the turnpike?"

"Geez." The woman in the background stopped screaming and I could actually hear my sister's eyes roll.

Of course, how silly of me. Alas, The Marriage-Go-Round sells wedding *dresses*. Why settle for one of those when you can wrap yourself like a mummy in something straight off the bolt? Well, to each her own, I guess. I was never going to convince my baby sister that seams and hems had value, so I had best concentrate on the business at hand.

"Susannah, are you by yourself?"

"Well, I was—Ed, stop that—and I will be again, just as soon as you say yes."

"I don't have time to play games with you, dear. I have a parlor full of paranoid veterans who insist on doing just that."

"Ah, Mags, you're no fun. You know that?"

"Get to your point, dear."

"Well, it's like this, Mags. I need you to call The Material Girl and speak to a woman named Brenda. Tell her who you are and that you'll pay for my purchase."

"Will I?"

"Come on, Mags, you're my sister. Think of this as your wedding present."

"How much cloth are we talking about here, and how much is it per yard?"

"It's silk, Mags. And it's sky blue. You'll love it, I promise."

"How *much*?"

"A mere fifty yards."

I gasped, and the pilot lights went out on both my hot water heater and my stove. Just ask Freni if you don't believe it.

"It's on sale, Mags. It's been marked down to $29.99 a yard."

"How much is the regular price?"

"$54.95."

"Okay," I heard myself say, "but this silk better be something special."

"Really? You'll call her? Oh, Mags, you're the very best sister a girl could have. Did I ever tell you how much I love you?"

"No. Susannah—"

"Because you know I do, don't you?"

"Well, I guess so. I mean, I've never given it a lot of thought."

"Do you love me?"

"Don't be ridiculous. You're my sister."

"Then say it, Mags. Say 'I love you.'"

"I—uh—well—it's got to be as plain as the nose on my face." I mean, how much more obvious can something be?

"Say it, Mags!"

"Just say it," Naughty Eddy purred in the background.

"I love you!" I shrieked. "There! Are you happy now?"

"Oh, Mags, you're such a teddy bear, you know that?" There was the sound of muffled voices, and I waited. "Mags, dearest, Naughty Eddy wants to speak with you."

"Me?"

"He says he saw you last week at the I.G.A. here in Bedford, and you were fondling eggplants."

"I was not!"

"Anyway, so he bought one, and now he wants to know what to do with it."

"Tell Naughty Eddy to stuff it."

Susannah giggled and said something to Naughty Eddy before speaking to me. "He wants to know where?"

"Susannah dear, I don't have time to chat about recipes. I already said you could buy the silk. Now I have a question to ask you."

"Fire away, favorite sis."

"Did you drive to Bedford in a blue Saturn?"

"It's no big deal, Mags. I didn't steal it. That nice Dr. Burk loaned it to me. Isn't it a beaut? Say, Mags, do you think the Saturn company could be a front for a religious cult? I mean, don't those weekend gatherings seem a bit suspicious?"

"Cult, shmult! Susannah, shame on you! How many times do I have to tell you not to borrow other people's cars?"

"Well, you won't let me drive your Beamer," she whined.

I thought of lecturing her on the concept of working for one's possessions, but decided to save my breath. Except for her brief stint naming paint chip colors, Susannah has never worked a day in her life. That's exactly why my parents in their wisdom left the farm to me. Of course there was a codicil stipulating that should the day ever come when Susannah pulled her own weight, half the farm would revert to her. Since that is about as likely to happen as the NFL requiring its member teams to take flower arranging, the PennDutch is *mine*. In the meantime I supply my slutty, slovenly, and slothful sister with three squares a day, a bed if needed, and assorted bolts of fabric for her back. This was the first bolt of *silk,* however. You can count on that.

"Did you *ask* to borrow Dr. Burk's car?" Susannah's definition of "borrow" tends to be looser than Webster intended.

"He offered. He came storming out of the inn as mad as could be—even madder than Melvin gets when I forget to warm his milk—"

"Skip that part!" I shouted.

"Well, and so he's heading for his car, right? And I'm about to ask him for a lift, but then suddenly he says"— she giggled —"shall I skip that part too, Mags?"

"Shall I forget to call The Material Girl?"

"Aw, you're no fun! Well, anyway, when he was done swearing he looked at me like he was seeing me for the first time and said, 'Here, you better take the keys. I'm likely to do something really stupid behind the wheel. So I took them."

"That's *it*?"

"Yeah, basically. Oh, he mentioned something about taking a walk to let off steam. At least that's what I think he said. He's got a really weird accent, Mags. Is he from Argentina?"

"He's from Minnesota, dear, but at least now we're getting somewhere. Did you see which direction he headed?"

"Nah. I was out of there like a bat out of hell."

"Don't use the *h* word," I said sternly.

"Oh, Mags, you're such a prude. But hey, I came through for you, didn't I?"

"You did fine."

"Great, because I have another teensy weensy little favor to ask."

"Don't even think it, dear, because I am not going to wrap myself in a silk bandage, like I was a five-foot, ten-inch wound."

"Oh, no, Mags. It's nothing like that. Besides, you'd wouldn't look good in a free-form dress."

"Yes, she would," I heard a man's voice purr.

"Tell Evil Eddy to put a lid on it, dear, and I'll choose to take that last remark of yours as a compliment." I sighed perfunctorily. "So what's this *final* little favor? You want me to snap a few photos of the happy couple?"

"Nah, that would be asking too much. We just want to know if you'd spring for our honeymoon on Aruba."

"What?" I tried choking the receiver on my phone, but the hard plastic wouldn't budge, much less give me the satisfaction of a scream.

"It's just for five days, Mags. Pweeze. Pwetty prweeze."

"Can the baby talk, toots! You have a lot of nerve even thinking such a thought, when you didn't even invite me to your pre-wedding party."

Susannah screamed as loud as she did the time Shnookums fell out of her bra and into a pot of warm cookie batter. "Who told you about the party?"

"Sam Yoder, that's who. He said Melvin had been buying the store out getting ready for tomorrow's shindig."

"But it was supposed to be a surprise," she wailed.

"For who?"

"For you, you idiot!"

"What did you say?"

"Oh, Mags, you've done so much for me over the years. Since Mama and Papa died you've been like— well, a mother. And all along I've given you nothing but grief."

"Oh, pshaw," I said, frankly rather embarrassed. "The day before I got married you were nice to me for an hour, and you were nice again for twenty-two minutes the day Aaron left."

"You see? That's what I mean! All I do is take, take, take, and I hardly ever give, so this party was going to be my present to you."

"It *was*?"

"Everyone's coming, Mags—even Freni."

"Freni doesn't know a thing about this, dear. She's as hurt as I am."

"Not anymore, Mags. I explained the whole thing, and she's coming."

"Our Freni is going to an English party?"

"She wouldn't miss it for the world, Mags. And it's not for me she's coming. She's coming for you. Everyone is going to be there on account of you."

"Oh, my. I don't know what to say."

"Say you'll come! Melvin and I were going to 'kidnap'

you, which would have been a lot of fun, but maybe not so wise. Now we don't have to."

"And lucky for you. Okay, I'll come. And you're *sure* the party is for me?"

"Don't be silly, Mags. Now, about Aruba—"

"In your dreams, dear," I said sweetly. I called the airlines just the same.

I had just gotten off the phone with The Material Girl when I noticed Samantha Burk standing in the lengthening shadows of my lobby. Of course I jumped. Who knew how long the concert pianist had been skulking about; little people have an unfair advantage in the art of espionage.

"Yes, dear, can I help you?" If my tone was not as sweet as my words, it's because the silk Susannah wanted was not on sale. Some bumbling clerk or prank-playing child had switched the signs on her beloved bolt of blue with one of black. There was no way my baby sister was going to marry decked out in the color of sin, even though it was eminently appropriate to her lifestyle. So, I just paid more for a dress—to use the term loosely—than I had for my first car. Perhaps it was fortunate my sister didn't plan to cut or stitch her swath, because I knew a good seamstress who, after the wedding, could turn those fifty yards into five or six *real* dresses. Perhaps I would even make a profit—*if* my sister didn't spill anything, and if the mangy mutt minded his manners.

"Miss Yoder, here are the books you wanted from Mystery Lovers Bookshop."

"Thank you, dear. How much do I owe you?"

"Consider them a gift. I mean, sort of a thank-you for driving me around before."

"Well, that's very nice of you, dear. Just don't expect me to come down on my rates."

She smiled weakly. "Miss Yoder, have you heard anything about John?"

"Well, actually I have. Your husband didn't drive away in a fit of anger—"

"But the car! It's gone, and I heard it tear out of here, tires squealing and everything."

"That was my sister Susannah off on a shopping spree. Apparently your husband loaned her the car."

Her small brow puckered. "Are you sure? I mean, John's not in the habit of lending anything to anyone."

"I'm positive. Susannah might lie like a politician, but not when she's about to ask for a favor. And she just asked for a doozy. No, it seems your husband decided to cool off by taking a walk."

"A walk? John hates being outside."

"Well, that's what he did," I said firmly.

"Where would he go?"

I shrugged. "The woods? The pond across the road? There's lots of nifty places to explore here."

"John isn't in to exploring."

"I see. What *is* he in to?"

"History."

"Well, like I said before, there is that old grist mill on the Berkey farm, and Settlers' Cemetery is a very interesting place."

She shook her head, and not a hair stirred. "John is a student of the classics."

"I thought you said he was a professor."

Dainty lips parted. "He was. But the pursuit of knowledge is a lifelong passion for him."

"Perhaps you should have taken your vacation in

Greece," I said, secure in the knowledge that my no-refund, "a head laid is a dollar paid" rule is pinned to each of my guests' pillows.

"We were there just last month doing researching for a book John's writing on the military campaigns of Antigonus Monophthalmus."

"Gesundheit, dear."

She frowned. "John was looking for someplace quiet and relaxing to write up his notes. He wasn't counting on being carjacked."

Every hair on my bun bristled. "*Carjacked?* I told you my sister borrowed your car. In fact, your husband insisted she take it."

She stepped back deeper into the shadows. "Well, that is most unlike John, I assure you."

"Could we possibly be in denial, dear?"

"I beg your pardon!"

"Obviously you and your husband had more than just a tiff."

She said nothing.

"Look, dear, I want to help you."

Silence seemed to be her strength. I flipped the switch on the wall beside me, and she looked like a fawn caught in my Beamer's headlights.

"Oh," she gasped.

"You do want my help, don't you?"

She nodded. "Miss Yoder—uh—this is so personal."

I tugged on a lobe. "These ears have heard just about everything."

"Yes, but—"

"Look dear, I have a sister who's slept with more men than Richard Simmons. And did I mention the fact that half of Hollywood has spilled their guts to these babies?

So you see, there's nothing on this good earth that would surprise me. Now them"—I nodded in the direction of the parlor door, behind which the veterans congregated—"they might have their water glasses pressed up against the door as we speak. Far be it from me to speak ill of paying guests, but that bunch in there is one of the weirdest I've had stay here yet."

Samantha took a tentative step forward. "Really?"

"Oh, yes. The men, near as I can tell, have been huddled in there all day, and the women seem to have been banished somewhere else."

"Where?"

"Who knows? Bedford? Somerset? They took their rental cars and fanned out across the country. Well, I'm assuming they did. Not that they consulted me before they left, although it would have been a good idea. I have some lovely and informative brochures I could have given them. Full-color, you know."

"Miss Yoder, I have a confession to make."

"Confess away!" I said, perhaps too gaily.

"I lied before."

"I knew it! I knew those pitiful paws of yours couldn't even span an octave. You're not really a concert pianist, are you?"

"Oh, but I am! I lied to you about my husband."

I beckoned her closer. "Do tell!"

"Miss Yoder, I think my husband is a spy."

Nine

"**D**o tell, dear!"

I steered her into the dining room, which is on the opposite side of the lobby from the parlor. The vexing veterans were going to have their work cut out for them if they expected to eavesdrop on us now.

"Have a seat, dear." I pointed to a ladderback chair adjacent to a quilt stretched cross a six-foot frame. It is my custom to keep a "quilt in progress" at all times for my guests to try their hands at. If their stitches are reasonably small and neat, I allow the work to remain. If the stitches are sloppy, or too large, I sneak out to the dining room in the middle of the night and redo them. Not only do these quilts function as a form of therapy for my clientele—many of whom are deeply disturbed—but they are a tidy source of income for me. I ship the finished quilts to Lancaster County, where they are snatched up like hotcakes by the swarms of tourists who converge on that Amish community looking to exchange cash for culture.

I threaded a needle for her. "Now, dear, tell me everything."

"You swear you won't breathe a word of this to a soul?"

"Amish and Mennonites don't take oaths. But if it will

make you feel any better, I promise to stick this needle in my eye and hope to die if these lips blab a single syllable."

That seemed to satisfy her. "I don't think my John is the kind of spy like in the James Bond movies. I mean, he doesn't have any fancy gadgets that I know of, and as for the women—well, I already told you I thought there was no chance of that."

I waved a hand impatiently. "I don't watch movies, dear. Tell me what kind of spy your John *is* like."

"I think maybe he's C.I.A."

"Really?" I learned forward. I hadn't heard such a juicy piece of gossip since my first inn blew down.

She paused dramatically, but at least they weren't wasted seconds because she made a couple of stitches as well.

"Well, something like that. He won't discuss it, of course. It's probably only for my safety, you see. But he makes secret phone calls and sometimes, like when we're traveling, he disappears for a few days."

"Give me details," I begged.

Her fingers flew with the needle. "Well, there was that time I gave a concert in Vienna. No sooner had we checked into the Hoffman House—it's a small but exquisite establishment—when he just up and disappeared. If he hadn't done the same thing in Belgium the year before I would have been really worried."

"Ah, so you're used to this strange behavior of his. Why then all the concern now?"

She looked up from the quilt. "Because Vienna and Brussels, that I can understand. Those are places one would expect spies to operate—or whatever you call what they do. But Hernia, Pennsylvania?"

"I see, so we Herniatites are unworthy of being spied upon."

"Well—"

I tapped the quilt, and it vibrated, stretched taut as it was. "Those last few stitches of yours look like the tracks of a drunken chicken, dear—and you a concert pianist! For shame."

She flushed and reached for the stitch-ripper. "I didn't mean to offend you, Miss Yoder. It's just that I think my husband is an international spy, and Hernia is practically in Pittsburgh's backyard."

"We're two hours away, and besides, you have no idea how many of the world's most powerful people have stayed in Hernia."

"You're joking, right?"

"Wrong. And every one of them stayed right here." That was true in at least one sense, wasn't it?

She glanced up at me, and I could tell there was new respect in her eyes. "People like Tony Blair?"

"Bony Tony, I call him." That's quite true, although I'd never met the man.

"Of course, there aren't any famous people here now— besides myself, I mean?"

It still amazes me how someone so small could be so full of herself. "You, my dear," I said, making a cross-stitch, "are in a class by yourself."

Samantha beamed. "Maybe I'm being too concerned about John. He is, as you've pointed out, a grownup, and quite capable of taking care of himself. It's just that after so many years—well, he's a fixture of my life. Even though ours is a less than perfect marriage, I'm rather used to him."

I ripped out the cross-stitch. There was no use tempting

fate, after all. Besides, she really was right. Even if John Burk was a spy—about as likely as Susannah being a closet nun—there really was no reason for him to be snooping around Hernia. Not anymore.

"If he doesn't show up for dinner, I'll see what I can do about organizing a search party. Folks around here are very helpful—well, except for our chief of police. But speaking of dinner, I encourage folks to dress up, and since I like to set a good example, I'd best be going." I anchored my needle and stood up. "Tonight's going to be very special. We'll be serving SPAM® luncheon meat."

Samantha's eyes lit up like a jack-o'-lantern with twin candles. "Oh, I adore SPAM®. I have this wonderful recipe for SPAM® Western Bean Soup. Do you think your cook would like it?"

"Oh, I'm sure she would, dear. Just be careful how you go about it. Freni can be a mite on the sensitive side."

Samantha smiled. "Just you leave it to me. I have lots of experience dealing with sensitive people."

"But there is only one Freni," I muttered under my breath. "That woman is touchy with a capital *T*."

Truthfully, I said it so softly that a bat with a hearing aid wouldn't have heard a thing if it was hanging from my nose. Tell me, then, why it is that Freni, who is supposedly hard of hearing, came flying through the kitchen door.

"I heard that!"

"My, my, we have selective hearing, don't we, dear?"

"Magdalena, do you want I should quit?"

"Been there, done that," I said, borrowing a phrase from my sister. I know, it was absolutely foolish; but I wanted to appear "cool" in Samantha's glowing eyes.

"Yah? So then I quit! You are impossible to work for."

"But it's less than an hour until dinner!" I wailed. I realize it now, although I didn't then; wailing is seldom cool.

Freni stomped one of her sturdy little brogans. "Dinner sinner," she said, also borrowing from Susannah, "I'm outta here."

"And good riddance."

"Excuse me," Samantha said, gliding sideways toward my impossibly steep stairs. "I think I may have left the water running in my room."

"Yes, dear, go check on it," I whispered.

Freni, who had been staring at Samantha open-mouthed, whirled. "What did you say to me, Magdalena?"

"I said, 'good riddance.' And you mean *Big* Magdalena, don't you?"

"Ach!"

"So that's what everyone calls me, is it?"

Freni flapped her arms uselessly, like a bird with broken wings. "It's just a nickname. It means nothing."

"I see. That would explain why you're called Merry Freni."

"Ach!"

"Tell me, Merry Freni, how long *have* the Amish been calling me Big Magdalena?"

Freni hid her face in her apron and muttered something incomprehensible.

"*Excuse* me? I didn't hear that."

"Since you were three."

I gasped. "Well!"

"Of course I saw it the day you were born. I assisted the midwife, you know. I told your mama not to name you Magdalena—that there were too many already by that name, and all the good nicknames were already taken. I told her to name you Freni Yoder—there were only three of those in Bedford County, and one in Somerset, and the one in Somerset was already named Big Freni."

"Is that so? Well then, what nickname might I have gotten instead?"

Freni shrugged. "Slow Freni, maybe. You never were very quick at learning things."

"You didn't just quit," I wailed, "you're also fired!"

One of these days I'm going to hire a butler to answer the door for me. Of course my butler would have to dress like an Amish man, to fit in with my Pennsylvania Dutch theme. Unfortunately, a real Amish man would not pretend to be something he was not. Perhaps there was a nice young man at Bedford Community College who desired a job in show business, and was willing to buttal, not just rebuttal. Ask and you shall receive, the Bible says. Believe me, I do my share of asking, and I've done a lot of receiving, but there does not seem to be a fifty-fifty ratio. At least not in my life. In fact, my last three prayers had gone unanswered. Still, I decided to be a faithful Christian and give it one more try.

"Oh Lord, please send me one young good-looking and obedient young man from the drama department at B.C.C. It would be helpful, Lord, if he already has a beard. Those fake beards they sell for Halloween at Walmart don't look very convincing to me. And nice white teeth, Lord—guests don't like looking at tobacco and coffee stains. And it wouldn't hurt if he brought his own costume. I don't have time to do any sewing now."

Before I could even say "amen" there was a knock on the door.

"Thank you, Lord!"

I strode over to the front door, caught a glimpse of an Amish face through the peephole, and flung it open.

"Ach," Strubbly Sam squawked, clearly startled.

"You!"

"Yah, it's me, Big Magdalena—"

"Don't you Big Magdalena me!" I tried to slam the door on Strubbly Sam, but the man has feet the size of continents, and one of them, South America, I think, was firmly placed on the doorsill.

"Here." He thrust a hand the size of Belgium through the crack. In it was a package wrapped in brown butcher paper.

Never turn away a man bearing gifts until you've had a chance to examine the offerings. I opened the door grudgingly.

"Somebody leave that on my doorstep?"

"Ach, I brought it myself. It's fresh butter. Three pounds of it."

I'm no fool, so I took it. "Thanks. Say, Strubbly Sam, are you trying to court me?"

He blushed, from the brim of his straw hat to the V of his white cotton shirt. "Would that be so bad? I've been very lonely since my Amanda, God rest her soul, passed on."

"But Strubbly, dear, I'm Mennonite, and you're Amish. Doesn't the Bible warn us against being unevenly yoked in marriage?" Frankly, if I was going to be yoked again, it was going to be with someone to whom deodorant was not a worldly vice. Preferably, it would be to someone closer to my own age—like Mel Gibson or Harrison Ford. Even Brad Pitt would do in a pinch.

"Ach, Magdalena, there is such an easy solution."

97

"There is?"

"Yah, I could speak to the new bishop. It would be a simple thing for you to join the Amish church." He chuckled at his little joke. "After all, your ancestors were all Amish, weren't they?"

"Indeed they were, dear, but they obviously took issue with some things and left that denomination. Who am I to argue with their wisdom?"

We were still standing in my lobby, and Strubbly Sam was still wearing his straw hat. A more hospitable woman would have invited her guest to take the load off his feet—not that tootsies that size couldn't support just about anything—but the parlor was occupied, and I was afraid that if I invited Strubbly Sam into the dining room, he might invite himself to supper.

Strubbly Sam seemed quite content to stand. "And doesn't the Bible say that God created Eve so that Adam wouldn't have to be alone? So that he would have a helpmate?"

"You're quite right, dear. But it says nothing about we women needing company. Indeed, had the Good Lord created Eve first, there would have been no need for men."

"Ach!" Strubbly Sam glanced up at the ceiling, perhaps expecting to see a lightning bolt.

"You see why I wouldn't make a very good Amish woman?"

He finally had the nerve look away from the ceiling and at me. "You believe in this—this—"

"Equality of the sexes?"

"Yah, that."

I shook my head vigorously. "No way, dear. It is a biological fact that women are *superior* to men."

He gasped.

"Well, maybe not in terms of brute strength, which, if you ask me, is the only reason we're not in charge of things. But we live longer, are more resilient, and of course we whine a lot less when we're sick. Oh, did I mention that we are just as intelligent, if not more intelligent, than you?"

Strubbly Sam, now the color of powdered sugar, was swaying like a birch in a thunderstorm. Had it not been for South America and Africa beneath him, he might well have pitched forward, possibly even adding to the death toll of these premises. It was clear that Big Magdalena now stood a snowball's chance in you-know-where of ever becoming the next Mrs. Strubbly Sam Berkey.

"You don't suppose your new bishop would agree with me?"

"Ach!"

"Well, I guess that settles that then, doesn't it? But I hear that Anna Yutzy is already twenty-three and still unmarried. That's a real shame, you know, because she makes the best pie crust in the county, and with hips like those—well, there could be a whole new generation of Strubbly Sams running around the Hernia area."

Once again, duo continents kept my visitor upright. "Ach! Anna Yutzy is—is—"

"Now, be kind, dear. And don't think you're too old to procreate. If Clint Eastwood can, you can too. And I just happen to know that Anna Yutzy loves children."

He mumbled something about his horse being more attractive than Anna, which normally would have offended me, but in this case it was all too true. The poor dear has one of the ugliest faces and weirdest shapes of any filly around—and yes, I'm speaking of Strubbly Sam's horse.

"Yah, I must always try to be kind. I will confess this sin to the congregation next meeting Sunday."

"Don't you dare. That will only humiliate poor Anna. Besides, you didn't mutter your unflattering remark to another Amish person. Just to these worldly ears of mine—and believe me, what goes into one, goes right out the other. So consider your nasty little comment unsaid."

"Yah. You are a wise woman, Magdalena."

"Feel free to change my name to Wise Magdalena, dear. And of course spread the word. Maybe someday folks will refer to me simply as the Wise One. I've never been too fond of Magdalena, you know."

Strubbly Sam looked doubtful, but having learned his lesson, held his tongue.

"Well—thanks again for the butter." I tried edging him back to the door. It must take a lot of energy to uproot two-sevenths of the earth's land surface, because he remained as immobile as Lot's wife *after* she turned around for one last glimpse of Sodom.

"Do you need a gentle push?" I asked sensibly.

He blinked. "Ach, I was just thinking."

"There's a first time for everything, dear." I don't mean to be cruel, but Strubbly Sam has another nickname: Slow Sam. Don't take my word for it, either. Ask anyone in Bedford and Somerset counties. Strubbly Sam Berkey is not the fastest mare to pull a loaded buggy.

Strubbly Sam smiled. "I understood that joke about thinking. It's because I'm from Australia, yah?"

Australia! So that was it! Who would have thought there were Amish down under? Did they, perchance, hitch kangaroos to their buggies?

"G'day mate!" I said, pleased to give him a gentle

push. "Take care crossing the billabong, and when you get home throw a few shrimp on the barbie for me."

Strubbly, or Slow Sam—take your pick—had grown roots. "You really must be going, dear."

"Ach, Big Magdalena, are you all right?"

"It's Wise Magdalena now, remember? And I'm peachy-keen. What makes you ask?"

"You seem so eager that I should leave."

"Silly me. I guess I just hadn't considered the possibility of a live Amish coatrack. Do you do hats as well? Of course you must, you're wearing a hat!"

"That was sarcasm, maybe?"

"Very good, dear, and so is this."

I am ashamed to say that the poor man's face looked like a souffle after the oven door has been slammed. I hate treating anyone badly—except for the truly deserved, like Melvin Stoltzfus—and especially an old defenseless Amish man like Strubbly Sam.

"Big Magdalena, if you are in any kind of trouble—if anything is wrong—you can turn to me. Maybe there is something I can do to help."

"*Really?* Well, in that case, my cook just quit, my slutty, slovenly sister is marrying a mantis, and one of my guests is missing. Now fix that!"

Strubbly Sam grinned. "I can fix all three things."

Ten

SPAM® Western Bean Soup

✦

1 cup chopped onion
1 tablespoon vegetable oil
1 cup sliced carrots
3 (10 ½-ounce) cans condensed chicken broth
1 (14 ½-ounce) can tomatoes, cut up
1/3 cup chili sauce
3 tablespoons firmly packed brown sugar
3 tablespoons cider vinegar
2 teaspoons Worcestershire sauce
2 teaspoons prepared mustard
2 (15 ½-ounce) cans pinto beans, rinsed and drained
1 (12-ounce) can SPAM® Luncheon Meat, cubed
2 tablespoons chopped parsley

In 5-quart saucepan, saute onion in oil until golden. Stir in carrots, chicken broth, tomatoes, chili sauce, brown sugar, vinegar, Worcestershire sauce, and mustard. Mash half of beans with fork; add mashed beans and whole beans to soup. Blend well. Bring to a boil. Cover. Reduce heat and simmer 30 minutes or until carrots are tender. Stir in SPAM® and parsley. Simmer 2 minutes. Serves 6.

NUTRITIONAL INFORMATION PER SERVING:

Calories 331; Protein 22g; Carbohydrates 34g; Fat 13g; Cholesterol 46mg; Sodium 2263mg.

Eleven

"**G**et out of town!"

Strubbly Sam looked like a sheep who had just been asked an algebra question.

"It's an expression of incredibility, dear. So tell me, how are you going to fix my life? Can you cook?"

He nodded. "Yah. I cook every day now that my Amanda is gone."

"I thought cooking was women's work."

"Yah, it is, but God looks the other way when there is no one to help."

"Hmm." If that were indeed true, maybe I should see about buying a new Hoover with *all* the attachments.

"Do you think you could follow a recipe for SPAM® jambalaya?"

"Ach, my favorite!"

"You'd be cooking for war veterans."

Strubbly Sam blinked. "Soldiers?"

"Ex. But nonetheless mysterious, mumbling men who spend all their time huddled together in the parlor, no doubt scheming to take over the government."

"God gives everyone a second chance, Magdalena. Why shouldn't I?"

"Well, okay, but what about the mantis?"

"You mean Melvin Stoltzfus, the chief of police, yah?"

"You got it. Incidentally, what nickname do you Amish have for him?"

Strubbly Sam found new interest in my ceiling. "Handsome Mel."

"What?"

"I too think he looks like a praying mantis, but the others"— he shrugged—"they think he's very handsome. Not that one should be proud of such a thing, mind you. It is a gift from God."

I decided to move the conversation along before I said something uncharitable. My tongue may not cut cheese, like Irma Yoder's, but it has been known to slice butter into neat, uniform pats.

"So how are you going to stop Susannah from marrying Melvin?"

"Does your sister know that Handsome Mel—"

"Please!"

"Does she know that Elvina's son is adopted?"

"Say what?"

"Elvina found him on the front porch the morning after a caravan of Gypsies passed through."

"Get out of town!" I'd known Melvin his entire life and had never heard that story. In fact, I clearly remember seeing Elvina Stoltzfus pregnant. Still, the tale had a certain ring of truth. Leave it to Melvin to be *left* by the Gypsies, not stolen.

The sheep smiled, now that he knew an equation or two. "Elvina couldn't have any children herself, see, so she and Amos—may his soul rest in peace—took the little boy in and raised him as their own."

I sighed. "That's all very interesting, dear, but it isn't

going to stop her. Nor should it. There's nothing wrong with being adopted."

"Yah, this is true." He scratched is head while the straw hat bobbled. "Ach, now I know!"

"Do tell, dear. Time's a-wasting."

"Handsome Mel only has one."

"One what?"

Strubbly Sam clamped a hand over his mouth, but that didn't stop the words from leaking through his fingers. "His head wasn't the only place that bull kicked him."

"So what?" I wailed. "Susannah's slept with the man! That isn't going to be news to her. You can't stop this wedding, can you?"

"Ach, maybe we should go to the third thing on your list. Did you say someone was missing?"

I nodded miserably. "One of my guests. A man named John Burk. What do you propose to do, Strubbly Sam, organize a posse?"

The sheep drew a blank again.

"A search party, dear. Because if—"

"Yah, that I can do."

"You're kidding, aren't you? I mean, it's planting season—how are you going to get anyone to join a search party for a missing Englisher?"

The straw hat was a blur. "There's Strong Jonathan, Small Ben, Two-Horse Miller, Lefthanded Ed, and Strubbly Pete. They're all retired like me. They'd be happy to help."

"Are you sure, Sam?"

"We can find this guest, Magdalena."

"You forgot the 'Big.' "

"You forgot the 'Strubbly.' "

We grinned like a pair of Cheshire cats, and in that moment an unlikely friendship was born.

I expect my guests to gather in the parlor between six and half-past every evening. At the very minimum, gentlemen must wear shirts, pants, and shoes. I will not tolerate shorts at the dinner table. Ladies may wear slacks—although dresses are preferred—and they too must wear shoes. Neither sex may wear sleeveless apparel. After all, there are parts of the body the Good Lord intended for us to keep private, and any place where odor is a problem is on that list. I do encourage my guests to go beyond the minimum code, and am sometimes rewarded by smartly dressed diners who appear to have stepped right off the society page of *The Philadelphia Inquirer*.

At any rate, I collect my guests promptly at six-thirty and lead them to the dining room where I personally assign their seats. Anyone rude enough to be late risks being seated next to me, within poking range of my fork. By the second day tardiness is no longer a problem. Occasionally—and this happens, or I should say *used* to happen, with the Hollywood crowd more than any other group—someone will fail to appear altogether. If I have not been notified in advance, and food has been prepared, the culprit is treated to a thorough tongue-lashing. Perhaps this might not seem like the Christian thing to do, but neither is wasting food—not when there are all those starving children in India.

This particular evening, since the men were already gathered in the parlor, and the women not the sort who gussied up a lot, I didn't anticipate any problems. Neither did I anticipate what happened. At twenty-nine minutes after six, just as I was about to rap on the parlor door, it opened and Tulsa Bob stepped out, looking like the cat who'd swallowed the canary.

"Ah, Miss Yoder, you're just the woman I want to see."

"Well, here I am, as big as life and twice as ugly." It was a phrase I'd picked up from Susannah and which I intended to be humorous. A sporting person would have laughed, and contradicted my obvious joke.

Bob, however, merely nodded. "Yeah, I'm glad we got this chance to talk before dinner."

I glanced at my plain, but very accurate watch. "You have thirty-nine seconds, dear."

"Ma'am?"

"Make it fast," I said crossly, "or I'll have to shorten the table grace. You don't want me to cheat God, do you?"

"No ma'am. It's this—we won't be needing the parlor anymore. As a conference room, I mean."

That announcement did little to improve my mood. "A deal's a deal, dear. We agreed on fifty dollars a day."

His eyebrows merged, like two storm clouds coming together. "Ma'am, it's not like you'd really be losing money on it. Would you? Our deal didn't stop you from renting it to anyone else, did it?"

Okay, so he had a point. But never let someone off the hook unless you have *something* to reel in. Otherwise you risk snagging yourself.

"How about a new deal?"

"What kind of deal, ma'am?"

"Well, it would appear that one of my guests is missing—"

"Missing, ma'am?"

"Well—and this is strictly confidential—I think it's more likely he ran away."

"Is this a child we're talking about?"

"Hardly. He's at least your age, dear. But"—I lowered my voice—"his wife's a little strange. She has this crazy idea he's a spy. Says he's gone missing all over the world. She's a concert pianist, you see, and travels a lot, but just between you and me, these musician types tend to be high-strung. My guess is the poor guy just needs a break now and then. Anyhow, I promised her I'd organize a search party tomorrow and we'd comb the woods around here."

"Isn't that something the authorities are supposed to do?"

"Not this early in the game, and not without compelling evidence of foul play. And frankly, I'd be hesitant to jump in to somebody else's business except that—well, enough said."

The storm clouds lifted and parted. "Ma'am?"

"It's just that I have a reputation to uphold." There was no need for him to know that a few previous guests had gone missing, only to be found on the premises as corpses. I don't mean to sound heartless here, but if John Burk was found dead, it had better not be on my property. The kind of folks who might be attracted to stay in an inn where multiple deaths had occurred were not the folks I wanted as guests.

"I see. Well, ma'am, me and the guys sort of had plans."

"Are those plans worth two hundred dollars? Because that's what you'd owe me through Friday."

Bob grinned. "Ma'am, I was in sales in civilian life. I sure could have used a woman like you on the team."

"What did you sell, dear?"

"Previously owned cars."

I wrinkled my nose, which given its length, takes a few seconds. "Well then, do we have a deal? I'll let you out of the agreement if you help me look for John Doe—I mean, John Burk."

"Deal," he said and thrust out a hand for me to shake.

While I'd just as soon pick up someone's pair of dirty undies than shake their hand—both things have been in the same place, after all—I grabbed the proffered paw. I've been told I have an uncommonly strong grip, thanks to my penchant for pinching pennies. Contrary to rumor, I cannot squeeze blood out of a turnip. I can, however, force a few tears.

The hedgerows came together again, this time in a wince. "Yes, ma'am, you and I would have made great teammates."

I patted my bun with my free hand. Flattery can get me to do many things, but selling used cars is not one of them.

"Say uncle, dear, and hurry up before I have to cut the grace out altogether."

We all agreed that an organized search should wait until the morning. Samantha seemed calmer now that she had shared her suspicions with me about John being a C.I.A. agent. And Zelda, bless her little overly made-up face, had promised to keep a painted eye open for any suspicious Englishers skulking about Hernia. As for Sam, not only was he a dynamite cook, he was a whole lot more pleasant than Freni.

Dinner was served around a massive table that was built by my great-great-great Grandfather Jacob "The Strong" Yoder. The table was constructed of solid oak and can seat twenty people—twenty-six in a pinch. It and Grandma Yoder's bed were the only pieces of furniture to survive intact during the tornado. Frankly—and this is just between you and me—I wish Granny's bed had sailed away to Oz. Sure, I was born in that bed, but Granny died in it. And while I'm not about to confess that I believe in ghosts, I have seen Granny in that bed on several occasions since she left her earthly body. Unfortunately it is the same bed I feel compelled to use—after all, Granny wouldn't be happy with a stranger sleeping on top of her.

At any rate, Sam made an excellent butler and he hovered over us like a mother hen, pecking at each little worm and flinging it to the neediest chick. Of course that's a bad analogy, because Sam was an excellent cook. Even better than Freni, if the truth be told.

The guests seemed delighted by a butler liveried in livery clothes, and were altogether in high spirits—except for Sandy Hart, who was at her other pole, and as quiet as a can of worms. Her husband, Bob, however, more than made up for her silence.

"Excellent meal, Miss Yoder."

I nodded graciously at the bobbing butler. "Thank Sam. You didn't know that Amish men could cook, did you?"

"No, ma'am."

"My sugar plum can cook," Doris Hill cooed. "He learned it in the army."

I arched one brow, to signify that I was displeased at her interruption. "Did he now?"

"Oh, yes! He learned to cook in that horrible prisoner-of-war camp he was in"—she ran chubby fingers through her husband's hair—"what was the name of that, dear?"

"*We* called it the Black Hole," Bob said before Jimmy Hill could as much as part his lips.

"Prisoner-of-war camp? Black Hole? Are we sure this is proper dinner conversation?" I asked gently. Actually, I was dying to hear more, but in a one-on-one situation. It is *my* dinner table, after all, and I should be the mistress of conversation.

"Oh, it's just history," Bob said without missing a beat. "You see, it was during the war—WW II, that is—and we were in an armored tank regiment in the Tunisian desert."

"Is that so? You know, the king of Morocco stayed here once. He brought seven of his wives with him—or were they harem girls? Anyway, I said I wasn't going to allow any hanky-panky with girls wearing hankies. Made him put them up at a motel in Bedford."

"Well, this was Tunisia," Jimmy said needlessly. "It's two countries over."

"And the capital is Tunis," Doris hissed. I think she meant to purr.

I rolled my eyes politely. That is to say, I kept at least a smidge of iris showing at all times.

"I'm quite good at geography, dear. I haven't traveled much personally, but my guests have. Did you know that the shape of Tunisia has often been compared to the hull of a ship?"

"Isn't that interesting," Bob said, his voice straining, as if to change gears. "I guess I was too concerned with the shape I was in to be noticing the shape of the country. You see, we were fighting Rommel in the desert—the temperature was like a hundred and forty in the daytime. At night it was freezing."

"The highest temperature ever recorded was one hundred thirty-six point four in the shade, and that was in Aziz, Libya," I said instructively.

Bob barreled on. "Our unit was destroyed by a division of Panzers. There were only seven survivors. We four"—he waved a hand at the other men present, excluding Sam—"were there. We all escaped into the dunes, and they didn't bother to follow.

"I got off easy—just some shrapnel in my left leg. But others—like Frank over there—were hit pretty bad. Frank, show Miss Yoder here your scars."

"I don't think so, dear."

"Anyway, we went three days with just one canteen of water between us—nothing to eat, of course—and then we were found by a tribe of Bedouin. They're nomads—"

"I know all about the Bedouin, dear."

"I'm sure you do, Miss Yoder. Anyway, these were the nicest folks. They didn't have as much as a Bandaid, but at least we were safe until *he* showed up. Well, that's what we thought."

"Until who showed up? Rommel?"

"I wish. No, ma'am, I'm talking about the Butcher of Tunis, and his sidekick, the Scorpion."

"Hernia's too small to have its own butcher, but there's a good one over in Bedford."

"Not that kind of butcher, ma'am. This one butchered humans."

"How fascinating, dear." I turned to Samantha, who had remained silent through the meal. "Who is your favorite composer?"

Bob's bushy black eyebrows merged in a hedgerow frown. "Beg pardon, ma'am, but the story is just beginning. And it ain't a pretty story like that *Casablanca* movie. The Germans were in control in Tunisia, not the wishy-washy Vichy government of France. And there wasn't anything like Rick's bar in Tunis—well, not the part that I saw, at any rate.

"You see, the Butcher of Tunis was in charge of a prisoner-of-war camp just outside the city. We called it the Black Hole, because that's just what it was. Nothing but a pit under a building, where there were twenty-five of us, crammed together like sardines in a can. We couldn't even lie down. And it was hot in that hole too—hotter than in the desert, I think. And the smell, ma'am—"

"*Please!* Can we get back to the Bedouins?"

"Yes, ma'am. That's where the Butcher caught up with his brother. His brother, the Scorpion, was an S.S. agent whose job it was to round up Allied troops who had escaped capture behind enemy lines. Anyway, the Scorpion had this network of spies and unfortunately one of them was a Bedouin. His name was Achim—"

"Bless you, dear."

"No, that was his name. A very personable fellow in his early twenties. The only one in the camp who spoke a little English. Anyway, the minute the Butcher and his brother, the Scorpion, showed up, our lives were hell."

"I do not allow swearing in this establishment," I said firmly.

"I wasn't swearing, Miss Yoder. Just stating a fact. The Butcher and his gang of sadists starved and beat us. I wouldn't do that to a rat. For six months we lived like that—may as well have been six years; it seemed like a lifetime. Three of my regiment—Eddy Dalton, Bill Easley, and Jackson Hayes—didn't make it. I swore that if I ever got out of there alive I was coming after the Butcher of Tunis. The Scorpion and Achim too."

"And did you? Go after them, I mean. You're obviously very much alive."

"You better believe it, ma'am. We all did. Frank there even hired a German private investigator."

"What did you learn, dear?" I said, turning to Frank, and then immediately wished I hadn't. Anyone that old and still having sex is unstable if you ask me—like Doris and Jimmy Hall. If by the time we reach our dotage we're not free of the urges of the flesh, then there's no hope for our redemption as a species. Besides, in heaven there are only single beds. Read your Bible if you don't believe me.

"The Butcher disappeared without a trace. However, the Scorpion left a short trail in Italy. I think he was murdered—I should say executed—by the Mafia. No doubt something to do with a money-laundering scheme gone awry."

"And what about Achim, dear?" It was fun just saying the name.

"Now that's a good one. He was kind of a big guy, but he ended up as a belly dancer in Newark. Went by the name of Fatima."

"Oh, dear."

"Well, Miss Yoder," Bob said, eager to take over the reins again, "that's all going to be water under the bridge soon. In a few years there won't be any of us left—"

"Speak for yourself!" Marjorie Frost had placed a protective hand on her husband's arm.

"No offense, little lady. It's just that Frank there is—well—he's my age, and I don't plan on hanging around forever.

"We do," Doris cooed and nuzzled her husbands neck.

"Please, dear," I said, "not at the table."

"The truth is," Jimmy said as his wife blissfully ignored me and nibbled her way up to her chubby hubby's ears, "I consider myself lucky. No one in my family—on either side—has lived past sixty-five. Heart attacks on my father's side, cancer on my mother's."

"Yeah, but Jimmy works out and watches what he eats," Doris grunted, her mouth full of lobe.

"That's true, babe, but I'm still going to die."

"Then I'm going to die with you." Doris ceased her naughty nibbling long enough to look pointedly at Marjorie. "Jimmy and I are only six weeks apart."

"Well, my Frank is in better shape than any of you," Marjorie said, her eyes blazing. "He'll live to be a hundred and ten."

"And how old will you be then, dear?" I asked pleasantly. "Thirty?"

"I'm twenty-four, and Frank's seventy-six. I already told you that!"

Dixie Montgomery cocked her large, pleasant head. "It's hard for the young to accept death," she said, in her charming Minnesota accent.

"I have no problem with death," Marjorie practically screamed. "It's you old fossils that drive me crazy."

Clearly it was time for me to intervene, and trust me, it is something I'm quite skilled at. "Please, dear," I said to eager Bob, "regale us with more of your war stories."

Bob beamed. "Be happy to, ma'am. Did I mention—"

The doorbell rang and I nodded at Sam to get it. He responded immediately, which was no surprise, because he had been butling beautifully all evening. To think that I had been missing out on such service all these years . . . perhaps if I offered him Susannah's room, now that she was moving in with Melvin—she *was* moving out, wasn't she? My heart raced. My sister hadn't said a thing about that. Still, they couldn't possibly be thinking of *him* moving in here! Susannah knows that Melvin gets under my skin like a chigger in June, and that if he were to move in I would surely kill him and end up you-know-where. There is no shortage of double beds in that place. Even a few triples, I've heard. That would of course appeal to Susannah, but . . .

"Magdalena," Sam whispered in my ear, "that woman is here to see you."

I shook my head to clear my brain of cobwebs. "Which woman?"

"The one who meddles."

"You mean Freni's back?"

"Ach, not her. The Mennonite preacher's wife."

"Ach!" I squawked. "Lodema Schrock?"

Sam nodded soberly.

Twelve

"**P**lease," I begged, "let's go into the parlor. It's so much more comfortable than standing here in the foyer."

"Comfort is but a worldly illusion," Lodema snapped. The woman should know. She looks like she's never been comfortable a day in her life. Although only in her early fifties, our pastor's wife could pass for his mother—except that Reverend Schrock's mother is really much prettier. Lodema has a hard, pinched look about her that can be obtained only through extreme suffering or by religious zeal.

"Oh, no, dear, my furniture is quite real. After the tornado I replaced all that stark wooden furniture of Mama's with upholstered pieces. I even have a sofa now."

"Soft furniture, for soft minds. It will only lead to laziness and idle hands, and as we all know, idle hands are the devil's playground."

I clasped my hands as if in prayer. "Well, perhaps we could step outside then."

"It's chilly out there, Magdalena. Do you want me to catch my death of cold?"

I bit my tongue.

"So, what is this I hear about you harboring criminals?"

I rearranged my size elevens into a more comfortable stance. I was going to need that sofa when Lodema left.

"There aren't any criminals here—not to my knowledge, at any rate."

"I've heard otherwise. I've heard they're hardened killers—the lot of them."

I small sigh escaped me. "They're war veterans, dear. Heroes."

"But they've killed other men, right? And women and children, too?"

I rocked slowly on my heels. "I didn't ask them for a body count."

"No, of course not. *You* wouldn't. If their money is green, you'll take it, right?"

"The Bible tells us not to judge, dear."

"Magdalena, you are a Mennonite. All your ancestors were either Mennonite or Amish. Do you know what that means?"

"That I have fifty percent fewer genes than the average American?"

"It means that we are pacifists," she hissed. "We shouldn't have anything to do with the warring English."

The Amish may refer to outsiders as English, but we Mennonites seldom, if ever, do. But somehow, Lodema Schrock—perhaps because she is the pastor's wife—has elevated herself to a higher level of exclusivity without having to make the accompanying sacrifices.

I gave Lodema's pinched hardness the once-over. "Those cheap plastic combs you wear in your bun are from Walmart. Ditto for your faux turtleshell eyeglass frames. And that dress you're wearing isn't homespun, is it? Looks more like polyester. And those leatherette shoes—where did you get them? Payless? Chances are they were made by the English in China—"

"Okay, I get your point. Just don't blame me if something terrible happens this week in Hernia."

"I won't."

"Because something evil is going to happen. I can feel it in my bones."

"It's probably just a touch of arthritis, dear."

"And I'm not talking about that so-called wedding that your sister is having Wednesday."

"Oh?"

"It won't count in God's eyes, Magdalena—you do realize that, don't you? In the Lord's eyes your sister will be an adulteress."

That did it. Susannah might be the bane of my existence—well, Freni aside—but she is my baby sister. No one has the right to say anything critical about her except for me. And who was Lodema to tell me that God would disapprove of Susannah's second marriage? The woman's husband was doing the knot tying, for pete's sake.

"Tell that to your husband, the reverend," I said.

"Oh, Reverend Schrock will not be officiating. You can be sure of that."

"Of course he will. Susannah might have defected to the Presbyterians, but that was years ago, and she's learned her lesson since then. Besides, Melvin is still a Mennonite—well, loosely speaking."

Lodema Schrock's smirk can spoil milk. "That may be so, but the reverend is out of town."

"That's silly. I saw him at church yesterday."

"But that was then, and this is now, like the young

folks say today. No, I'm afraid the reverend is off fly-fishing in West Virginia until Friday."

"But he can't be! Susannah is getting married Wednesday out at Elvina Stoltzfus's place. Just ask anybody. Ask Freni Hostetler!"

The smirk swelled, becoming a full-fledged grin. "There's no need to ask anybody. I already know about the so-called minister your sister has lined up."

"Oh, Susannah brought in a woman minister? Well, there's nothing wrong with female clergy, dear "

"Oh, this one's a woman, all right, but she's definitely not clergy."

"Then what is she? The pope's pajamas?"

"She's Diana Lefcourt."

My heart sank into my stomach, which in turn sagged until it bumped against my knees. "The same Diana Lefcourt who changed her name to Sister Anjelica Houston?"

"The very one."

"Who heads a commune in Bedford called Convent of the Broken Heart? *That* Sister Anjelica Houston?"

"Yes, except now she goes by the title Mother Anjelica Houston."

"Oh." There was nothing else to say. Diana Lefcourt, a.k.a. Mother Anjelica Houston, is to New Age religion what Shirley MacLaine is to we Mennonites. She's so far out on that limb that there's nothing left to cling to but twigs and leaves. Diana actually believes she is able to call forth into the present, via channeling, the very person of Pharaoh Tutankhamen. It started out as a scam, but tragically progressed far beyond that. Now, not only does Diana swallow her own bunk, but she bunks with the buried. That is to say, on those nights she's not Mother Anjelica Houston, Diana sleeps in a sarcophagus.

"Even you wouldn't approve of a marriage performed by that nutcase, now would you, Magdalena?"

I humbly mumbled something.

"What was that? I'm afraid I didn't hear you."

"I said I'd talk to her, dear."

"You do that. The Good Lord knows that girl would be so much better off if only she had a proper mother."

"She's in her mid-thirties," I wailed. "You can't accuse me of child neglect."

"Just the same, if your mother was still alive, your sister would not be getting married by the high priestess of some satanic cult."

I avoided Lodema's taunting eyes. "You've made your point, dear. Now if you'll just skedaddle, I have guests to attend to."

"Magdalena, are you giving me the bum's rush?"

"Truer words were never spoken, dear." I gave her the gentlest of pushes.

"Why, I never! Just wait until the Mennonite Women's Sewing Circle hears about this."

They say that the best defense is a good offense, and I can be quite offensive if I put my mind to it. "Believe me, they *will* hear about this—from me. You see, I have a phone right here, and you, dear, don't have a cellular phone. By the time you get home everyone in the circle is going to know about your visit—and that of your dear friend, Lady Marion."

"Don't be ridiculous. I don't know anyone by that name."

"Formula number twelve—*Peach Bark,* I believe the color is called."

Lodema stifled a gasp. "I don't know what you're talking about."

"Sure you do, dear. Under those cheap plastic combs of yours is a mop of hair that hasn't been its true color for years. What *is* the true color, dear? Asphalt gray?"

"Why, I never!"

"Sure you do, dear. What is the schedule? Once every six weeks or so?"

Lodema's hands flew to her head. "How did you know? Are my roots showing?"

I leaned closer. "Why, yes they are."

She turned the color of her hair, which was more the color of cigar ash. "You—you—won't tell anyone, will you?"

"That depends, dear. Can you get Reverend Schrock back in Hernia by Wednesday?"

The ashes lightened. "He fishes in the mountains, Magdalena. In *wilderness*. I really have no idea where he is or how to reach him."

It occurred to me that my pastor might possibly be partying in Parkersburg. No, that was on the Ohio River. More likely, he *was* in the mountains—the Reverend is smart enough to stick close to the truth—and was having a highland fling with a lass with even fewer forebears than I. Of course, I kept my suspicions to myself. There is no point in wasting ammunition, after all.

"Doesn't your husband usually fish with Hugh Gingerich?"

"That's who he's with now, but—"

"Give Hugh's wife a call, dear," I said, giving her another gentle push. "Maybe she knows, and even if she doesn't, she might have some clues that the two of you could piece together. If Reverend Schrock ties Susannah's knot, not a word about the devil's dye will pass these lips."

Lodema can move pretty fast for a woman with half a century under her belt.

Speaking of women in their golden years, that night I dreamed Freni came crawling back to me on her hands and knees. I mean that literally. She was even wearing garden knee pads and gloves. I should have known it was all a dream when Freni not only apologized for leaving me in the lurch, but offered to lick my muddy shoes. After all, I never wear muddy shoes.

At any rate, I guess I had Freni on my brain when I went to sleep. Sam had been the perfect butler and had even helped me wash the dishes afterward, but he moved at half the speed of Freni. The gangly Marjorie had tried to pitch in, but after she broke her third plate, I kindly showed her to the kitchen door. Samantha went straight to her room after supper, and as for the others—well, if that new sofa in the parlor sprung a spring, someone was going to pay. So, I guess I'm going to have to come right out and say it: There is no one on God's green earth quite as efficient as Freni Augusta Hostetler.

"Lick the left one a little more," I instructed kindly. "Up along the tongue."

"Ach!"

"I don't know what the big deal is, dear. You licked my right one until it sparkled."

"For shame, Magdalena! How you talk!"

I opened one eye, which by rights should already have been opened. Cautiously I opened the other eye. Binocular vision only confirmed Freni's presence. Indeed, my squat bulky cousin was sitting on the bed, just inches from my face.

I popped up faster than a jack-in-the-box. "Freni! What on earth are you doing in my bedroom? And what in heaven's name are you doing on my bed?"

"Ach, I was just trying to wake you up. You're like a bear in hydration."

"That's hibernation, dear, and that still doesn't explain why you're here."

"Me? Explain? It's you who should explain, Magdalena."

"I don't think so, dear. You're the one who was fired, and now it seems you've stooped to breaking and entering."

"Ach! I quit before I was fired, so that doesn't count. And I didn't break anything, Magdalena."

"That's a legal expression—it deals with trespassing."

"Ach! Me trespassing? I was here when you were born, Magdalena. Right in this room, right in this bed!"

"Well technically, dear, it wasn't this room. After the tornado—"

"But it was *this* bed, Magdalena. And I remember it like it was yesterday. Your mama was a skinny thing like you with no hips to speak of. Ach, you should have heard her scream—like a sow being led to the butcher stand. 'Push,' I kept telling her. 'Push harder.' But it was thundering and lightning so bad, she couldn't even hear me. Of course I could hear her. Rachel Kreider said your mama's screams put the cows off milking for three weeks. But what could I do? We were alone in the house—just your mama and me—"

"And me."

"Yah, and you. Your papa, you see, had gone off to get

the proper midwife, and old Doc Shaffor—well, his wife had just died and he was—ach, such a shame to say it—"

"In his cups?"

Freni frowned. "He was drunk, Magdalena."

"So he was, dear," I said graciously. "Go on."

"So what was I to do? 'Freni,' I said to myself, 'what would your Mose do if he was here, and not off buying horses in Lancaster?' Then I remembered that pincher thing."

"Mama's food tongs?"

"Yah. Mose uses big ones just like that when he births horses. So, I ran to the kitchen to get the pinchers and when I got back, there you were, lying on the bed—all eight and a half pounds of you—and screaming even louder than your mama."

I must have heard the story a million times, but it never failed to warm the cockles of my heart. "And wasn't I just the cutest thing?"

"Ach, such a red, wrinkled face! Like a shriveled apple."

"But a very large apple, right?"

"Yah, a very large, *shriveled* apple. So, Magdalena, do you want your breakfast now?"

"What?"

"I could serve it to you in bed, even."

"What are you talking about?"

"Buckwheat pancakes—real maple syrup, of course— melon, and some delicious fried SPAM® luncheon meat."

"Don't be ridiculous, dear. Mama always said it was a sin to eat in bed, and if I remember correctly, you always agreed."

"Sin, shmin, what your mama doesn't know won't hurt her."

I braced myself against the hard wooden headboard of Granny's bed. If American scientists could harness the energy created when Mama rolls over in her grave, we would never again be made impotent by Middle Eastern potentates. This time, however, I didn't feel as much as a quiver. Perhaps it was lunchtime in Heaven.

Freni noticed the uncommon stillness too, and took advantage of it. "Your mama, rest her soul, was always too hard on you. Give my Magdalena a break, I used to say. You remember all those times I stuck up for you, yah?"

"No."

"No? Well, maybe I should have. But you were always a queer bird, Magdalena—but a nice queer bird. Don't get me wrong."

"Aha, I get it! Freni, you're playing the sycophant, aren't you?"

"I am doing no such thing! I feel perfectly well, Magdalena. Here, feel my forehead."

"You just want your job back, that's why you're being so nice."

"Ach, is that such a terrible thing to want?"

"You tell me, dear. I thought I was *impossible* to work for."

Freni gulped. She was still wearing her black traveling bonnet, and I could see the bow bob under her chin.

"Ach, I—"

The loud rap at the door was sure to summon Mama back from lunch.

"Come in, dear," I called bravely. For all I knew it *was* Mama. Even in my theological circles, physical resurrections have been few and far between, but if the Good Lord starts sending mortals back on a regular basis, you can be sure that Mama will be among the first. Simply put, Heaven would be a more peaceful place without her.

"*Gut marriye,* Magdalena."

"Sam!" I jumped back into bed and pulled the covers up to my chin. "Freni, you know Sam, don't you? Of course you do! I've heard you say such nice things about him."

Freni colored. "What *is* he doing here?"

I glanced at the clock on my night stand. "What *are* you doing here, Sam? It's only six-thirty. I told you this bunch of English all said they like to sleep late. Except for Mrs. Burk—she's the one whose husband is missing— they don't want their breakfast until eight."

"Yah, I remember, but last night Mrs. Burk said she wanted her breakfast at seven."

I groaned. "This would never have happened with the celebrities. They never ate breakfast before noon."

Freni hopped off my bed. "Breakfast? Why are you talking with this man about breakfast?"

I smiled sweetly. "Because he's my new cook. Don't you worry, dear, I'm sure Sam wouldn't mind rustling up a little breakfast for you too."

"Ach!"

"Oh, that's right, you already made buckwheat pancakes. Well, since I'm not particularly hungry this morning, would you mind terribly if Sam serves my share to Mrs. Burk?"

Freni's mouth opened and closed with the regularity of a pump valve, but no sounds came out.

"Yes, dear?" I asked patiently.

Like the pump she started to sputter, and then the words came pouring out in a torrent. Since my cousin is a god-fearing Amish woman they are all repeatable, but I won't waste your time. Besides, they were in Pennsylvania Dutch. Suffice it to say, Mama would have approved of every one of Freni's admonitions, and even Lodema Schrock would have little to add.

When Freni was quite through she bustled her broad back out of my room and slammed the door behind her. The way the house shook I knew that Mama was adding a few vibrations of her own.

"Magdalena," Sam said quietly as the last bit of plaster drifted down from the ceiling, "maybe you go too far."

"*Et tu*, Brutus?" I wailed.

Samuel looked like a possum caught in the beam of my flashlight. It was time to bring him up to speed.

"She brings it on herself, dear. Last night was the fifty-second time she's quit since I opened the original inn. Now, don't just stand there, dear, *tempus fugit*."

"Ach!"

"You're wasting time," I explained kindly. "After breakfast we have that search to organize, remember?"

Sam shook his head.

I sat bolt upright. Unfortunately, this sudden action allowed three inches of my flannel nightgown to show. Poor Sam's face turned the color of Susannah's eyes the morning after her senior prom.

I clutched the blanket to my scrawny bosom. "You're not backing out of your offer, are you, dear?"

Sam looked graciously away. "No, I will help with the search. But now we must search for two people."

"*Two* people?"

Sam nodded, still focused on some dust bunnies in the corner. "Yah. It is terrible news what I must say."

Thirteen

"**S**ay it," I wailed. "It's Susannah, isn't?"

I am ashamed to admit this, but Susannah has gone missing more times than Freni's quit her job. Some might say that gal suffers from wanderlust, but between you and me, it's just pure lust. That's right, it's nothing more than sex that has inspired my sister to visit every roadside rest and truck stop in the lower forty-eight. As far as I know, Susannah has never been to Hawaii—or had sex there—but she has been to Alaska, and it is rumored that her passion was responsible for melting several igloos. But just for the record, she was *not* responsible for El Niño.

"No, it's not your sister. It's Mrs. Yoder."

I drummed on the blanket with my long, slender fingers. Yoder is the most common surname in both the local Mennonite and Amish communities.

"It's Irma Yoder," Sam said quickly. "Old Irma."

Ah, now we're getting somewhere. There are many old Irma Yoders in the area as well, but only one *Old* Irma Yoder. At one hundred and two she isn't the oldest woman around, but thanks to that cheddar-shredding tongue, she is the most memorable.

"So, Old Irma's gone missing, has she?"

"Yah. I stopped by on my way here to give her some milk. She wasn't at home."

"Maybe she's off visiting relatives. Or maybe she went shopping." I shudder to say this, but Old Irma still drives. Not that I have anything against the elderly drivers, mind you, but when they pull out on to a major highway, they should at least be going the speed of lava.

"Ach, she was there last night. I asked her if she needed anything, and she said she could use a little milk. I promised to drop it by this morning on my way to work. Six o'clock, I tell her."

"You're two-timing me with Old Irma?" Of course I was only teasing.

"Ach! The Bible says to give what we have to the poor, and I have lots of milk."

"I know, dear, I was only pulling your leg. Maybe Old Irma forgot about your appointment. Maybe she was sleeping in." Both Amish and Mennonites are notoriously early risers. I wouldn't be surprised if Mama still gets up at five, even in Heaven.

"Yah, first I think maybe that is so, because her car is there. But then I remember Old Irma can't hear so well. Maybe she has not put in the—uh—uh—"

"Hearing aid?"

"Yah. That's what I think to myself, so I knock even louder."

"And?"

"The door opened."

"So you checked inside, of course." The fact that the door was unlocked was irrelevant to our conversation. Nobody in Hernia locks their doors—except for me. And even I would probably not be doing that if Little Eddy Beiler hadn't wandered in one fine afternoon when I was alone and with a flip of his topcoat proved to me that he was misnamed.

"Yah, I went in and checked. No Old Irma."

"Hmm. Maybe she went out for a walk and just didn't shut it tight behind her."

Sam scratched his sparsely covered chin. "Yah, maybe so. Except for one thing."

"Yes?"

"Maybe it is not such a big thing."

"What is it?" I practically screamed. "Do I need to get a crowbar to pry out this morsel?"

Sam looked like a sheep who correctly answered his algebra question. "Uh—"

"Just tell me!"

"Old Irma left the water running in the kitchen sink."

"That is serious." I wasn't being facetious, either. Not only can Old Irma lacerate lactose with her lingua, she can pinch a penny until it screams. It was clear to me that Hernia's most acerbic centenarian was not just missing, she'd been abducted.

"Maybe you should call Melvin," Samuel said quietly.

"Definitely so," I said, and reached for the phone.

"Good. But be patient, Magdalena. Melvin Stoltzfus is sometimes a difficult man."

"*Sometimes?* The man was a breach birth, for crying out loud, and he grows into a bigger pain every day. But don't you worry about him—Vee haf our vays."

Sam laughed nervously while I dialed.

My nemesis picked up on the first ring. "You have reached 555-9247," he said in a monotone. "I'm sorry we're unable to come to the phone right now—"

"Melvin, I know that's you!"

"So please leave your message after the beep."

I waited until the beep. "Melvin is a big fat idiot," I shouted, my mouth pressed against the receiver.

"Ach! Ach!" Sam was flapping his arms in distress, so I motioned him out of the room. Apparently some of my ways are a little too English for the Australian.

"Melvin! This is official police business and if you don't stop this nonsense I'm telling your mama what you did last night."

His gasp flattened my ear against the receiver. "Yoder, is that you?"

"Is that Mags?" I heard Susannah whisper in the background.

"Of course it's me. Who else would be foolish enough to call you at this hour of the morning?"

"You won't tell Mama, will you, Yoder? I mean, we're getting married tomorrow, and we only—"

"Can it, Melvin. I don't want to know what you and Susannah did, or didn't do. I want you to hop into your official police car and drive on out to Irma Yoder's place. That's Old Irma out on Kuntzler Lane."

Melvin gasped again, and my ear practically disappeared into the phone. "What for, Yoder?"

"She's disappeared."

"You mean she died?" He sounded hopeful.

"I don't know. She's missing from her house. Sam— Strubbly Sam—says he was supposed to deliver milk to her this morning, and no one was there."

"That means nothing, Yoder."

"Perhaps. But her car was there—and the water was running in the kitchen sink. Melvin, this is something you should check out."

"Don't tell me my job, Yoder."

"Do I detect a hint of fear, dear? Old Irma may have a gouda-gouging tongue, but you're still bigger than her."

There was a moment of terrified silence. "I'm *not* afraid of her, Yoder."

"Of course not, dear, I didn't think you were. So, you'll check on her."

"Yes, damn it."

"Don't you swear on my phone line," I snapped, and hung up. Hard.

I am a God-fearing woman, and dress like one. No strumpet-scarlet or prostitute pink for me, thank you very much. Ditto for yuppie yellow. The Good Lord created black before any other color—just read your Bible—when he created the darkness upon the face of the earth. Then came blue for the sky and sea, and green for plants. These are the colors he prefers us to dress in, if you ask me. But when it comes to cars, I'm sure the kind Creator looks the other way—at least He never seems to have penalized me for my red BMW.

At any rate, Tuesday morning, the day of my sister's shindig, I carefully selected a navy blue dress that would take me through to the evening and a pair of comfortable black brogans. Of course my dress sleeves extended beyond the elbows and my skirt length well below the knees. Even the Lord isn't fond of looking at those.

When I was decently attired and had my hair neatly swept into a bun and covered with an organza prayer cap, I stepped out into the hall. Now, I consider myself to be a calm, sensible woman, so you can imagine how startled I was by the looming shape of Scott Montgomery when I tell you I literally jumped out of my shoes.

"What on earth are you doing lurking outside my bedroom door?" I demanded.

To be honest, he seemed every bit as surprised as I. Fortunately for him, he had laced his shoes tighter.

"Oh! Uh—well, I was coming to see you."

"You were?" I must confess to feeling vaguely titilated. The tall, comely Minnesotan was by far the most attractive male guest in residence.

"Yah," he said in that charming land-o'-lakes accent. "I was wondering if you might have a county map we could borrow."

This certainly piqued my interest, but before somebody peeked into the downstairs hall, we needed to relocate to a more public spot. To be caught standing just outside my bedroom with a handsome man was one way to put a feather in my prayer cap, but it would ruin my reputation. Folks might start expecting me to wear fuchsia and coral. Prudently I shepherded him into the lobby.

"Yes, I do happen to have a county map—and a very detailed one at that—but why, may I ask, do you want to borrow it? Are you planning to join the search party? If you are, you needn't worry about getting lost. That's Buffalo Mountain in the distance across the road, and Stucky Ridge is behind us. Slave Creek runs right in between and passes just on the eastern side of Hernia. The PennDutch is less than five miles north of the center of town."

"Thanks for the pointers. I'm sure they'll come in useful."

"You still haven't answered my question. Why do you need the map?"

He smiled, revealing a few wispy cobwebs clinging to

the overhead light. "The guys and I like to play these silly little games. Reconnaissance missions, strategy maneuvers—that sort of thing. A good map helps with the planning."

"I see. So, you weren't planning to help with the search?"

"Actually, we'd like to incorporate it into our war games."

I flinched. "Please, no three-letter words in this house."

"Excuse me?"

"You see, we're pacifists and—oh, never mind. I'll get you the map right after breakfast."

"Thank you. That's awfully kind of you. May I please ask one more favor?"

"Ask away."

"About the map—could we keep it a secret from the others?"

"But why? That wouldn't be fair, would it?"

A second smiled exposed the dust bunnies in the far corners of the lobby. "That's exactly why."

"I don't get it."

"You see, part of the game is to outsmart the other players. I bet none of them have thought to ask you for a map, have they?"

"You're right about that." I grinned, but genetics has determined that I have yuppie yellow teeth. I couldn't light up a jack-o-lantern on the dark side of the moon.

"So, you won't say anything, will you?"

"These lips are sealed, dear." I meant it, of course, but I kept my fingers crossed behind my back just to be on the safe side. They say that all is fair in love and you-know-what, and that being the case, I didn't want to put

my soul in jeopardy in case an even smarter player decided to grease my palms with the color of nature.

Alas, no one offered to even touch my palms, much
less grease them. Perhaps they thought the grease Sam
served up with breakfast was enough. The man should
have stuck to his menu and served SPAM® as the only
meat, but oh no, in a grandstanding effort to secure Freni's
job for himself, my busy-bee butler plied my guests with
platters of thick slabs of bacon, sausage patties, sausage
links, and generous slabs of fried scrapple.

"Hey, what's this stuff?" Frizzy-haired Sandy Hart
jabbed a wedge of scrapple with a fork that had already
been licked.

"That's scrapple, dear."

"What's that?"

"It's ground liver pudding cooked with corn meal and
flour and then fried."

"Yuck. And you have the nerve to charge us big bucks
for that?"

I groaned behind the privacy of my napkin. Now I had
a manic on my hands. If she didn't put a lid on it real
soon, one of us was going to be very depressed.

"It's authentic, dear. The Amish eat it all the time."

"Big deal. I don't want to do *everything* the Amish do,
just the fun stuff."

"And what would that be?"

"Go to barn-raisings and quilting bees. That kind of
thing."

"You just missed a barn-raising, dear." Much to my
surprise, my eyes had filled with tears. The old barn had
seen many good times—a couple of murders and an ill-
fated wedding notwithstanding.

"And buggy rides. The brochure you sent had a buggy on the front, but you don't even have one, do you? Now that's false advertising, if you ask me."

"Nobody did, hon," Bob said gently.

Sandy turned on her husband like a pit bull on its handler. "Hey, whose side are you on?"

"Yours, hon."

"No, you're not. I can tell by the way you look at her that you've got a thing for her, don't you!"

"Sandy!

"Well, you do! And don't lie about this one, Robert. I know all about that bimbo of yours back in Tulsa."

"Bimbo? What bimbo?"

"Megan. You know, your so-called ex-secretary. The one who worked for you for fifteen years in the dealership. The one you called your *team*mate."

Teammate? I made a quick dab at my eyes with a corner of my napkin. One of the advantages of not wearing makeup is that there's nothing to run or smear. Unfortunately, when I wake up in the morning, that's as good as I'll look all day.

I jabbed at Bob with my fork. Of course I was careful not to actually touch him, because I had yet to complete my meal.

"You have a lot of nerve to suggest we'd make good teammates."

Sandy's eyes assumed the size of Sam's flapjacks. "He did?"

"He did."

Surely the swill that Sandy swore would have made a sailor swoon. I did my Christian duty and jabbed at her. Unfortunately I miscalculated the distance, and a tip of one tine brushed her sleeve.

Sandy shrieked, and swore again. This time the word *lawsuit* reared its ugly head.

"Sorry, dear, it was an accident."

She turned to the others. "Y'all are my witnesses. This crazy woman stabbed me."

"Don't be calling the kettle black, dear," I said calmly. "And besides, it's *him* you're mad at, not me."

"Nah, my little Bobby's bimbos don't really bother me, but this"—she rubbed her elbow—"really hurts."

There are times when it pays to have a sister like Susannah. Some of my best strategies come from my ethically-challenged sibling. I'm not saying it is any less wrong of me to copy her, but sometimes a gal's gotta do what a gal's gotta do. Besides, a few of Susannah's tricks— like divert and conquer—are not wrong, they're just highly effective ways to manipulate adults that every teenager knows, and most adults have forgotten.

"Did you say bimbos, dear?" I asked pleasantly. "Is there more than one tart on the Hart plate?"

"Sandy!" Bob barked.

She smirked and turned to me. "Well, it's true. Bob likes them young, and Megan is getting a little long in the tooth now. Lord knows, she must be nearing your age."

"Which is a good twenty years younger than *your* age, dear," I said, remaining calm. I'll take an insult over a lawsuit any day.

"Even so, Bob likes them young. Heather, now she can't be a day over twenty-one, and Angie, well, I have things in the back of my fridge that are older than her."

"I'm sure you do," I said kindly. Frankly, I was flattered that Bob had deemed me young enough to be his playmate—I mean, teammate.

Bob, however, was clearly taken aback. "You know

about Heather and Angie? Why haven't you said anything?"

Sandy shrugged. "Emil helps take my mind off things," she said to me in a low, conspiratorial voice. Apparently it wasn't low enough.

"Who the hell is Emil?"

"I don't allow swearing on these premises!" This time tines touched tissue.

It shouldn't have come as a surprise, but Bob Hart knew even more swear words than his wife. I poked him into submission and turned to Sandy.

"Do tell, dear." Now, lest you judge me, I must hasten to say that yes, Jimmy Carter was right, it is a sin to lust in one's heart. But I can find nothing in my Bible that says it's a sin to listen to the lust of others.

Sandy sat back in chair and smiled. "If Bobby can have his bimbos, then I can have my boytoy. Right, Miss Yoder?"

"What's good for the gander is good for the goose, dear." I wasn't condoning her behavior, mind you, since geese of both sexes seldom die of natural causes on my farm.

"Yeah, you hear that, Bobby? Miss Yoder here sees things my way."

"Not hardly dear. For one thing—"

Bob Hart held his elbows clamped against his sides, but his gaze was on me. "You see what you've done?"

"Me?"

"I told you she was ill, Miss Yoder."

Sandy stood, and in the process managed to knock over Samantha's water glass. Although perturbed, the petite pianist was apparently far too polite to protest— although perhaps she was simply afraid.

"And that's another thing," Sandy screamed. "You're always telling people that I'm ill. Well, there is nothing wrong with me! I am not a manic-depressive. You're the one with the problem, not me."

"Shut up, Sandy."

"Don't you tell me to shut up! I want everyone here to know that—"

"They are invited to a party tonight!" Trust me, I can scream louder than Sandy. When you're five foot ten, your lungs are like boats.

"A party tonight?" someone echoed. I think it was Dixie Montgomery, because I heard traces of that delightful Minnesota accent.

"That's right, a party. My sister Susannah is getting married tomorrow, and tonight's the celebratory bash."

It would serve Susannah right to have a bunch of senior citizens crash her party. Besides, my guests, who had for the most part been transfixed by the domestic discord, needed a new and even bigger diversion.

"Ooh, Cuddle Buns," Doris cooed obscenely to her tubby teddy, "a Mennonite party! Doesn't that seem like fun?"

Sandy sat. "Will there be buggy rides?"

I looked meaningfully at Sam, who had been lurking quietly in a corner. While it's not true that a glance from me can turn small animals into stone—Mama's could, you know—some of my stronger stares have produced remarkable results.

"Yah, buggy rides," Sam said, shaking his head.

"I forget what they call it," Doris said, disengaging herself from her hubby for the purpose of illustration, "but will they throw us up in the air and catch us on a quilt?"

"That's the Eskimos, dear, and I believe they use walrus hides." I kindly refrained from pointing out that anyone throwing a seventy-year-old, overweight woman into the air had best catch her on an ambulance stretcher.

"Horseshoes," Scott said, his accent just as charming as his wife's. "I hope they play horseshoes. I haven't had a chance to play in years."

"Scott was the state champion back in 1956," Dixie added proudly.

"My Frank was the Missouri state champion in 1956 and 1958," Marjorie said in a less charming accent, although she did have a strong, clear voice.

Dixie nodded. "That's right. I remember. Scott and Frank played against each other in the nationals."

Marjorie turned to her husband. "You did? You never mentioned that. Who won?"

"Oh, that's right," Sandy sniffed, "that would have been before your time."

"*Way* before," Doris said and giggled.

"I won," Frank said. I do believe those were the first words I'd heard him utter since checking in the day before.

"You *did*? Honey, that's wonderful. How come you never told me that?"

"Because he cheated," Dixie said. You might think it impossible to sound vehement in that lovely lilt, but believe me, it isn't.

I was running out of diversions. "Well, now, are we all ready to begin the search?"

"What search?" Marjorie asked.

"Honestly," Sandy said, "doesn't your husband tell you anything?"

I tapped on my water glass with my knife. The fact that

I got melted butter and maple syrup on the glass did little to improve my mood.

"Breakfast is over, dears. Now go to your rooms, brush your teeth—do whatever you need to do—and meet me in the parlor in half an hour. Just make sure your beds are made and your rooms are swept first."

"That's ridiculous," Sandy snapped. "She's treating us like we're children, instead of paying guests. Bobby, do something."

"She's magnificent," her husband mumbled.

"What did you say?"

The hedgerows rose to new heights in mock surprise. "I didn't say anything, hon."

"Yes, you did."

I tapped on my glass again. "The last one to leave this room gets to wash the dishes. And I *mean* it."

The room cleared in record time. Even Sam made himself as scarce as pearls around an Amish neck.

When I was quite alone, I loaded up my plate with another stack of pancakes and a couple slices of delicious fried SPAM® luncheon meat. After all, it is a sin to skimp on breakfast since that is the first meal Adam and Eve ate in the Garden of Eden. Okay, so maybe I don't have any proof of that, but neither is there any proof to the contrary. At any rate, what I should have done was gone back to bed and pulled the covers up over my head.

Fourteen

I ate fourteen pancakes. This is not something I do on a regular basis, but Sam's were the lightest, fluffiest pancakes I'd ever set teeth in. Plus, the man had the audacity to serve freshly churned butter and genuine maple syrup that had been heated and was still warm at the time of the grand exodus. I was feeling satiated, to put it politely, when the doorbell rang.

"Sam!" I yelled. How quickly one acclimates to luxury.

Alas, Sam was not forthcoming. After an irksome number of rings I waddled to the door and jerked it open.

"Yes?"

"Yoder!"

I stared at the repulsive face of my nemesis. That fact that he was just hours' away from becoming my sister's husband did nothing to mitigate my feelings of revulsion. All right, so the Bible tells us not to hate, but it says little about loathing.

You'd loathe Melvin too, if you knew him like I do. The man is a snide, arrogant, know-it-all who, like many of this ilk, actually knows very little at all. The only thing Melvin Stoltzfus excels at is getting under people's skin. Even if the Gypsy story isn't true, I know for a fact that

Elvina Stoltzfus took her son to Pittsburgh and tried to lose him on the subway. Unfortunately the city only has one line and for half the distance the train is above ground. Well, so much for last year's plan. Maybe Susannah will come up with something better this year.

"Hey, Yoder, you know that when you gawk like that, with your mouth wide open and everything, you look just like a turkey on a hot day? You even have those wattles under your neck."

The reasonable part of me wanted to slam the door in Melvin's face and pretend the wind did it. "This better be official business, dear."

"Oh, it's official, all right. I'm here to arrest you for the murder of Irma Yoder."

I belched in astonishment. The mantis never ceases to amaze me.

"Does your keeper know you've figured out the trick to unlocking your cage door, dear?"

"Yoder, you have the right to remain silent. You have the right—"

"To call the wedding off!" I wailed.

He didn't exactly push his way inside, because I backed up voluntarily. The man has the hygiene habits of a hyena.

"Yoder, don't make this any harder than it has to be."

Not having an electric cattle prod handy, there was nothing I could do but scoot around and close the door. It was still chilly out and there was no need to heat up all of Bedford County.

"You've got thirty seconds to try and make some sense," I said, exhibiting the patience of a saint. "And that's only out of consideration for my baby sister."

Melvin's eyes function independently, like the shopping

cart wheels at Sam's Corner Market. His left eye, which is considerably larger than his right, appeared to focus on my face.

"Well, you were right, Yoder—of course you would be, you're the one who made the call."

"Right about *what*?"

"As if you didn't know."

"Spill it, knucklehead!" I screamed. "What was I right about?"

I know this may strike you as sacrilegious, but if Melvin had been alive in Jesus' day—okay, maybe that's going too far. But surely Ghandi would have grabbed a gun and added a few more holes to Melvin's cranial collection.

No doubt you are wondering how Melvin ever managed to get the job of police chief in the first place. Well, the answer is simple: *No one else wanted the job.* Besides, having a public official we can all legitimately hate has been the greatest unifying force our little town could possibly have. And barring a war on American soil, or some horrible natural disaster, we really don't need someone more competent. So we tend to think of our police chief as a malevolent but manageable plague. Outside of this, there are actually a few good things that Melvin does for the community, but I don't have time to think of them now.

Melvin took so long to answer my question that even Mother Teresa, God rest her soul, would have tried to strangle his scrawny, insectile neck. The Good Lord knows I had my hands poised and ready.

"Somebody finally got to Old Irma. But why am I wasting my breath?"

I gasped. "You found her body?"

"Of course not, Yoder. You're too clever. No corpus, no habeus."

I sighed. "Yes, dear, I remember. You flunked Latin in high school. So you didn't find a body. What makes you think somebody did her in?"

The left eye drifted, its gaze replaced by its smaller companion. "The blood. Yoder, how careless can you get?"

"Pretty careless, dear. I accidentally let you in, didn't I? Now what's this about blood? Strubbly Sam didn't say anything about that."

"You left blood on the kitchen faucet handles, Yoder. I got me a sample and I'm sending it in to Harrisburg. I should have the results back in three days. Now, if you'll just cooperate and give me a sample of your blood—"

I took a menacing, un-Mennonite step forward. "You want *blood*?"

Melvin took a Stoltzfus step backward. "Why did you do it, Yoder?"

"Don't be ridiculous—"

"Don't even try to deny it, Yoder. Both Mishler brothers say they saw your car parked in Irma's driveway Sunday morning. *Both* brothers, Yoder. And as we all know, you're the only one in Hernia with a red BMW."

"Which proves nothing. I was offering the woman a ride to church."

"Ha! She has her own car, Yoder."

"That she does. But a few of us are trying to see to it that she drives it as little as possible. The woman drives like a blind teenager on steroids. She's clipped more mailboxes than Freni's clipped coupons."

Melvin smirked. "Yeah, she helps me meet my ticket quota."

"Melvin, why do you do this to me? Why do you constantly accuse me of things you know I haven't done? Of things that haven't even *been* done?"

Melvin's mandibles moved silently for a full minute before the first sound escaped his lipless mouth. "Because you always have an answer."

"I *do*?"

"I'm only going to say this once, Yoder, but you're kind of smart."

"*What* did you just say?" I longed to sit, but the nearest chair was behind the check-in counter, and legs weren't going to carry me that far.

For just an instant both of Melvin's eyes met mine. "You're like the big sister I never had."

"Expound, dear." The brother I never had would have been *nothing* like Melvin.

"You always have the answers, Yoder. It's like you think, or something. Anyway, I just know I can always come to you for help."

"Is that what you call it? Accusing me of murdering a centenarian?"

"Don't be ridiculous, Yoder. I didn't say anything about a Roman soldier."

"Let me get this straight, dear. Your asinine accusations are merely your way of asking me for help?"

"This man has his pride, Yoder."

"If only this woman had a can of Raid. Melvin, you're pathetic, you know that?"

He actually hung his monstrous head in shame. For the first time ever I felt sorry *for* him, not just sorry that I knew him.

"Yoder, you'll help me, won't you?"

Okay, as a Christian woman it is behooving to me to

be totally honest, so I will confess that for a mere nanosecond I had the impulse to clasp his carapace to my scrawny bosom and give him the love Elvina obviously had not. Thank the Good Lord the impulse passed so quickly.

"Yeah, I'll help you."

"You *will*?" Both eyes rotated upwards in their sockets and I knew he could see my face even though his nose was pointed directly at the floor.

"But you have to agree to let me be in charge."

"Agreed."

"I mean *totally* in charge."

"Uh—okay."

"Great. Now go home, Melvin, and get ready for tonight's party, not to mention your wedding."

The huge head lifted slowly. "I can't do that. I mean, someone needs to keep an official eye on things."

"Then our deal is off—you're on your own. Swivel those orbs any direction you want, just not on me."

"Okay, Yoder, I'm going." He took a single step backward.

"Then be gone!"

"You drive a hard bargain, Yoder." Two more steps and he was almost to the door.

"Look, Melvin, we don't know what happened to Old Irma. Maybe she cut her thumb making breakfast, or maybe that's blood from a piece of meat. At any rate, I have a search party organized and—"

"You do? Wow, Yoder, I have to hand it to you. You're really on the ball."

"Thanks, dear." There was no need to tell my numb-skull nemesis that a guest of mine was missing as well, was there? After all, omitting information is not a sin.

Just pick your Bible if you don't believe me. There is plenty missing from *that* book.

I could tell by the way his arms were twitching that Melvin was coming dangerously close to hugging me. Since I would sooner dance naked in downtown Hernia, I gave him a helpful push and slammed the door behind him.

The next thing I did was dial Lodema. Thankfully, she answered on the first ring.

"Reverend, is that you? It better be, because I have an emergency on my hands. I probably don't need to tell you that it involves that old spinster, Magdalena. Big Magdalena, that is."

Of all things! Who would have guessed that the pastor's wife addressed him by his title in the privacy of their own home? My shock rendered me temporarily speechless. For the first time in months I could hear my heart pound.

"Reverend, are those bongos I hear in the background? Look, Reverend, you better not be up in Pittsburgh at your mama's house. I've told you a million times I won't stand for a mama's boy."

I kindly hung up and dialed again. "This is Magdalena," I said before Lodema had a chance to blink, much less speak. "I need your help."

"What? Magdalena, did you just call?"

"Don't be silly, Lodema. Did you get in touch with your husband?"

"Yes and no."

"I don't have time for riddles, dear. Pick an answer—just make sure it's the right one."

"Well, he's not at the motel where he said he'd be

staying, but I think he rang just a minute ago. Your call must have disconnected us."

"Think again, dear. We're part of the Bedford calling area now, and it's all computerized. Did you check with Esther Gingerich?"

"Hugh didn't go fishing," Lodema said in a tiny little-girl voice. "He has the flu."

"Oh. Well, that's too bad, I'm sure." Now *that* was a lie. But an understandable lie, of course. You see, after my bogus marriage to the bigamist Aaron became public knowledge, Hugh had been one of my most vocal detractors. If Hugh had had his way, I'd still be picking feathers out of my teeth and scrubbing tar from between my toes.

"Is that all you wanted, Magdalena? To nag me about getting the reverend home in time for your sister's wedding? Well, I'm doing my best. It's not my fault he gave me the wrong motel phone number."

"Of course not, dear. And I didn't call just to nag. You are a multifaceted woman, after all. I thought we might explore another facet of you."

"Now who's speaking in riddles? Get off the phone, Magdalena. The reverend might be trying to call."

"Okay, but I need to ask you a quick question."

"You can buy formula number twelve at Sam Yoder's Corner Market. But you already knew that, didn't you?"

"This has nothing to do with hair dye, dear. It's about Irma Yoder. Old Irma."

"What about her?"

"How well do you know her?"

Lodema's sigh rustled the thin blond hairs on my arm. "The woman has a tongue that could slice Swiss. You don't want to get on her bad side. I can tell you that."

"Does she have any enemies?"

"Do you?"

"Touché, dear. But I mean real enemies, somebody who might want to do away with her—never mind, I get your point. Just tell me this, did Old Irma have any plans for today? Anybody expected to drop by—maybe pick her up and take her shopping someplace? Or to the doctor?"

"How should I know? I'm not her social secretary."

"Indeed, you're not, but you are her pastor's wife. You might have overheard some conversation that might give a clue as to her whereabouts."

"Well, I didn't. Why the sudden interest in Old Irma?"

"It isn't sudden, dear. You know good and well I sometimes pick her up for church."

"Magdalena Portulacca Yoder, you should be ashamed of yourself."

"I beg your pardon?"

"You're not dealing with an amateur, here, Magdalena. I know you want information on Old Irma, but I can't be of any help unless you get to the point."

"Okay! Old Irma is missing, and so is one of my guests, and there's blood on the sink and the water was running, and since you're the nosiest woman in the county, I thought if anyone would know anything, it would be you."

I would not have been surprised if Lodema had chosen that moment to shatter my eardrum. Instead she was remarkably cooperative, which made me highly suspicious. Perhaps the reverend hadn't gone fishing after all, but merely around the bend. Perhaps he had a gun pointed at his wife's dyed head and was forcing her to be nice for a change.

"Old Irma is not who you think she is, Magdalena," Lodema said without a trace of sarcasm.

"Give me a break, dear. I don't believe for one second that tired old rumor that Old Irma Yoder is really Milton Berle."

"Well, you must admit that was rather creative of me. Remember those old TV shows with Uncle Miltie?"

"I don't watch television, dear, and as the pastor's wife, neither should you."

"The reverend says that nature shows are a testimonial to the Creator."

"Can we please get back to Old Irma?" I wailed.

"Ah, yes, the mystery woman. Well, for starters, she's not one hundred and two."

"Yes, she is—"

"She's one hundred and three. I checked her baptismal record. It's on file in the church office."

"Well, the nerve of the woman!"

"Exactly. But oh, Magdalena, there's much more. And I mean really juicy stuff."

"How juicy?"

"This will knock your socks off, as the young people say."

Always a cooperative soul, I slipped off my shoes. "Sock it to me, babe."

Fifteen

Hearty SPAM® Breakfast Skillet

✦

2 cups frozen diced or shredded potatoes
½ cup chopped onion
¼ medium green bell pepper, cut into 1-inch thin
strips
¼ medium red or yellow pepper, cut into 1-inch thin
strips
2 teaspoons oil
1 (12-ounce) can SPAM® Luncheon Meat, cut into
julienne strips
1 (8-ounce) carton frozen fat-free egg product,
thawed, or 4 eggs
¼ teaspoon dried basil
¼ teaspoon salt
⅛ teaspoon pepper
6 drops hot pepper sauce
¼ cup shredded Cheddar cheese

In large nonstick skillet, cook potatoes, onion, and peppers in oil over medium-high heat 5 minutes, stirring constantly. Add SPAM®; cook and stir 5 minutes. In small bowl, combine egg product, basil, salt, pepper, and hot pepper sauce; blend well. Pour over mixture in skillet. Cover. Cook over medium-low heat 8 to 12 minutes or until set. Sprinkle with cheese; remove from heat. Serves 6.

NUTRITIONAL INFORMATION PER SERVING:
 Calories 294; Protein 17g; Carbohydrate 17g; Fat 18g; Cholesterol 50mg; Sodium 725mg.

Sixteen

Is it a sin to salivate at the mere promise of juicy gossip? If so, call me the Whore of Babylon. You may even call me Lucifer, if you must, because I was drooling like a three-month-old baby with a tooth coming in.

I have tried to be a good Christian neighbor to Old Irma, the Good Lord knows I have. But the woman is *impossible* to like. Even Papa, who had the soul of a saint, prayed daily for charitable feelings toward the old crone.

There is no way getting around it; Irma Yoder is mean. True, it was Lodema Schrock who spread the word about the breakup of my pseudo-marriage with Aaron, and who tried to drum me out of the Mennonite Women's Sewing Circle, but it was Irma who stood in the doorway of Beechy Grove Mennonite Church and whacked me with her cane.

"You sitting down, Magdalena?" Lodema asked.

"Yes, and I'm bracing myself against the check-in counter. Let me have it."

"Well, you're never going to believe this, and I promised the reverend that I would never repeat confidences he shares with me, but this one I overheard by accident, so strictly speaking, I'm not obligated to keep it to myself, am I?"

"Spit it out, dear!"

"Okay, hold your horses. I just want to do the right thing." Lodema sounded dangerously hesitant. "I mean, this is the right thing, isn't it?"

I refrained from telling Lodema to have her tongue surgically removed. "The right thing is to find the old gal and make sure nothing has happened to her. Who knows what information might be useful?"

"That's what I thought. So, here goes. Old Irma, when she was not so old, was once a cabaret singer in Paris."

"Get out of town!"

"I beg your pardon? You said you *wanted* to hear everything."

I am constantly reminded that, thanks to a worldly clientele, I am far hipper than your average Hernian. "That's just an expression, dear. Is this on the level?"

"I heard her tell the reverend myself. You see, sometimes I do secretarial work for him—the church doesn't have a secretary you know, even though Elm Hill Mennonite has a full-time paid secretary, and they're only half our size—"

"Get back to your story, dear. Please," I was careful to add. Lodema wouldn't hesitate to hang up on God.

"Well, the wall between the reverend's study and that little closet I get stuck in is only made of plywood. You can hear everything through it. So anyway, there I am, typing away on the Sunday bulletin, and I hear Irma Yoder tell the reverend that back in the early 1930s she worked in Paris. He asks what kind of work she did—maybe she was a missionary or something because you know, the French are Catholics and in need of salvation—but oh no, she says she worked as a dancer in something called the 'follies' and then when her legs started looking old, she switched over to singing. Sang in what they call a cabaret. Sort of smoky nightclub, I guess, where they had variety acts. You ever been to any kind of show, Magdalena?"

"Is this a trap?"

"Oh, come on, you can tell me!"

"No, I haven't," I said honestly and quite emphatically. "Have you?"

"Once. I wasn't born a Mennonite, you know. My folks were Methodists."

I gasped. That was certainly news to me. Methodists were just spitting distance from Presbyterians who, everyone knows, are practically Unitarians except that they believe in the Trinity.

Lodema sighed, ruffling my arm hairs again. "I was eighteen. For my high-school graduation present my folks took me into New York City—to a Broadway play! *West Side Story,* can you imagine that? There was dancing and even a little swearing!"

"Any nudity?"

She sighed again. "No. But there were some awfully tight jeans."

I was torn between begging her for details and getting on with my business. Reluctantly I decided that Lodema's sordid past would have to take a back seat to Irma's.

"How did Irma Yoder get on that slippery road to you-know-where? You did say she was born a Mennonite, didn't you?"

"Oh, yes, but when she was still very young she was jilted by her fiancé. He literally left her standing at the altar. Walked out during the middle of the ceremony.

"The very next day Irma left Hernia and went to Pittsburgh, where she got a job as a waitress. Then one day a customer heard her singing and offered her a job at a nightclub. Well, we all know that the road to hell is wide and slippery, and Irma Yoder slid straight from Pittsburgh to Paris. I saw an old newspaper story on her once. It said she was really quite good. Not only could she sing, but she played some sort of horn. A trumpet, I think. Some kind of brass instrument, at any rate."

"Imagine that, a Mennonite girl in Paris."

"Well! She was no *longer* a proper Mennonite by then, was she? Lydia Shoemaker says she heard from Veronica Rickenbach who heard from Anna Lichty that Irma took lovers."

"Get out of town!"

"Why, Magdalena, I thought—"

"It's just an expression!" I wailed. "I already told you that. Now get on with your story."

"Well, if you insist. Where was I?"

"Lovers," I hissed. This was not prurient interest, mind you—well, maybe it was, but I was properly appalled as well. Still, the very word *lovers* intrigued me. Except for Melvin, Susannah had never had any lovers—just boyfriends and what she called one-night stands; the dregs of society gleaned from rest areas along the interstate and cafés where the flies piled on the windowsills with each passing year. I need not tell you that *I* had never had a lover. A lover was—well, it was almost literary. But still a sin, of course.

"Ah yes, Irma Yoder's lovers. Aristocrats, most of them. Men with titles, or important government positions. She was a great beauty, you know—in the worldly sense of the word. Anyway, it is even rumored that she was Charles DeGaulle's mistress for a while.

Supposedly he dumped her because—well, there really is no decent word for it, Magdalena."

"Say it anyway!"

"Uh—okay, but I'm only repeating what I heard. Irma was *insatiable*."

"A strumpet with a trumpet!"

"Of course that rumor is pretty tame compared to some of the others."

Lodema paused. Whether for dramatic effect, or to catch her breath, it doesn't matter. While she paused, I prayed. If the Good Lord didn't strike me dead or smite me with a plague for being on the receiving end of such juicy gossip, I would donate an extra thousand dollars to the foreign missions fund for each additional rumor Lodema shared. That way some impoverished missionary in Africa could benefit from my penchant for the prurient.

"Tell me the other rumors," I begged. I owed it to the missionaries, after all.

"Well, there was the rumor she had an affair with one of the German high command during the early days of Vichy France."

I gasped. "Irma did the nasty with a Nazi?"

"Apparently she was very much in love with him, but not he with her."

"That seems to be the story of her life. Tell me more about the floozy with the flugelhorn," I said, helping to spread God's word in Africa.

"Well, I haven't even got to the best part. They say she had a baby by the Nazi. Actually, some folks say she had two babies—twins. A boy and a girl."

"Oh, my." Fornicating with the devil was one thing, but having his litter quite another. The missionaries were going to make out like bandits.

"Well, how do you like them apples?" Lodema's voice rose with every syllable. No doubt the woman was high on hearsay.

I swallowed hard. Sin might be tasty, but it has a putrid aftertaste. "I must say, dear, that this is one of the most incredible things I've ever heard. A horny hornist from Hernia as Hitler's harlot—"

"Don't be ridiculous, Magdalena. It wasn't Hitler—it was some other high muckety-muck. Franz something, I think his name was."

"Even so, I've known Irma Yoder all my life, and she doesn't have any children."

"They say she gave the baby—or babies, as the case may be—up for adoption. One story says they were placed in a French orphanage, another that they were brought back here and adopted by a Mennonite family."

It took me only a few seconds to do the math. I wasn't born until well after WWII, and I didn't have a brother—that I *knew* of. Still, I've always had the feeling I was adopted. Never mind that I'm the spitting image of Mama when she was my age. Surely my *real* mama would have relented and allowed me to go to the senior prom, even if there was dancing.

"Why is it Mennonites are not allowed to have sex standing up?" I asked bitterly.

Lodema cleared her throat. "They're not?"

"Of course not," I snapped, "it might lead to dancing."

"Must you always be so tawdry, Magdalena?"

"*Me*? You're the one who started yapping about a tuba-tooting tootsie who did the hootchy-cootchy with half of France."

"Well, she *did,* and like I said, I think it was a trumpet."

"Trumpet, crumpet, it just doesn't seem like her. She may have a tongue that can dice dairy, but other than that, the Irma Yoder I know is the most devout member of Beechy Grove Mennonite Church, present company excepted."

"Thank you, Magdalena—"

"I mean *me*!"

"Always putting yourself first, aren't you, Magdalena? Well, just remember that you lived with a married man who was not your lawfully married husband."

I gasped, and had to spit out a mouthful of Lodema's hair. "That is *so* unfair of you! I didn't know Aaron was married."

"Well, that's what you say, at any rate."

"Let's not forget Formula number twelve!" I screamed. "And you know what? I think you made all that stuff up about Irma Yoder. I mean, what did she do, suddenly have a religious conversion?"

"Exactly," Lodema said, cowed by my threat.

"I still think that's ridiculous. I know people can change, dear, but that *much*?"

"Converts can. They're twice as zealous as everyone else."

"You should know, dear. Didn't you just say you were once a Methodist?"

Of course I deserved to get the receiver slammed in my ear, but to be absolutely honest, it should have happened earlier in the conversation. No doubt Lodema was genuinely worried about her missing husband, which would explain why she was off her stride. At any rate, I could feel that someone was watching me so I casually laid my receiver back in its cradle. Trust me, a face-saving gesture is not the same as a lie.

* * *

I scowled at young Marjorie Frost. Contrary to what Susannah says, one *cannot* plant corn in my creases.

"Doesn't a gal deserve a little privacy?"

The earnest hazel eyes met my gaze without blinking. "You told us to gather here at eight-thirty, and it's eight-thirty-two. I thought you valued punctuality."

"Don't get fresh with me, dear," I said sternly. Frankly, I admired the child. I wouldn't have dared be that forthright at her age. It wasn't until my thirtieth birthday, when I realized I had nothing left to lose, that I began to be candid. I said as much to Marjorie.

"I was a real woose," I added.

"That's wuss," she said with a faint smile. "Miss Yoder, I'm afraid my husband won't be joining us on the search."

"What do you mean your husband won't be joining us on the search?"

"Frank says he has some business in town."

"Which town? Hernia?"

Marjorie shrugged. "My husband is a busy man."

"Well, I hate to burst your bubble, dear, but there is no one in Hernia to do business *with,* except Sam the grocer and those folks over at the feed store."

"Then maybe it was that other town."

"Bedford?"

"Look, Miss Yoder, I happen to trust my husband. He's not like that horrible Mr. Hart."

"Did I hear my name spoken in vain, little lady?" Bob was standing in the door between the parlor and the lobby, and, much to my relief, he was alone.

"Indeed you did, dear. It seems that your little band of followers is deserting me."

"How's that?"

"Well, young Marjorie here tells me that her husband has backed out of the search party."

"Don't call me young Marjorie," she snapped.

I nodded. "Sorry, dear." I turned to Bob. "Is it true you're a master tracker?"

Black bushy brows lifted in surprise and then settled on a happy face. Flattery, I have finally learned, will get you just about anywhere you want to go. At least with me. Tell me I'm beautiful, and I'll let you ride in my BMW for free. And although, in some cases, flattery might well be a distant cousin of deceit, it doesn't have to be a flat-out lie.

"As a matter of fact, Miss Yoder, I am a good tracker— if you mean it in the sense I think you do. I do a lot of hunting back home. Shot me a buck with a record rack last year."

"Perfect! We could use a good tracker."

"Excuse me, ma'am?"

"Oh, not for deer or anything like that. I mean people."

"Well, ma'am, I don't know as how I'd be so good at that. That professor fellow disappeared yesterday, didn't he? Them footprints might be pretty messed up by now. But now my daddy, he coulda done it. His mama was a full-blooded Cherokee. Only Daddy's dead now, you see. Died twenty years ago in a terrible accident. Happened right here in Pennsylvania, as a matter of fact."

"Oh?"

"Yes, ma'am. In that long tunnel between here and a town called Somerset. Two trucks boxed a car in and, well, the driver of the one truck pushed the car into the back of the first, and the car just sort of folded up. Like an accordion, they say. Anyway, my daddy was a trucker, and he was way past retirement age. That was supposed to be his last haul, you know."

Every hair on my head stood up—well, tried to. Fortunately I was wearing it in a bun, but the bun became as hard as yesterday's roll.

"*When* exactly did this happen?"

"It was exactly twenty years ago August thirteenth."

"*Which* truck was your daddy driving?"

"An eighteen-wheeler rig with a double cab."

"What was it carrying?" I screamed.

"Sports shoes, ma'am."

Thank God I was still sitting on my stool behind the check-in counter. As it was, I swayed and lost my balance, and had it not been for Bob's quick reaction, might have gashed my forehead on the counter.

"Ma'am, you all right?"

"No, I'm not! Your daddy killed my papa! My mama too!"

"*Ma'am?*"

I jerked away from his steadying hand. "My parents were in that car that got folded like an accordion. Your daddy rammed into them from behind, and squished them right up against a milk tanker. What was he, drunk?"

Perfectly round patches of color formed on Bob's cheeks. "My daddy was a God-fearing, born-again Baptist, ma'am. He never drank a day in his life."

"*Oh really*? Then what was he trying to do? Purposely run over a poor Mennonite couple?"

The patches faded slowly while Marjorie and I watched in silence. Finally Bob spoke.

"Ma'am, they didn't tell you the whole story, did they?"

"Of course they did. Why wouldn't they?"

"Ma'am, your daddy—I mean, the car your parents were in—it passed my daddy's truck."

"*So?*"

"He—I mean, it—passed in the tunnel. Seconds later another car zoomed around from behind my daddy's truck and got in front of the milk truck. The driver of the milk truck—he was the only one to survive the accident—said it looked like the two cars were playing tag. Anyway, he had no choice but to slam on the brakes."

My head pounded. "That's preposterous!"

"Ma'am, it's all in the sheriff's report."

"And you've read this?"

"I have a copy in my desk in Tulsa. I'd be happy to send a copy to you."

"Why didn't anyone show me that report?"

"Maybe they were trying to protect you, ma'am."

For approximately six seconds I entertained the possibility that Papa would have done something that foolish. Sure, he was ahead of his time in that he occasionally exhibited signs of road rage, but who hasn't? Just last week I honked at a car that cut me off on my way into Bedford. No, Papa was a sensible, loving family man. He would never have risked his or Mama's life to play a stupid game of one-upmanship.

I straightened. "There's no need to. I know it isn't true. Besides, what happened to the car in front? The one Papa was supposedly playing tag with?"

Bob had the audacity to look me straight in the eye. He didn't even have the decency to blink.

"According to the sheriff's report, the car—which was a blue Nash Rambler—sped up and just drove away. The driver of the milk truck didn't have a chance to get the license number."

"A likely story." Either Bob was a pathological liar, or the sheriff had been trying to frame Papa. Whichever the case, I had neither the time nor energy to deal with it at the moment.

"I'm really sorry to have taken you by surprise, ma'am. I had no idea you lost your parents in that accident, or I wouldn't have brought it up."

"Yeah, yeah, whatever you say."

I struggled to my feet. Someday I would make it a point to ask Freni what really happened in the tunnel. Or Sam. Or Irma Yoder, if we could find her. One of these three would undoubtedly have heard something—assuming there was anything to hear. What a pity Lodema Schrock hadn't been around back then. Well, in the meantime I needed to pull myself together, find two missing people, and watch my baby sister marry the meanest mantis in all God's green creation. Sure, I was at the end of my rope, but lucky for me, I have long arms.

Then, just when things couldn't possibly be any worse, the doorbell rang.

Seventeen

"**W**e're not buying this morning, dear," I said and tried to slam the door.

Diana Lefcourt was as slippery as an oiled slug—either that or she used her magical powers. The next thing I knew she was standing in the middle of the lobby, which by then was filling up rapidly.

"What are you doing here *now*?" I wailed. "The wedding's not until tomorrow."

"I sensed you needed help." She said it with a straight face, despite the fact that she was dressed like an Egyptian pharaoh. Fortunately for propriety's sake, she was dressed like a female pharaoh.

"Where's Tutankhamen, dear? All I see is Nefertiti."

"My name is Ankhesenamen. I am the wife of Tutankhamen, Queen of all Egypt, the Sudan and Nubia."

I curtsied. "Welcome, Your Highness."

"Go ahead and laugh, Magdalena, but I can see you are in trouble. Your aura is sick."

"My *what* is what?"

"It's all gray and deflated. It's hanging from you like a shroud."

I rubbed my arms. I felt nothing unusual—well, actually I did, but it wasn't hanging from me, it was emanating from a four-thousand-year-old queen. In Susannah's words, I felt bad vibes.

"Don't make a fool of yourself, dear," I said kindly. "Everyone's staring. Now if you'll just hop back into your chariot, we can get on with our day."

The woman formerly known as Diana, a.k.a. Mother Anjelica Houston, and whose new name I couldn't pronounce on the pain of death, nodded. "Yes, of course—the search."

"I don't know what you're talking about, dear." I wanted nothing more than to shove the interloper back onto the porch.

"Yes, you do, Magdalena. There are two missing presences."

"Don't be ridiculous," I hissed. "A missing presence is a contradiction in terms. Besides, who told *you*?"

"It's all over the county—Magdalena has lost two guests again."

"Old Irma is not a guest!"

"Just be grateful Susannah called me."

"Susannah!"

"Of course, even on my own, I would have eventually known there was trouble. I can feel the magnetic misalignment of these two missing presences. Like you, they have sick auras."

"Can the New Age mumbo-jumbo, toots." I glanced helplessly around. "Sorry folks. This woman is an escapee from the County Home for the Rationally Impaired."

"No need to apologize," Dixie said in her charming accent. "This is all very interesting."

"Yah," her husband said in his charming accent, "this sure is nothing like Minnesota."

"Ooh, I just love her outfit," Doris cooed. "Do you think we could get his-and-hers outfits like that?"

Jimmy Hill nipped nauseatingly at his wife's left ear. "Not back home in Arkansas. Maybe it's a Mennonite thing."

"We're not all like this," I wailed. "And she doesn't have a drop of Mennonite or Amish blood in her. Not a single drop!"

Diana held up a wrinkled brown hand in which she held a wooden staff with a serpent's head. In her younger days she had been a devoted sun worshipper. Now she was married to the sun's earthly representative.

"Actually, I do. My grandmother was a Kauffman."

Young Marjorie was staring at the faux pharaoh as if she was Santa Claus, the Tooth Fairy, and the Good Lord all in one. It was downright sacrilegious.

"Totally awesome," she finally managed to mumble.

Even Sam seemed mesmerized by the vamp in veils.

It was time to step in and share a little perspective. "The woman's a nut," I said not unkindly. "Normal people do not claim to be dead Egyptians. Okay, I know my sister dresses sort of like that, but she doesn't wear a black wig with a gold cobra on top. And yes, she wears a lot of makeup, but with all that kohl around your eyes, you look like a raccoon that's been in a fist fight. Now listen up, people, we have a search to conduct. You"— I pointed at the amorous Arkansans—"will search as a team. Same thing for you," I said to the charming couple from Minnesota. "Sam here has a couple of Amish buddies to help him—"

"Ach, Magdalena, it's spring planting—they are younger men and so busy. I will search alone."

"Fine, dear, you know the area." I turned to the others.

"Since she's not here. I'm assuming Mrs. Hart is not up to the task this morning, so, that leaves just you and you." I nodded first at young Marjorie, and then at Bob. "And don't even contemplate making her into a teammate."

Bob blushed, as well he should. Young Marjorie merely giggled.

"Now you be careful, dear."

"Don't worry, Miss Yoder. I'm a big girl, I can take care of myself."

I smiled kindly. "I wasn't talking to you, dear." I turned to Bob. "Be careful. The girl's like a bull in china shop."

Marjorie took step forward and tripped on an untied shoelace, but to be honest, made a remarkable recovery. "Hey, I resent that. And what about you? Who's going to be your partner?"

"I will," Diana Lefcourt said in a voice that could part the Red Sea.

I smiled patiently. "In your dreams, dear."

Diana, a.k.a. Ankhesenamen, smiled back. Now, I know what I'm about to describe doesn't make a lick of sense. And I must warn you that the mumbo-jumbo, hocus-pocus aspect of it is not in keeping with the great Judeo-Christian tradition. In fact, it feels like a sin to even remember what happened. But forewarned is forearmed, right? So consider yourself indebted to me if you are able to resist the Diana Lefcourts of this world, and their bags of tricks from the netherworld. Alas, I had no such alarm sounded for me, and found myself carried along like flotsam on the sea of sin.

One moment I was Magdalena Portulacca Yoder, Mennonite mistress of my domain, and the next I was nothing

more than a pathetic puppy yapping at the flapping sandals of a phantom Pharaoh. Even Mama with her bag of
seismographic tricks was unable to stop me.

Of course, no one could stop Diana. She assigned the
search areas with the authority of General MacArthur.

"You and I will check out the old Miller homestead
across the road," she said after the others had departed.
"It's been unoccupied for months. It would be the perfect
place for someone to hide."

"Nobody is hiding, dear. Two people are *missing*."

"Yes, but consider the possibility that one of the
missing presences might have abducted the other, and
has stashed her or him, as the case may be, in the Miller
house."

"Old Irma has a formidable tongue, but she couldn't
abduct her own shadow. She's over a century old, for
Pete's sake. But even if you're right, I can't go there."

"Why not?"

"Well, because—well, you know. That's where my
Aaron used to live."

"Get over it, Magdalena."

"Yes, ma'am."

We lit out in a light rain. Okay, so maybe it was only a
mist, but I hate getting my shoes grass-stained, and even
though I wear my hair in a bun, a *wet* bun doesn't look
good even on me. Nonetheless, since galoshes and bum-
bershoots were not in vogue in the eighteenth dynasty, I
had to do without—never mind that Her Highness arrived at the inn in a 1968 Volkswagen beetle. A bright orange bug, no less.

I trotted obediently at her heels as she crossed Hertlzer
road, and ignoring the long driveway that leads to the

Miller farmhouse, strode across the greening pasture. At least there were no cows—wet cow pies can be treacherous—now that the Miller farm is defunct, but there were plenty of memories for me to rehash. Miller's pond, set smack in the middle of the pasture, is the scene of my most poignant memory.

My Pooky Bear and I met when we were children, but I fell in love with him on the banks of Miller's pond. Aaron Miller is storybook handsome, and as glib as an itinerant preacher. I gave my heart to the man, and later, after we were supposedly married, I gave him the *rest* of me. It all started one warm sunny day when Aaron literally dropped at my feet. You see, I had been daydreaming in the shade of a tree at the water's edge, quite unaware that hidden up in the foliage was God's gift to women. Don't ask me what a grown man is doing up in a tree, but when Aaron miraculously appeared, I took it as a sign from above. Although I have since learned that not everything that falls from trees is good, or necessarily from God, the sight of this particular tree still plucks the strings of my pathetic heart.

"There's the tree," I moaned.

"Yes, and it's a fine tree," Diana said. Despite her claims of psychic ability, the woman didn't have a clue.

"That's where I met Aaron."

"Ah, yes, Aaron. I dated his brother Moses, you know."

"Not *that* Aaron! Aaron Miller."

Diana tossed her head in disdain. Unfortunately, the black wig stayed snugly in place. The gold serpent slipped a bit however, but she didn't seem to notice.

"Moses—now there was a real man! He drove the fastest chariot in all of Goshen. All the Hebrew girls were crazy about him, but of course we Egyptians got first dibs. And since my daddy was the pharaoh—well, I'm not at liberty to say what went on in the bulrushes."

"You're a raving lunatic, dear," I said gently.

"That's exactly what I said to Moses when he threatened Daddy with the plagues. Then they started to happen. Now, I didn't mind the first plague so much—we women can deal with a little blood, right? But those frogs!" She stopped and pointed at the pond. "Are there any frogs in there?"

"It's chock full of the critters, dear."

Diana grabbed my arm and yanked me away from the water's edge, away from the tree that changed my life. "Those wretched beasts were everywhere," she croaked. "They were in my bed, on my pillow, even in my drinking cup."

"Hey, stop," I protested weakly, "I wanted to sit here for a moment. This is a very special place for me."

"Because of that silly tree?"

"So what if it is? After all, a gal has a right to lash herself with the whip of regret every now and then. Sure, it may leave unsightly welts, but the discomfort is nothing compared to choking down crow."

Diana had the talons of an eagle and she continued to drag me until we were well away from the pond. "Aaron broke your heart, didn't he?"

I unpeeled her fingers from my arm. "Maybe."

"Well, Moses broke mine. I heard he married a Midianite woman who wasn't half as pretty as I, nor a tenth as rich. It didn't matter—I still loved him. But then after that Red Sea fiasco I never saw him again. He just disappeared into the wilderness. I guess that shouldn't have come as a big surprise because he was always getting lost—never would stop and ask directions. At any rate, I suppose I should have made an effort to find him. But then what? I mean, what if I had convinced him to dump the Midianite and marry me? The truth is, I've never been much of a camper."

"Why didn't you just call him on your cellular?"

Pharaoh frowned. "Are you mocking me, Magdalena? Don't think I haven't heard all those nasty little asides of yours. You must think I'm stupid as well as crazy."

"If the shoe fits, dear, buy several pairs. Who knows when they're going to let you out again?"

Diana shook her head so hard the golden cobra went sailing, only to land at my feet with thunk. The black wig—if that's indeed what it was—stayed put.

"Before the day's over I'll prove to you that I *am* Ankhesenamen. I tell you what—what if I call up my husband, Tutankhamen? You'll like Tut—everyone does—even though he overdoes it with the jewelry."

I picked up the headpiece and handed it to her. It may not have been real gold, but it was remarkably heavy.

"That's okay, dear. I'll take your word for it. Sorry about the cellular joke."

She plopped the diadem back on with surprising carelessness. "No harm done. And you're right, it would have been so much easier with a cellular phone. Although I got a letter once—but both tablets were broken, smashed into smithereens—it was almost impossible to read. I had the court librarian reassemble it, but it was hardly worth the effort. I mean, the message was just was *so* negative. Anyway, I never wrote back."

I rolled my eyes the second she turned her head. Don't for a second think that I bought into her story. I may have been under some kind of a spell, but my chandelier wasn't missing any bulbs.

"Diana, dear—"

"Ah-ah-ah—I must insist that you address me as Your Royal Highness."

"I thought you were a queen. And what ever happened to Mother Anjelica Houston?"

"I jettisoned Anjelica. And I *am* a queen."

"Well, shouldn't you be a majesty, as opposed to a highness?"

Diana sighed. "Well, maybe. English is such a difficult language."

"They say the same thing in Oakland, dear. Anyway, I just wanted to ask you a simple question."

"Oh, all right, what is it?"

We had left the pond far behind and were only a pyramid width from the house. "I wanted to know if you knew Irma Yoder before the war?"

"Which war would that be? The war against the Greeks or the war against the Romans? Tut, you know, had this thing for Cleopatra, and she wasn't any better looking than that Midianite Moses took up with."

"Stop it," I wailed. "At least get your facts right."

"I beg your pardon?"

"King Tut never hankered over Liz."

"He didn't?"

"Not in his lifetime, at any rate. And it was Ramses the Second who oppressed the Hebrews, and his son who finally let them go."

Diana blinked rapidly. It may have been only misting, but the kohl was oozing down her face like dozens of miniature lava flows. I suspected that there were tears involved as well.

"Are you sure?" Her voice was suddenly weak.

"Reasonably. Many scholars seem to think so. And oh, by the way, you look just like a Rorschach inkblot test." Trust me, it really was an attempt to cheer her up.

"What?"

I rubbed my index finger along her cheek. Along with some kohl deposits, I scooped up a good inch of putty-like foundation.

"My gracious, is that Jimmy Hoffa under there?"

She jerked her face away, the black wig slapping me in the face "Go away," she said in a little girl's voice.

I am not the mean, overbearing woman some folks have accused me of being. It broke my heart to see King Tut's tootsie tearing up like that.

"Diana, can we talk?"

"What's there to talk about? You think I'm crazy."

I prayed for an understanding heart and a gentle tongue.

"*Don't* you?"

"Well, we're all entitled to our eccentricities, so let's just say that you are more blessed in that department than most."

The black wig whipped around again, narrowly missing my left eye. "Okay, you win. Sometimes the line between fact and fantasy blurs for me. Is that so wrong? I mean, just look at you."

"What *about* me?"

"Well, there you are, a good Mennonite girl, practically never been kissed—"

"Oh, I've been kissed, sister! I've had the full monty." Okay, so I never saw the movie, but Susannah did. Frankly, she was disappointed that she didn't see the *full* monty.

"What I mean is, you live this virtuous, restricted life, based on your religious beliefs, of course, but you're in the minority."

"What's wrong with that?" I wailed. Don't think for a minute that I doubt who I am, or what I believe—well, okay, but doubt is a perfectly natural component of faith. Reverend Schrock said so in his last sermon.

"Oh, there's nothing wrong with it, it's just that you might consider loosening up a bit. You know, live into your fantasies."

"Is it profitable?" I asked sensibly.

Diana smiled. "Spoken like a true Yoder. It can be."

I ignored her insensitive generalization. "Okay, so you're no longer Mother Anjelica Houston, but you still heading up the Convent of the Broken Heart in Bedford?"

"Yes, but now we call it a retreat. We offer psychic adjustment and spiritual travel. You'd be surprised what folks can be talked into spending their money on, just so long as they think it's something really special, something not available to the hoi polloi."

"So *that's* where my clientele went! And all this time I thought they were in Montana frolicking naked with wolves."

"Heavens, no! Montana and Wyoming are passé now. No, Magdalena, I'm happy to say that the Retreat of the Fractured Soul is now *the* watering hole of the rich and blameless."

She turned and strode toward the farmhouse. Despite the twenty years she has on me, I practically had to run to keep up.

"Are you trying to tell me that Babs and John and Shirley now hang out in that dump of yours?" I knew that it was only a matter of time before Travolta would bolt, but not those two.

"Well, not Shirley. Not anymore. She didn't like Sister Agnes's cooking and left this morning."

"Oh, so that's why you're really here. You came to steal Freni from me. Well, I've got news for you, dear. Freni quit!"

"I don't care about Freni. She doesn't cook vegetarian anyway. Like I told you, I came to help you find the missing presence—I mean, people."

I lagged a cautious step behind. "Which is it, dear? Are you as nutty as Grandma Yoder's fruitcake, or a pragmatic businesswoman?"

"Both."

"Come again?"

She stopped abruptly and I nearly slammed into her. "You wouldn't understand."

"Try me."

"Sometimes I *am* Ankhesenamen, and sometimes I'm me, Diana Louise Lefcourt. Yes, I know, I have a grown son living in Johnstown, Pennsylvania, but I had *three* children in Egypt. They're dead now, of course, but I can remember them just as clearly as I can my son in Johnstown."

She was right. I didn't understand.

"Well, you don't say!" Better a little gentle sarcasm, I figured, than an outright harsh remark. Trust me, Irma Yoder, bless her aged missing heart, would not have shown such restraint.

"I knew you wouldn't understand. But that's how it is. Some days I'm more one than the other. I don't seem able to control it much anymore."

"Oh?"

"It wasn't like this in the beginning, you know."

"Oh?" What else was there to say? I had prayed for a charitable tongue, and was still waiting for the Good Lord to send me the replacement. Until it arrived, it was best to say as little as possible.

"I started the convent, as I called it back then, as a place where women could gather and express themselves freely. The channeling thing was just a lark—something to amuse us in the evenings. But then gradually it became real to me. Tutankhamen—well, I was never really him, but something made me pick him as the channeler, and then later Ankhesenamen."

"Could that something have been the devil, dear?"

"Magdalena, you don't still believe in a devil, do you? All red with horns and a tail?"

"You forgot the pitchfork, dear." It was meant to be facetious.

"You do, don't you? Of course you do! How charming."

I blushed devil red. I know I'm a dying breed, but there you have it. I do believe in the devil. Of course I don't believe he—and indeed he is male—necessarily has a tail and horns. Or carries a pitchfork. More likely he is a wiry little thing with bulging eyes and wears a police chief's uniform.

"Well, at least I believe in God too," I mumbled.

"So do I, Magdalena. But we are all God. Don't you get it? Every one of us is a component of the universal godhead."

Again I thought of a wiry little man with bulging eyes and a police chief's uniform. "Wrong!"

"Oh well, I guess there is no point in trying to enlighten you."

"Likewise I'm sure, dear. So, you went chasing after

false prophets and caught up with one. Well, let's see, I don't think Reverend Schrock performs exorcisms, but the priest over in Bedford might."

Diana grabbed both my wrists. Her extraordinarily strong grip was certainly a testimony to the power of fruits and nuts.

"Look, we can stand here in this miserable wet cow pasture and argue theology and the state of my mental health, or we can do something to save your life."

"*My* life?"

Diana nodded. "I wasn't going to tell you this unless I had to, because I knew it would freak you out. But I had a dream last night in which you were killed. I've had three of these dreams in the past, Magdalena, and every one of them came true."

Eighteen

There is power in a crazy face. While I didn't for a minute believe that Diana was a mummy's mommy, I wasn't about to discount her dream. Not without more details, at any rate. After all, Granny Yoder dreamed about my parents' death fifteen years before it happened. Never mind that Granny got a few of the details wrong—Mama did not drown in a vat of milk, and Papa was not squashed by a giant tennis shoe. But you see, Granny had the basic components, and in her dream my parents died on the same day.

"Where, when, and how?" I demanded.

Diana had let go of one of my wrists, but she was pulling me along by the other. "The where is the hardest part. It's someplace close and familiar, but I can't get a clear picture. Someplace round, I think. Or near something round."

"Someplace *round*? The earth is round, for pete's sake, or haven't they learned that in Egypt yet?"

Diana gave me an extra strong tug and I nearly fell flat on my face. Thank heavens there were no longer any cows on the old Miller spread.

"Of course we know the earth is round. For your information it wasn't Columbus or even the Vikings who discovered America."

"I know, silly, it was the Asians—although now we call them Indians, or Native Americans."

"Yes. But I mean from the west."

"Oh, so now you're going to tell me that folks from Cairo founded Rio?"

"I wish—even though it wasn't Cairo in my day. Alas, it was the Phoenicians who made that great sea voyage to the New World. But I can assure you, it wasn't my fault for lack of trying. I kept nagging Tut to invest in overseas exploration, but oh no, the man was obsessed with stockpiling his tomb. You *can* take it with you was his motto, you know."

"How inspiring, dear. But can we get on with what happens to *me*?"

"Yes, well, like I said, the place wasn't very clear, but as to how—are you sure you can take this?"

"*How?*" I wailed.

"You get crushed."

"*Crushed?* What does that mean?"

"You know, like flattened. Rolled over with something?"

"What kind of something? A steamroller?" I knew the county was getting ready to resurface the highway into Bedford. In fact, I had lobbied hard to get the levy passed, and had come up against some rather strong opposition. I will admit that at times the debate got a little bit heated, and I may have let a few things slip out that I shouldn't have. And while I wouldn't have been surprised to find myself tarred and feathered as a result, tarred and painted with a dotted yellow line was going too far.

"It couldn't be a steamroller," Diana said gravely, "because you're in some kind of building."

"Ah, yes, the one with the round rooms."

"Are you making fun of me again, Magdalena?"

"Not at all, dear."

"Good, because you shouldn't look a gift horse in the mouth, and I came here to save you. I tried warning those silly Trojans, you know, but—"

"Save away," I wailed, "but can you spare me the history lesson?"

Diana's grip on my wrist tightened. Fortunately I am ambidextrous.

"I told you I dreamt you would die in a round space—or near a round shape. I didn't say it was a room. It could be anywhere. This pasture, even."

"This pasture isn't round, dear."

"Maybe, but that pond back there is."

My pace quickened. Now it was me pulling her.

"Come on, dear. Get a move on it, before a meteor hits."

"Oh, I don't think it's going to be a meteor. No, this is something man made. Maybe one of those jumbo jets with huge tires is going to land on you. We never had to worry about that in Egypt."

I glanced at the sky. No planes in sight.

"When?"

"Today," she said calmly. "Tomorrow at the latest."

A shiver ran down my spine. "You really and truly dreamt this?"

"Would I be wasting my time, here, on a day like this, if I hadn't?"

"Okay, let's say you dreamt it, and that your dreams do

come true. What does this have to do with the missing presences—I mean, people?"

"They're somewhere on this property, Magdalena, and like you, they're in great danger."

"Then we should be going home," I wailed. "I don't have to help Melvin. We can call in the county sheriff."

"No."

"What do you mean 'no'? Unlike you, I only get *one* life!"

"Because I had two dreams, and in the second dream you did something and it saved not only your life, but theirs."

"What did I do?"

"I don't remember."

"What do you mean, you don't remember?"

"I'm not perfect, Magdalena. Sometimes I forget my dreams—just like you do."

Boy, was that a laugh. Ever since the day Aaron called me from Minnesota to tell me that we weren't legally married after all, and that he had reconciled with his *first* wife, I've had the same reoccurring nightmare. I won't bore you with details, but it involves that telephone call, our wedding night, a tub of low-fat whipped topping, and a large orange balloon. Just believe me when I say that every detail of that dream is crystal clear when I wake, and remains with me the rest of the day.

"Anyway, Magdalena, in the second dream you took matters into your own hands and saved the day. And you saved the benign presence."

"Shouldn't we have at least brought along a shovel? Or a pickax?" Just because I'm a pacifist in life, doesn't mean I plan to *die* peacefully. My great-great-great-great-grandmother, a Hostetler, was stabbed in the back and scalped by the Delaware, while her husband did nothing to defend her. I had no intention of repeating her hair-raising experience.

Diana laughed. "Magdalena, it's your mind that is needed, not some garden tool."

"My mind?" I asked dangerously.

"You're one of the brightest, sharpest people I know. I have every faith in you."

"You do?"

"Of course! I'm nowhere near ready to die again. Just between you and me, it's not all it's cracked up to be."

"So practice doesn't necessarily make perfect?"

"Not in this case. Take that time on the *Titanic,* for instance—"

If I had to die that April day, it wasn't going to be from boredom. "Race you to the Miller house!" I cried.

Despite a breakfast of pancakes and bacon, I could still outrun Diana Lefcourt.

I never have liked the Miller house. It spooked me even as a child. Constance, Aaron's grandmother, was a pretentious woman who eschewed traditional Pennsylvania Dutch farmhouse architecture in favor of Victorian gingerbread. Unfortunately, the humble Mennonite laborers she hired didn't know gingerbread from banana bread, and the result was a pseudogothic structure with more towers and turrets than Windsor Castle. Susannah tells me it looks like the Addams family's house, which, since it isn't in Bedford County, I have yet to see.

At any rate, Aaron's father did little to improve his inheritance. He had the cheerful yellow exterior of the house painted gray, and his wife Rebecca hired a heterosexual interior decorator from Pittsburgh. Enough said.

"I feel some vibes from the barn," Diana said, "but most of them are coming from the house."

I stared at the dismal behemoth. Even I could feel the vibes. They were almost as strong as the vibes coming from Granny Yoder's room the day she died. Every now and then I can still feel them when I crawl into bed.

"Maybe we should start with the barn," I said.

"Magdalena, are you scared?"

"Don't be ridiculous, dear. It's just that the barn isn't locked, and it would be easier for someone to hide in there, if that is indeed what John Burk and Irma Yoder are doing."

"You *are* scared, aren't you?"

"Of course not, dear!" That lie just slipped out. All the same, I was going to have to be careful, or pretty soon I could eat my supper out of anthills. And anyway, there is nothing wrong with cowardice, as long as it is for self-preservation. Fear is a God-given instinct, after all.

"Well, *I'm* scared, Magdalena."

"You *are*?"

"I told you, dying isn't any fun. Of course some ways of getting your ticket punched are worse than others. Take the Hindenberg, for example—"

"No thanks, dear." I flipped over the soggy doormat and retrieved the key, which I knew all along would be there. There isn't a Mennonite worth her bonnet who would think to hide her house key anyplace *but* under the front mat. Rebecca Miller had been no exception, and Aaron Senior, bless his dotty heart, was not the type to mess with tradition. As for Aaron, Jr., my former Pooky Bear, to put it kindly—well, since when do weasels lock their dens?

That the key was rusty, and so was the lock, didn't

make a lick of difference because the heavy oak door swung open with a creak the second I touched it. For a moment I peered into the gloom. Then, like the intelligent woman I am, I flipped on the foyer light switch.

"Let there be light," I said.

And there was light. Now, I don't mean to be sacrilegious. My point is that even though the Miller house was unoccupied, it still had electricity. Earl Whitaker of Hernia Realty has been trying to sell the Miller farm for months. Walmart expressed a brief interest, as did a Japanese firm, but so far no one has even made an offer. Last month a well-to-do Amish family spent several days examining the fields and inspecting the barn. Most likely they even took a peek inside the house, because the last I saw of them they were headed north on Hertlzer Road, their buggy wheels a blur. Like I said, the place has bad vibes.

"Earl!" I called. "You in there?"

There was no answer. Earl, Ali Baba, and a hundred thieves could have been hiding on the ground floor alone, and I never would have known it. This branch of the Millers is genetically incapable of discarding anything, and since Rebecca was a Miller on her mama's side, the foible was only compounded. No doubt the heterosexual decorator had been able to convince Rebecca to part with a few things, but in the fifty intervening years nothing brought into the house ever left.

I must admit that there are certain advantages to clutter—one need never worry about dusting or sweeping, and new introductions to the melange always match with *something*. Diana and I timorously wound our way around stacks of yellow newspaper, piles of vintage clothes, and towers of musty books. Those were the more normative things. The eight defunct bathroom scales and twenty-six broken manual typewriters were harder to explain. And why would anyone keep five shoeboxes filled with rubber bands so old they were fused to each other? Or six boxes of half-empty sewing machine bobbins? Or nine shoeboxes of old pens, their ink long since dried up? And what about the literally hundreds of empty plastic two-liter bottles, their labels carefully removed? Of what use were they? Not to mention the large garbage bag filled with the cotton packing removed from medicine bottles. And are any of you wondering where your wire hangers have disappeared to? Well, look no further. The bad news is they took a vacation to the Miller house; the good news is they have been engaging in nonstop procreation since then. Or is it the other way around? At any rate, you are welcome to come to Hernia and collect your wire coat hangers and their progeny. As of this moment they fill up the entire Miller dining room and spill out into the hallway.

"Looks like somebody could have used a garage sale," I said kindly. I didn't say a word about a garbage truck.

Diana nodded. Her eyes were wide, no doubt a mixture of fear and wonder.

"Possession is a primitive need that we at the retreat seek to eliminate."

"I'm sure that's so, dear. Eliminate Babs's need for possessions and she turns them all over to you, right? Well, just remember, she promised me that Art Deco Tiffany lamp she travels with."

"Magdalena! How terribly crass of you."

"Oh, no, she didn't already give it to you, did she?"

"I don't know what you're talking about. Besides, you're just wasting time."

"I am not! Earl! Earl! Are you here?"

"You see what I mean? You keep calling for Earl, and he's not one of the two presences."

"Earl is the real estate agent," I snapped, "and anyway, how do you know he isn't one of the two missing people? You haven't even asked their names."

"He wasn't in my dreams."

"Well, who was?"

"I don't know—but I'll recognize their names when I hear them."

"I can't believe I'm here," I moaned. "For all I know you abducted poor Irma Yoder."

"Ah, Irma! Of course. She has a very strong aura. I can feel it everywhere."

"Sit by her in church on Sunday morning and you can smell it, too," I said matter-of-factly. "It's enough to make you pass out, especially if it's summer. Why is it that so many older folks think they no longer have to bathe?"

Diana wasn't interested in Irma's hygiene habits. "Now tell me the other name."

"Arthur."

"What? Magdalena, are you playing games with me?"

"That's one way of putting it, dear. I prefer to think of it as a little test. For all I know, you have no psychic skills."

"Okay, Magdalena, if that's the way you want it. But it's just another waste of time. I'll know the right name when I hear it."

Maybe she would, or maybe she wouldn't. "Horatio."

"That's not it."

"You're right. It's a woman's name—Dorothy."

"That's not it, either."

"Mr. Burk?"

"Yeah, that's it. I can feel his aura too. He's been in this room."

A chill ran up my bony back. We were in the smaller of Rebecca's two parlors then, ringed by foothills of worn-out shoes, which in turn were surrounded by mountains of empty cereal boxes, lampshades, and cheap vinyl clothes hampers. Mr. Burk could well be hiding—or stashed as a corpse—behind any of the refuse piles.

"Is he alive?"

"Don't be ridiculous, Magdalena. The dead don't have auras."

"So where is he? Is he still in this room?"

Black flaps of faux hair swung from side to side. "I'm not picking it up strong enough for that. Here"—she stepped out into the main hall, catching her heel on a wire coat hanger—"and there." She pointed to the stairs.

I shook my head, but my damp bun didn't budge. "Don't look at me, dear. I'm not going up there. It's spooky enough down here. Besides, Mr. Burk is a big guy. He can take care of himself."

"Magdalena, you must go up there."

"That's what you think, dear." I turned and headed for the front door. At least, that was my intention. And while I do not, for a moment, ascribe any special powers to the demented Diana, I found myself inexplicably turning again and heading for the stairs.

"Why me?" I wailed as my feet carried me up two treacherous flights. The Miller stairs, while not as impossibly steep as mine, were an obstacle course of precariously stacked junk and slippery surfaces.

"Don't worry, Magdalena. Like I said, in my second dream you survive."

"What if your dreams mean nothing?"

"Don't be ridiculous. And besides, I'm right behind you."

Those were the last words I heard before the lights went out in my head.

Nineteen

I moaned, I groaned, and I phoned.

"Nine-one-one? This is Magdalena Yoder. A 747 just landed on my head."

"She's coming around now," an angel said.

"Nine-one-one? Forget I called. I made it up *there* after all."

"Miss, are you all right?"

I gazed up at the angel through a fine mist. Brown eyes, dark curly hair—okay, so he wasn't your typical Renaissance angel, but in heaven anything is possible. Even a male angel. And this angel was definitely male; he was wafting male pheromones like pollen on a spring breeze.

"What happened to your wings, dear? Did you send them out to be cleaned?"

"You see? She talks nonsense."

I tried to focus on the second speaker who, while not the devil, was certainly his female counterpart. "Get behind me, Satan," I moaned.

"Ach, such nonsense! Didn't I tell you?"

"Freni? Freni is that you? Did you make it to Heaven too?"

Before my fickle cook could answer, the mist cleared

and I found myself staring into the eyes of Irma Yoder. "Oh, no," I wailed, "not the *other* place!"

"Stop it, Magdalena! Stop it this second!"

I tried to sit up, but a second jumbo jet came in for a landing, flattening me in the process.

"Where am I?"

The dark-haired angel laid a well-manicured hand on my forehead. "Lie still, Miss. You may have had a concussion."

"Concussion, my eye! Can't you feel the tread marks?"

Irma Yoder snorted. "She always was as fruity as a plum pudding."

I ignored her and concentrated on the angel. He was a superb specimen of celestial manhood—tall, lean, broad shouldered with narrow waist and hips. He was even around my age, which frankly struck me as rather odd, considering he was an angel. I mean, according to the Bible angels have been around for thousands of years. Assuming they had a choice in the matter, and didn't want to look several millenniums old, why would an angel pick forty-six? Why not twenty-six? Or more sensibly, sixty-six? If you're shooting for character, why not go all the way?

"What's your name, dear?"

"Gabriel."

"Of course. How long have you been around?"

"About ten minutes. Look, Miss—"

I struggled into a sitting position. Let another plane hit me. I could have been sitting on Runway 1 at Pittsburgh International Airport for all I cared.

"Just *ten* minutes?"

Old Irma stuck her craggy face between Gabriel's and

mine. "And he wouldn't have come at all, if I hadn't screamed. Isn't that right?"

"The Lord works in mysterious ways, dear."

"It wasn't the Lord who screamed, Magdalena. It was me."

"Is that so? Now be a good girl, Old Irma, and wait your turn in line to register. You've had oodles of chances to go to Heaven, and you couldn't be bothered."

"Why, I never! Such a tongue you have, Big Magdalena." She turned to my angel. "Her tongue can slice salami, you know."

"It cannot!"

Gabriel seemed as amused as he was confused. "How does your vision seem?"

"Never been better, dear."

"How many fingers do you see?" he asked, holding up a victory sign.

"Four very handsome tanned fingers, dear."

"Four?"

"Well, not including a very handsome tanned thumb."

Gabriel smiled and laid two of those handsome fingers on my pulse. "Now just relax, if you can."

"The last man who said that to me is living in Minnesota with his *real* wife. You're not married, are you? Of course not—how silly of me! Angels don't get married."

Gabriel frowned. "Your pulse is a little fast. Maybe I should run you into town. We can run an MRI and see if there's a hairline fracture."

"Run me any place you like, dear, but not back down to earth. I'm not saying I've had an especially hard life, but it hasn't been a picnic either. Besides, I've covered all the bases I'm ever going to cover. My papa used to say that"—my pulse raced—"hey, is he here? And Mama? Again, those are such silly questions. Of course they're here. Mama's probably driving God crazy telling him what to do."

"Nuttier than a squirrel's pantry," Old Irma said, shaking her ancient head.

The angel smiled again. "Miss—uh, Magdalena—I'm sorry to have to tell you this, but you're not in Heaven."

For the first time I looked past God's messenger and at my surroundings. They looked remarkably similar to the Miller house. Perhaps God also loved to collect and had hired a straight decorator.

"Please don't tell me I'm in a musty Mennonite museum. Because it's either that or I'm you-know-where."

Old Irma cackled. "I've got to agree with her on that one. Those Millers have always been packrats, and Rebecca never did have an ounce of taste."

I blinked rapidly, hoping to erase the house and Old Irma, but keep the angel. Alas, it didn't work.

"Okay, so I'm still here in this horrible gray house. But where's Diana Lefcourt, and what's *he* doing here?" Confidentially, I was afraid to look at Gabriel now that I knew he was all man. It's one thing to lust after an angel, since, as everyone knows, they are above carnal needs, but a man—no way! Never again.

The sharpest tongue east of the Mississippi wagged at the speed of light. "Diana's gone for help. A pity how that woman's turned out—a sin even, pretending to be Potiphar's wife. But what else can one expect from the product of a mixed marriage? I told Diana's mama not to marry a Methodist. They're just one step away from Presbyterians. Elizabeth Mast married a Catholic, for

crying out loud. You can be sure *she's* you-know-where."
Old Irma turned to Gabriel. "What church are you?"

"I'm Jewish."

Her eyes widened, but she nodded slowly. "Well, at least your people are mentioned in the Bible. Methodists aren't."

"Neither are Mennonites, dear."

Old Irma glared at me. "Don't argue with your elders, Big Magdalena."

Fortunately for my soul, Grabriel intervened. "We haven't officially met. My name is Dr. Gabriel Rosen— although my friends call me Gabe—and you are—?"

I sneaked a quick peek at the man. He was still an angel.

"Magdalena Portulacca Yoder," I said in a loud, clear voice, "proprietress of the PennDutch Inn."

"I'm delighted to meet you."

"Likewise, I'm sure." Truer words were never spoken, and just to show that I wasn't the slightest bit prejudiced, I held out my hand. The handsome tanned fingers felt just as nice belonging to a man.

"Well, Magdalena, you certainly have a good grip."

I grinned foolishly and dropped my hand. "So, Doctor— I mean, Gabe—what brings you to our neck of the woods, and to this dump in particular?"

Old Irma had fingers too, but they were far from handsome. One of them, just as crooked as a pretzel, waggled in my face.

"Enough with the small talk. That man tried to kill me."

"Don't be ridiculous, dear."

"And he would have killed you too, if I hadn't screamed and scared him away."

I had gotten over my reluctance to gaze upon Gabe.

Since lust is a sin, I'll know I'm truly dead when I see Jimmy Carter.

"You're talking gibberish, dear. This man is not a killer."

"Not *him,* you nincompoop. Johanne Burkholder!"

"And you had the nerve to call me nutty! Dr. Rosen, you aren't a psychiatrist by any chance, are you?"

"I'm afraid not. I'm a heart surgeon—well, I was. I don't practice anymore."

The waggling pretzel poked me in the chest. "I don't need a doctor, Big Magdalena. I need someone with a lick of sense who will listen to what I say."

"We're listening," Gabe said gently.

"Yes, dear, we're all ears. Babble away!"

The pretzel jabbed harder, digging into my sternum. "You'll regret this, Magdalena. So help me, you'll regret that you let a Nazi war criminal get away."

I winced as another plane landed on my head.

Twenty

SPAM® Stuffed Potatoes Florentine

✦

Vegetable cooking spray
1 teaspoon butter or margarine
1 (12-ounce) can SPAM® Lite Luncheon Meat, cubed
⅓ cup chopped onion
½ (10-ounce) package frozen chopped spinach, thawed
  and squeezed dry
¼ teaspoon dried leaf thyme
6 baking potatoes, baked and kept warm
¼ cup skim milk
2 tablespoons grated Parmesan cheese
¼ teaspoon pepper
¼ cup shredded Monterey Jack cheese
¼ cup shredded Cheddar cheese

Heat oven to 350 F. Spray a shallow rectangular 2-quart
baking dish with vegetable cooking spray. In a large nonstick skillet, saute SPAM® in butter 3 minutes. Add
onion, spinach, and thyme; cook and stir 2 minutes. Set

aside. Cut a thin slice off the top of each potato. Scoop out each potato, leaving a ½-inch shell. Place shells in prepared baking dish. Place scooped-out potato in medium mixing bowl. Beat at medium speed 30 seconds. Add milk, Parmesan cheese, and pepper; beat just until combined. Stir in SPAM® mixture. Fill potato shells with potato mixture. Bake, uncovered, 25 to 30 minutes or until thoroughly heated. Top with cheeses. Bake five minutes longer or until cheese is melted. Serves 6.

NUTRITIONAL INFORMATION PER SERVING:
Calories 396; Protein 18g; Carbohydrate 54g; Fat 12g; Cholesterol 56mg; Sodium 704mg.

Twenty-One

"Tell me about the Nazi," I said weakly. Thank heavens gorgeous Gabe had the good sense to move us out on the porch. Still concerned that I might have a concussion, my guardian angel had carried me there in his arms.

Old Irma had walked. Having to use her God-given legs, while I used Gabe's, had not put the old biddy in a better mood.

"Some of us had *lives*, Magdalena."

"Tell me about it, dear. You may have lived longer than Methuselah, but Diana Lefcourt has you beat. She *was* Methuselah."

Old Irma pointed to her head and made a circular motion. "She was kicked in the head while trying to milk a bull," she muttered to Gabriel.

"I was not! That was Melvin Stoltzfus, and you know it. Are you going to tell us about your Nazi, or are *you* going to be the one who lets him get away?"

"He wasn't *my* Nazi. Although he did come to visit sometimes. Brought flowers to my apartment on Rue Ordener. My Nazi was much older."

I gasped. "So those stories are true! You were the Fuehrer's floozy!"

Old Irma made a face which, given the ravages of one hundred and three years, was quite a feat. "I never met the Fuehrer. My Nazi was Franz von Weimar, assistant chief of military intelligence in France."

"An oxymoron, dear. Even so, as Weimar's wench you were a traitor to your country."

"I worked for my country."

"You're *German*?"

"Don't be ridiculous, Magdalena. I was born right here in Hernia, the same year your granddaddy was born. If you didn't interrupt so much, you would know by now that I was an American spy."

"Get out of town!"

"That's exactly what Franz said when he found out. He loved me, you know. Of course I didn't love him. To the contrary, I hated him—hated what he stood for. But I had to pretend that the sun rose and set in his eyes."

Suddenly it all fit together. John Burk was really Johanne Burkholder, and he was Old Irma's illegitimate son. No doubt Burkholder had been Irma's alias, and when she had her baby, or babies, out of wedlock she gave them her fictitious name.

"Well, you liked him enough to have his baby."

"I most certainly did not!"

"Two babies, then—or was it three?"

"I never had a baby in my life!"

"That's not what I heard."

"Those silly rumors have been floating around ever since I returned from Europe. And just because I didn't talk about my life. Well, I assure you, I am nobody's mother."

"Then who is the Nazi? Who is Johanne Burkholder?"

"Johanne—although apparently he goes by the name

John now—was an acquaintance from my cabaret days. You see, I was a very accomplished singer. Very popular too, I might add, and—"

"And humble"—I clamped a hand over my mouth, lest I provoke her into silence.

"No, I wasn't humble. Not in those days. I had that certain *je ne sais quoi* that men found irresistible. But I wasn't the tramp you seem to think I was. I didn't sleep with anyone. I merely flirted. Held parties—open houses, really—that were both gay and intellectually stimulating. We called them salons in those days."

"We call them saloons these days."

"Bite your tongue, Magdalena. You have no respect for the older generation."

"Bite your tongue and your gums will bleed."

Gabriel placed a poker-hot hand on my shoulder. *"Please,* ladies."

"Oh, all right. Continue, dear," I said graciously.

Irma stuck her considerable Yoder nose in the air. There are Yoder noses, and then there are Yoder *noses*. Small planes could land on Irma's.

"Well, as I was saying before I was so rudely interrupted, Franz von Weimar was a great admirer of mine, and so was his protégé young Johanne Burkholder. I do believe the boy was even more in love with me than was his mentor."

"Tch, tch," was all I could manage before my angel gently covered my mouth with his hand. I would gladly have remained mute the rest of my days to keep that hand there.

Irma's nose made a quick dip, like a polygraph needle, but she scarcely paused. "Anyway, young Johanne was posted elsewhere, and of course I had no idea where, because he was a spy like me, you see. I did get the occasional letter, delivered grudgingly by Franz, who was getting rather tiresome. Then one day the State Department decided things had gotten too hot in the City of Light, and yanked me back stateside. Boy, was I ever relieved. Unlike some"—she glowered at me—"I would never have gone to bed with Franz von Weimer."

"Ahn wohad nawgh!" I wailed into Grabriel's palm.

"And then this morning. while I was making breakfast, he suddenly appears. Johanne, I mean, not Franz. Right there in my kitchen. Well, I was so surprised I cut myself." She held up her left hand, whose index finger sported a beige bandage.

"You better let me check that," Gabe said. Men can be such babes in the woods.

Fortunately my guardian angel had to remove his hand from my mug to examine the wound. I chose my words carefully.

"That's barely even a scratch, dear."

Of course I meant to be encouraging, and of course the old crone misinterpreted my tone. "Well, it bled a lot! And I was only slicing bananas with a table knife."

"Your skin is thin," Gabe said gently.

"Touché!" I can't tell you how delighted I was that Gabe had seen right through her.

Alas, my joy was short lived. Gabe, the babe, was definitely lost in the woods.

"No, I meant that literally. When people age, their skin becomes thinner, easier to cut and bruise. But you did a good job of cleaning the wound. It should heal nicely." He replaced the used bandage which, remarkably, stuck. Only insults seem to stick to me.

"Now *you're* interrupting, dear."

"Ah, so I am. Please. Miss Yoder, continue."

"Well, I recognized the boy right away. I know, he's not a boy now, but he still stands the same way he did all those years ago. Some folks think it's the eyes that stay the same, but that's not so. Eyes are like paper—life writes its story on them. Johanne's eyes told me he had seen things—*done* things—that no human being should do. He stood the same way, however. Slouched, with his neck kind of sticking out. It didn't matter that he'd gained a few pounds and lost most of his hair. I can recognize anyone by the way they stand."

"Ha!" I caught one of Gabriel's beautifully manicured hands and placed it over my mouth.

"You cut yourself," he said, seemingly oblivious to the fire in my face. "What then?"

"Well, like you said, I washed the cut. Then I invited Johanne to sit down and have a cup of tea."

"Weren't you afraid?"

"Afraid of what? This isn't Vichy France. This is my turf."

"Yes, it is. Yet you ended up here." He gestured with his free hand at the house. "Was that your idea?"

"Actually it was. Johanne said we needed to talk, but my place has turned into Grand Central lately." Old Irma pointed meaningfully at me with her proboscis, as well as her cane. "So I suggested we come here to talk. I mean, now that the Millers are gone, it's as empty as Lazarus's grave. Sure, I know, there is a 'for sale' sign outside, but that Earl Whitaker is so lazy, he once got fired from a job testing mattresses."

"You don't say," Gabriel said in his rich baritone. "Well, that's who I came here to see."

I pushed his hand gently away from my mouth. "*You* want to buy the Miller place?"

"As a matter of fact, I do."

"Thank you, Lord!"

Old Irma cackled again. "And she thinks I was loose!"

My face stung. I could actually feel the red as it concentrated in my cheeks.

"It's not what you think! I'm just glad someone—*anyone*—is buying this place. It's eerie to look over here night after night and see a dark farmhouse. Besides, we were talking about Johanne, remember? This is the same man who is married to a petite piano player named Samantha?"

"He did say he was married to a concert pianist, and that he taught history somewhere. Or was it mathematics?"

"Definitely history, dear. So you came all the way over here to talk about his job and marriage?"

"Don't be ridiculous, Magdalena. We talked about the old days. What fun it was—despite the political unpleasantness."

"That political unpleasantness cost me ten family members," Gabriel said much to my surprise. "All my father's siblings and both his parents died in Auschwitz."

Old Irma swallowed. "Well, that's why I was there. In Paris, I mean. Don't forget I was working for our side."

"While cavorting with the other, dear."

"Magdalena!" Grabriel said sharply.

I shrunk back, like a chastised puppy.

Gabriel touched the old woman's shoulder. "Is that all Johanne wanted? To talk about good times?"

"No!" She spit the word out like a rotten bite of apple.

"What did he want?"

"Ach, he was full of questions! Who did I see from the

old days? How was my German? Still good? I told him in German—that I could outtalk him any day."

"No doubt about it," I muttered.

Old Irma ignored me. Or perhaps she didn't hear.

"He has a funny accent now, you know."

"Like from Minnesota?"

That time she heard me and rolled her faded eyes. "A funny *German* accent. His English is much better now than when we met. We used to speak only in French."

I slapped my forehead in astonishment. Old Irma knew French? They must have taught that in U.S. spy school, because Hernia graduates would be hard pressed to say *bonjour* without a phrase book.

Gabriel should have gone into general practice instead of surgery. My doctor has never asked that many questions in the thirty years I've known him.

"I heard you shout at him, then he ran out the front door. Why were you so angry?"

Old Irma put down her cane. She attempted to point at me with one of her pretzel fingers, but thanks to sixty years of arthritis, she pointed at the doc instead. "Because he hit her—with a lamp base, no less. Magdalena may be as mean as a stepped-on rattlesnake, but she's family."

"I am *not!*" I wailed.

"Don't be ridiculous, child. Your granddaddy was my double first cousin, and both your grandmothers were third cousins once-removed."

"Which leaves one grandparent unaccounted for!" I said triumphantly.

"Yes, your mama's daddy. We were only fifth cousins twice removed."

"Aha! You see? We are *distant* cousins!"

Gabriel smiled, and I had to gasp for breath. "I think I'm going to like living here. Is everyone around here like you two?"

Before I could assure him that there were no other century-old citizens quite as cranky as Irma, a car came barreling up the long Miller drive and screeched to a halt amid a spray of gravel.

"Where's my husband?" Samantha Burk demanded. If indeed that was her name.

Twenty-Two

"That's what we want to know, dear." I looked at Diana Lefcourt, who had driven the motorized chariot. "Where's the rescue squad?"

"I didn't call 911 after all."

"What?"

"I knew you'd be all right, Magdalena. You already had a doctor with you. Besides, you Yoders have heads of stone."

I ignored the compliment. "Concert pianist indeed!" I said to Samantha. "I should have known you were a fake. Look at those itty-bitty hands—even a possum has a wider span. And a real concert pianist would have been begging me for a key to Beachy Grove Mennonite Church. We may not have a Steinway, but it's good enough for Lodema Schrock."

"Ach, Lodema!" Old Irma shook her head. "That woman couldn't play a radio properly if you gave her a month of lessons."

"Lodema is not the point," I snapped. "The point is your Nazi's wife."

"Johanne is married?"

"To her!" I pointed at the pianist imposter.

Samantha turned to Diana. "Is Miss Yoder—you know, *ill*?"

"She's a few spokes shy of a chariot wheel."

"Potiphar's calling the kettle black!" I wailed. "And you, Mrs. Burk—or is it Burkholder?—have a lot of explaining to do. The C.I.A. indeed! Your husband was a spy all right, but for the Nazis!"

Samantha had a disgustingly pert mouth, which she arranged into a mocking smile. "Has anyone bothered to tell Miss Yoder here that the war is over?"

Old Irma stepped forward with the help of her cane. "Leave the child alone. She's not crazy, she's merely flighty—you know, empty in the head. But in this case Magdalena knows what she's talking about."

Samantha gasped. "But that's impossible! My John was born and raised in Minnesota."

"No. If I recall right, it was Stuttgart."

"I've seen his birth certificate. It says quite clearly, New Bedford, Minnesota."

A bell rang in my head. As there was plenty of room in there, it came as no surprise.

"Aha! I remember now! Scott Montgomery, who is a *true* Minnesotan, says there is no such place as New Bedford."

"Well—uh, I'm sure he's mistaken. Minnesota is a large state."

"Not if you drained it, dear. Anyway, have you been to New Bedford?"

"No."

"And did you know your husband before the war? World War II, I mean?"

"No."

Old Irma nudged me aside with a paw as cold as a

Minneapolis winter. "Well, *I* knew your husband during the war. He was a shy young thing at first—until you got him singing. Let me tell you, Johanne could sing those beer-hall songs along with the best of them."

"*My* John sang? He never sings for me. Claims he can't carry a tune."

"I didn't he say sang on key. I said he sang with the best of them. Franz and Horst were the best. Sure, Horst had a smoother voice, but Franz had better diction."

"Stop it, both of you! We don't have time to yap about some drunken Nazis serenading the Fatherland. We need to notify the F.B.I."

"Ach," Old Irma said, covering me with spittle, "it's not the F.B.I. we should call, but the Department of Immigration."

Samantha blanched. "What for?"

"Because Johanne Burkholder is undoubtedly here illegally."

"And he was a Nazi," I hissed. "Who knows what heinous crimes he committed?"

"But that's just it. Neither of you has any proof that my husband committed any war crimes. And even if he did, he may have just been following orders."

I nudged Old Irma aside with a paw as hot as Hernia in the summer. "I don't buy that 'just following orders' line, sister. We all need to draw our own lines long before it gets to that point."

"Hear, hear," Gabriel said, his face grim. "If decent people had bothered to draw the line at decency, my Bubbe and Zayde might still be alive."

I nodded vigorously, despite my headache. "Millions of children—not just Jewish, either—would have survived to be alive today. The world might well have been a better place. Who knows, maybe we would already have a cure for AIDS. So you see, dear, following orders is not an excuse. And neither is ignorance. 'I saw nothing' is a phrase even the Swiss can't claim these days, and believe me, that hurts, because I'm one hundred percent Swiss. What's more, you don't seem terribly surprised to learn that your hubby was one of Hitler's henchmen."

"I am—I mean, I'm not sure he even was. Anyway, you can't prove a thing. And even if you can, well—I told you I suspected he was up to something. I wouldn't have brought that up if I had anything to hide."

"You have a point," I said grudgingly. "It would have been stupid of you to mention your husband's weird behavior."

"Or very smart."

We all turned to stare at Old Irma. The woman might have been Mennonite by birth, but singing in a Parisian cabaret had drained every drop of humility from her veins. Clearly, she still basked in the limelight.

"I did the same thing, you know—when I was a spy. I joked about being an American operative, just to throw people off my trail."

Samantha's tiny hands were rolled into fists the size of Freni's meatballs. "Well, I wasn't joking, and I'm not lying now. *If* my John was a Nazi, and *if* he was involved in any sort of horrible behavior, above and beyond that of any other soldier, I had no idea. I am innocent. I'm a professional—a concert pianist—I'm not in the business of hiding Nazi war criminals."

"Yeah, right," I growled. "If you're really a concert pianist then I'm a monkey's uncle."

"I am!"

"So prove it."

"How?"

"Play something for me."

"What? Where? Okay, I get it. I'll play at your church if that's what it takes."

"Forget the church, dear. I want you to play at my sister's wedding. You do know Handel's wedding march, don't you?"

Old Irma waved her arm like a schoolgirl—albeit a very slow school girl. "Can I sing 'O Promise Me'?"

"Yes, dear. In the shower whenever you please." I didn't mean to be cruel—honest I didn't—but who needs a one hundred-and-three-year-old ex-hussy warbling at her only sister's wedding?

Gabriel put a guiding hand gently on my shoulder.

"Okay," I wailed, "warble away!"

"I was about to say we have more company."

Indeed, there was second car barreling its way toward us in a spray of gravel.

"Freni, what are you doing here?"

"Ach! Like I told you, Magdalena, I rode with that couple—the ones with the funny accents."

"Yes, I know, the Montgomerys. That's how you got here. But what were you doing at the inn when they returned for a short potty break and found Diana's note?"

The day had warmed considerably and the grass was as dry as my cheeks the day *before* my Pooky Bear ripped the heart out of my scrawny chest and did jumping jacks on it. Therefore my elderly cousin—cum ex-cook—and I had elected to walk back. As for my oldest cousin, well, that gorgeous Gabriel had insisted on driving her home, from whence he would personally call the United States Immigration Service. But fear not, I had extracted a promise that he would attend my sister's party that night, and even the wedding itself the following day. As for the Nazi's wife, she had taken a shine to the faux pharaoh and was planning to stay with her until the business with Johanne was sorted out.

"Ach, Magdalena, why make such a federal box out of it?"

"If you're going to use Susannah's phrases, then at least get them right, dear. Now out with it."

"I came to ask for something."

"What's mine is yours," I said foolishly.

"Barbara doesn't want me in the house."

"What do you mean she doesn't want you there? It's your house."

"Yah, but she thinks I get under her foot."

I looked down at Freni. Barbara, like me, is vertically enhanced. Freni, on the other hand, is vertically challenged. But Freni is a heavy woman with an enormous bosom. She quite makes up for her lack of vertical visibility with her horizontal presence. It was unlikely Barbara literally stepped on her.

"So, you feel you are in the way in your own house? Is that it?"

"Yah, I make a simple comment, and this is the thanks I get."

"What comment was that, dear?"

"Nothing."

"Out with it!"

"Ach, it was not such a big thing. I just told her that now—since she is in the family way—there was no reason for her and my son Jonathan to be—well, you know."

"No, I don't."

214

"Ach, so dense, Magdalena. They were—you know."
Freni rolled her eyes.

"*That?* How do you know?"

"I have ears, Magdalena."

"You could *hear* them?"

Freni shook her head miserably. "Every day—sometimes more than once."

I clapped my hands over my ears. This was not a proper conversation to be having with someone Freni's age. With anyone of *any* age, for that matter.

"So what is it you want? Do you and Mose want to move in with me? Don't think I wouldn't like to help you, but this is where you need to put your own little foot down. It's your house, after all."

We walked in silence for few minutes. There is nothing quite as pleasant as a pieless pasture on a sunny spring day. My once-broken but now-healed heart wanted to soar with the chicken hawks, to sing with the starlings.

Leave it to Freni to intrude on my joy. "Ach, Magdalena, it's more than you-know-what."

"What is, dear?"

"My problem."

"Ah, that. Well, Sam sells the solution in a little tube. It will shrink those suckers in a New York minute."

"Ach!"

"Trust me. They'll practically disappear overnight."

Freni wrapped her stubby arms as best she could around her chest. "You always were jealous, Magdalena, but this is going too far. I'm happy the way God made me. I certainly don't want to look like you—flat as an ironing board."

"Hemorrhoids! I thought you were talking about hemorrhoids!"

"Yah, sure you were."

"But I *was*. And I'm not jealous. I wouldn't want— never mind. What's the favor?"

"My job." Flies landing on pudding are louder than that.

"You want your job back?"

"Are you deaf, Magdalena?"

I tossed my head. "Give me one good reason I should take you back."

"Ach, and this from the child I practically raised?"

I bided my time before responding. "I tell you what. I'll give you your job back, if you come clean with me."

"Such riddles, Magdalena. Of course I'll clean with you. Don't I always wash the dishes?"

"I want you to be honest with me about something. I'm going to ask you a question, and I want the truth, no matter how much it hurts."

Freni's beady eyes darted nervously from side to side behind her thick lenses. "So ask, already."

"The day Mama and Papa died in the tunnel—"

"Ach, a terrible day!"

"Yes, but whose fault was it?"

"The Lord numbers our days, Magdalena. You know that."

"Even so, we have free will, right? Did Papa do something foolish? Was he driving recklessly?"

Freni was as mum as Diana's mummy.

"He *was* driving recklessly, wasn't he?" Dim memories drifted back of Papa flying down the road, of Susannah and me huddled in the backseat as mailboxes fell like dominoes.

"Yah."

"Why didn't you ever say anything?"

"Ach—what was there to say? That your papa drove like a maniac? Everyone knew that, Magdalena."

"Yes, but I didn't."

Freni stared at me. The thick lenses needed a good scrubbing.

"You were a grown woman when your parents were killed—not a little girl. How was I to know you didn't remember? Or maybe didn't *want* to remember?"

I shrugged, tears filling my own beady blue eyes. "I guess, you wouldn't. I guess I liked to think of Papa as somehow perfect, and Mama as—well, you know, Mama."

Freni nodded. "Yah, your mama—she was something."

I smiled bravely and put my arm around her well-padded shoulders. "Well, you've been like a mother to me ever since."

I waited expectantly for her to tell me that I had been the daughter she had never had, and of course, wished she had. That it was I who put the bead in her eyes.

Nothing. Nada. Zip. My portly cousin plodded along as merrily as you please, but her lips were sealed tighter than a clam at low tide.

"*So*, Freni?"

"So, does that mean I get my job back?"

I sighed. "You really know how to hurt a girl—but okay, you can have your job back. A word of warning, however."

"Yah?"

"You get to quit only fifty-two more times, *and* you have to tell Strubbly Sam that I'm giving him the old heave-ho."

"Ach! And you not even married!"

"I'm letting him go, dear. I'm *firing* him. Surely that's a word you understand."

Freni slipped out of my awkward embrace. "Yah, but I won't have to."

"What do you mean?"

"I fired him already."

"*What?* You fired him? You can't be doing that! You're not his boss—I am! Well, now, this changes everything."

I tried to grab Freni by an apron strap, but she stepped deftly out of my reach. "I've been like a mama to you, remember?"

"Yes, like Mama." I gritted my teeth. I might have lunged for Freni and wrestled her to the ground had it not been for the glove that caught my eyes.

We were only yards from the pond now, and in one of the bushes that ringed the shore was a man's leather glove that had not been there earlier that morning. I don't have a mind like a steel trap—aluminum sieve is more like it—but the glove looked familiar.

I trotted over to retrieve the glove. Despite her age, Freni had no trouble keeping up.

"Ach, Magdalena, what are you doing?"

"I'm recovering what may be a valuable clue."

"An old glove?"

"A bird in the hand is worth two in the bush, dear, but a hand in the bush—now that beats everything."

"Ach, riddles again. Must you always talk in riddles, Magdalena?"

I reached the glove. I was wrong—it *had* been there a long time. It certainly didn't belong to Johanne Burkholder. It may even have belonged to Aaron Jr. I plucked it from the grasp of two stubborn twigs and turned it over. Sure enough, there was the rip in the palm from the time Aaron held a barbed wire down, so I could step over a fence. We'd been—well, never you mind.

"Life's a riddle, dear. There's got to be more to it than this."

Freni sniffed. "Ach, there's grandbabies."

"But I'll never have any," I wailed. "I'm thinking of selling the inn and becoming a missionary. To Africa, maybe."

Freni poked me in the ribs with a plump finger. "Yah, and if they still have cannibals, at least no one will eat you."

"Very funny, dear."

Freni sighed. "Ach, no sense of humor, this one. Well, I tell you, Magdalena, becoming a missionary would be a big mistake."

"Why? Don't you think I have a serving nature?"

"Service, schmervice, you won't be going anywhere."

I stamped one of my size elevens. Thank the good Lord there were no patties to watch for.

"Says who?"

"Says me," Freni said smugly. "I saw the way you looked at the English doctor back there."

"Wrong!"

But she was right. I know this is going to sound strange to you— maybe even worthy of Diana Lefcourt—but I could feel it in my bones. Dr. Rosen and I were destined for each other. Never mind that we had nothing in common. God works in mysterious ways, and sending a Jewish doctor to my faux-husband's former house was just one of many miracles. Sure, there would be obstacles to overcome, but—I shivered as a single puffy white cloud blocked the sun—there was nothing two people in love couldn't overcome.

Fortunately, I was blissfully unaware of an obstacle that lay right around life's next corner.

Twenty-Three

It was Susannah's fault. If she'd wanted a livelier party, she should have held it somewhere other than Elvina Stoltzfus's farm. Elvina is a seventy-five-year-old widow, for crying out loud, and a member of the Tulpehocken Hill Mennonite church, which is even more conservative than my branch. The woman is just a skip away from being Amish. I, on the other hand, am two skips and a hop away. Clearly, the party should have been held at the PennDutch.

"It's gotten cold again," I whined.

Gabriel gallantly removed his brown suede jacket and laid it across my shoulders. "There, see if that helps."

"I mean it's too cold to bob for apples."

"Oh, will we be doing that? It sounds like fun."

It didn't to me. If you had a profile like mine you wouldn't get it anywhere near fruit. Once when I was ten I bobbed for peaches, and much to my mortification speared one with my proboscis. Sure, the peach was overly ripe, and therefore on the soft side, but try explaining that to a group of fifth graders.

Gabriel had been late picking me up—he was a doctor, after all—and frankly, I was wringing my hands with despair when he showed up driving a gray Datsun of dubious vintage. When I saw the car he was driving, I wrung some more. We Mennonites might be a modest people, but since I'd already committed the sin of owning a red BMW, it would have been an even bigger sin to leave it home and disappoint my critics.

"I'd be happy to drive," I said, and headed toward my car. My guests had long since left for the party, and mine was on the only one left.

"No." He gently pulled me back.

"What do you mean 'no'?" I may be a traditional woman, but I won't stand for sexist treatment. Deep down everyone knows women are equal, if not superior, to men. After all, men were God's practice run. You can read about it in Genesis.

"I mean, I'm in the mood to drive tonight. Besides my car is already warm."

I meekly allowed myself to be led like a sheep to the slaughter. "That makes sense," I heard myself say.

Gabriel was a gentleman and opened the door for me. I don't mind that sort of treatment from a man, just as long as he knows I'm fully capable of opening my own door, and slamming it too, if need be. At any rate, the interior of the car smelled like cigarette smoke and there was a pair of fuzzy dice and a pink lace garter hanging from the rearview mirror.

"My nephew's," Gabriel said, reading my mind. "He's a college student."

"Uh-huh."

For the record, Gabriel Rosen is the slowest driver I've ever met. I could have pushed the car to Elvina's faster than he drove. Not that I'm complaining, mind you. There are worse things than being cooped up in a

222

small car with a handsome man. I could do without the cigarette smell, however.

"So," Gabriel said, looking intently at the road, "you own and operate a bed and breakfast."

"Well, in a manner of speaking. I prefer to think of it as a cultural exchange program. I give my guests a sample of Pennsylvania Dutch culture in exchange for a whole lot of cash." I laughed pleasantly at my little joke.

He nodded, but said nothing for the longest time. Since the devil is quite willing and able to fill silence, I saw it as my religious duty to jump in.

"So, Gabriel, are you really a doctor?"

"Please call me Gabe. And you mean because of the car, don't you?"

"Well, Gabe, you must admit, it isn't your typical doctor's car."

He glanced at me and smiled. He didn't have perfect teeth like Aaron, but they were close enough for me.

"It really is my nephew's car. I'm just borrowing it for a few days. In the meantime he gets to drive my Porsche."

"Get out of town!"

"I beg your pardon?"

"That doesn't make a lick of sense to me."

"Well, I didn't want to draw attention to myself, you see. Rich tourist in a fancy car—that kind of thing."

"And you don't think fuzzy dice and ladies' underpinnings draw attention in Hernia? Besides, thanks to the PennDutch, we're used to rich tourists."

"That's a shame—what I mean is, I'd much rather be driving my Porsche."

"At thirty-five miles an hour?"

He chuckled. "I'm used to city driving."

"We're not in the city now, dear."

We crept up to forty, which is about the speed fall color spreads south.

"You mean you're a *spy* too?"

He laughed. "No, I'm not a spy. You see, I've always had this dream—oh, incidentally, the Immigration Service is sending someone out to investigate, but it may take a couple of weeks."

"A couple of *weeks*?"

"Like you said, Magdalena, God works in mysterious ways. The government, however, works very slowly."

"But in the meantime—"

"In the meantime, would you like to hear about my life's dream?"

"Do tell, dear." Perhaps I was in it, wearing white—no, it would have to be off-white now. Darn that Aaron!

"I've always wanted to write."

"Write what?"

"Novels."

"What kind of novels?"

He shrugged. "I don't know—good novels. Mysteries, maybe."

"Wow!" I'd met many writers before—all of them guests—but none who could inspire me to a single-syllable exclamation.

"And I was thinking of writing them here."

"In your nephew's car?"

He smiled kindly. "No, here in Hernia. On that farm where we met today."

My heart tried to claw its way out of my chest. "So you were serious? You really want to buy the Miller farm?"

"Dead serious."

"But what about your practice, or whatever surgeons call it?"

"I've given it up. I've retired—I want to exchange it for a slower pace."

"I see. You're sort of like my guests, then. You want to exchange a large amount of cash for a taste of country life."

"Yeah, only I won't have to pay extra to clean my room."

I gasped. "Who told you?"

"Vee haf our vays," he said in the worst German accent I'd ever heard.

"Old Irma told you, didn't she? Why that garrulous old crone! I ought to wring her scrawny neck!"

"Now, now, be kind. A beautiful, talented woman like you can afford to be generous."

"Were you just describing *me*?"

"I hope you don't mind me saying so, but you are the most intriguing person I've ever met."

"Ditto, dear."

We glanced awkwardly at each other, and back to the road. What was there to say next? I surely wasn't going to be the first to speak. Thank the Good Lord after all that Gabriel was driving at a snail's pace. That way I could count the dashes in the broken white line that ran down the center of Hertzler Road.

"So," he said finally, "what sort of music do you like?"

"Hymns, of course. *Onward Christian Soldiers* is my favorite." I clapped a hand over my mouth.

"That's all right. We're allowed to have our differences. I'm rather partial to *klezmeir* myself."

"What's that?"

"Think of it as Jewish hymns. Lively Jewish hymns."

225

"I like Mozart," I said out of the blue.

"No kidding? So do I. What about art?"

"I can take him or leave him."

"You're funny as well as beautiful."

"Go on, dear."

"I meant it."

"I know. That's why I said 'go on.' Go on and tell me more."

"It would be my pleasure. Let's see, you're intelligent, resourceful—"

Unfortunately even snails get to their destinations, and we were at ours. I would have loved nothing more than to creep on past the Stoltzfus spread, while my rich Jewish doctor regaled me with a list of my attributes, but alas, my only sister was getting married, and this party was for her.

"Turn left into the next driveway," I said, "but don't forget where you left off."

Gabriel winked. "No need to worry about that."

I felt like Monica Lewinsky at a journalists' convention. Susannah, Sandy Hart, and Lodema Schrock descended on me like a flock of chickens on a June bug.

Susannah was the quickest. "She's my big sister. I get to speak to her first!"

"Well, *I'm* a paying guest!"

"That may be, but *I'm* the pastor's wife."

It didn't take the wisdom of Solomon to figure this one out. "Everyone, this Dr. Gabriel Rosen. And ladies, since you've already introduced yourselves, there's no need for me to do so further. You"— I said to Susannah —"show the good doctor around."

"It would be my pleasure," Susannah purred.

"Now you," I said to Lodema Schrock, "are the best cook in all of Hernia, and I just know you brought some goodies to contribute to the party. So why don't you fix a plate a plate of food for our guest? But no ham." I turned to Gabe. "You don't eat ham, do you?"

He smiled. "I'm not kosher, but I prefer not to eat ham all the same."

I turned back to Lodema. "Then pile on the three-bean salad, dear. I know that's one of your specialties." After all, there is nothing quite like a plate of gaseous fiber to test a man's manners.

"Do you like chocolate cake?" Lodema asked coquettishly. "I heard there's chocolate cake coming."

Gabe graced her with a grin. "It's my favorite."

"Now," I said to Sandy as I dragged her aside, "what's this all about? I don't change the towels every day, you know. If you want clean towels, you'll have to wash them yourself, and that will be a dollar fifty extra for hot water."

"It's not about your ratty, threadbare towels. It's about Bob."

"Don't tell me—he's already had too much of Lodema's three-bean salad?"

"Bob is missing."

"What?"

"I've looked for him everywhere."

"Everywhere? Even Elvina's outhouse?"

Sandy's frizzy blonde head bobbed like a fishing court on Miller's pond. "I said everywhere, didn't I? Anyway, when we first got here, we decided to split up and meet in half an hour at the horse-and-buggy rides. Well it's been forty-five minutes, but he ain't there. And speaking of which, you lied."

"I did?" Subconsciously I touched my nose.

"You said there was going to horse-and-buggy rides, but there ain't."

"Nonsense, dear. Look right over there."

"Them ain't horses, Miss Yoder, them's mules."

I peered into the dark. They looked like horses to me.

"Horses," I said.

"Mules. Them's too big to be horses."

"We grow them bigger in Pennsylvania, dear. Now, shall we continue debating livestock, or shall we look for your husband?"

We looked high and low, but found neither hide nor hair of the gregarious Bob Hart. No one even remembered seeing him.

"Are you sure your rental car is still here, dear?"

"Of course I'm sure. It's that hideous blue thing over there."

"Way over there on the edge of the field?"

I gasped as someone touched me on the shoulder. Contrary to what else you may have heard, I did not scream and spook the horses. They spooked much later in the evening when Gabe's beans repeated on themselves.

"Freni!"

"Ach, you'll be the death of me yet, Magdalena."

"*Me?* You're the one who sneaks up on people. What is it you want?"

Despite the darkness, and the layer of flour and lard covering her lenses, I could see Freni's eyes dart to Sandy and back to me.

"Freni, this is—"

"Yah, yah, we met at the inn. Magdalena, can I speak to you alone?"

"Well—"

"Oh, my God!"

I whirled just in time to see the gangly Marjorie climb out of the backseat of the Harts' rental car. Bob, still buckling his pants, tumbled out seconds later.

"I guess we found him, dear," I said sympathetically.

Sandy uttered words that Mennonite and Amish ears are genetically incapable of hearing and charged off to battle Sodom and Gomorrah.

"Ach, the English," Freni muttered, shaking her head.

I said nothing, lest Freni equate my mock marriage with this situation. I was an inadvertent hussy, not a strident strumpet like Marjorie. And let us not forget that, in both sets of circumstances, men were half the equation.

"So, Freni, what sort of bee do you have in your bonnet now?"

"Ach!" Freni slapped at her head.

"That's just an expression, dear. What is it you wanted to talk to me about?"

"Strubbly Sam."

"We settled that, dear. You fired him, remember?"

"Yah, and I told him he could come to Susannah's party."

"You did? Why, that was very nice of you."

"Ach, think nothing of it. But" — she spread her stubby arms — "he's not here."

"Can you blame him? Why would that dear, sweet man want to go to a party the same day he was fired?"

"Yah, but—"

"Freni, out with it!"

"He promised to bake three chocolate cakes for Elvina if I let him come to the party."

"If you let him? Why Freni Hostetler, shame on you!

Just because Elvina is your best friend gives you no right to take advantage of the guests."

Freni hung her head, but given that she has a thick, squat neck, she never truly looks repentant. "There's more, Magdalena."

"Yes?"

"Mose and I stopped by Strubbly Sam's house on the way here—to pick up the cakes—and he wasn't there."

"So, then he's here already. What's the problem?"

"He isn't here, either. Magdalena, I'm not superstitious—you know that—but something has happened to Strubbly Sam. I feel it in my bones. You must find him, Magdalena."

"What am I?" I wailed. "The lost and found bureau?"

"Ach, such riddles! Will you help me?"

"I'll do what I can," I said.

More stupid words were never spoken.

Twenty-Four

I love Rhythm. That's rhythm with a capital R, and it's the only kind we Mennonites know. It's also our wildest party game. Everyone sits around in a big circle and slaps their hands on their knees. Then they clap their hands once, snap the right thumb and forefinger, and then the left. As the finger snapping commences the player who is "it" shouts out first his assigned number, and then the assigned number of another player. This is all done, of course, without breaking the group's rhythm. Any player breaking the group rhythm is excluded from the circle, as is any player who, in the heat of battle, forgets his own number. Eventually only two players will remain, and the speed picks up dramatically. The staccato slapping, clapping, and subsequent barking of numbers would surely bewilder an English observer.

Susannah finds Rhythm boring, but that's only because she doesn't have any *rhythm* and is always knocked out of the game in the first round. Even though tonight there were one hundred and sixty-two people forming one giant circle inside the barn, my baby sister was the first out.

"Oh, Mags, it's *so* boring."

"Not your average night at a truckstop, is it, dear?"

"You can say that again!"

"So, dear, why are we playing?" I said this all without breaking rhythm, mind you.

"It was Melvin's idea."

"Twenty-nine—eighty-six! Figures. What are going to do next, sing?"

"How did you know?"

"Twenty-nine—thirty-six." Someone in the group was picking on me. "Just a lucky guess. Besides—twenty-nine—one hundred and eight!" Oops, the group was ganging up on me. Undoubtedly it bothered them to see someone could carry on a conversation and maintain a zippy beat.

"And Mags, you wouldn't believe the songs he's picked."

"Yes, I will—twenty-nine—thirty-six. Try me."

" 'She'll Be Coming 'Round the Mountain'! He wants us to sing it in rounds."

"Well, I rather like—twenty-nine—thirty-six!"

"And that's not all, Mags—"

"Twenty-nine—thirty-six!"

" 'Down by the Old Mill Stream,' if you can imagine that."

"Yes, I can—twenty-*one*—thirty-six!"

The barn seemed to explode with laughter as I crashed and burned. Thanks to number thirty-six I was out. But of course the game went on, most folks not missing a beat.

"Ooh, Mags, did you see who thirty-six was?"

I stepped out of the circle. "No, dear, I was too busy being pestered by you."

"It's that gorgeous doctor."

"What?" I couldn't seem to get the song titles out of my mind.

"Gabe, silly. Oh Mags, you're so lucky, you know that? Here I am, about to marry *Melvin,* and you've got one hot stud muffin just—"

"That's it," I cried. "The old mill stream—the old grist mill! That's where you'll find something round!"

Susannah had the temerity to sniff my breath. "You been drinking, Mags?"

"And the old grist mill is on Stubbly Sam's property."

"You're nuts, Mags, you know that?"

I had much better things to do than stand around and be insulted by a woman who wears her dog in a bra. "See you later, dear," I said calmly, and went out for a walk.

Susannah gets no credit for scheduling her party to coincide with the full moon. The girl doesn't even know her own cycle, if you get my drift. It was the Good Lord who provided the moon that night and made the walk from the rear of Elvina's property to Strubbly Sam's a piece of cake. The two farms abut, after all, and from Elvina's barn it was all downhill to the stream. Sure, there is woods most of the way, but it's primary growth and there is very little underbrush. I got to the millstream with nary a scratch, but crossing it was another matter.

The grist mill is on the *other* side of the stream, and although Slave Creek is not exactly the mighty Susquehanna, it is not something you want to wade—especially at night, after the temperature has dropped.

"Couldn't somebody have built a bridge?" I wailed.

I could see the old two-story stone mill, its wheel steadily turning, but there was no way to reach it. Not without removing my shoes and stockings, and hiking my dress up to my waist. Believe me. I went so far as to search the bank for vines with which to swing across. Tarzan was from Africa, and there are Mennonite missionaries there, so it is not as far fetched a thought as one might suppose. To be frank, I would have given up had I not seen a flicker of light in one of the lower-story windows.

I am a woman of prayer, and pray I did. "Oh Lord, don't let me faint from the cold," I moaned as I staggered across the rocky stream bed, my skirt bunched up beneath my armpits. And believe me, it was a miracle that I made it across. The mossy stones at the bottom of Slave Creek are as slippery as Freni's memory, and the current as strong as her resolve.

Once across, however, I felt strangely warm and confident. How else can I explain the fact that, after dropping my skirt, I marched straight up to the side door and peered in.

"Why, come on in, Miss Yoder. I've been expecting you."

I jumped, banging my head on the stone lintel.

"Don't tell me you're surprised." The speaker lit an oil lamp.

"Johanne!"

"Ah, so you know my real name. Good, that will save us some time." He turned and the lamp illuminated Sam's *strubbly* features.

"Sam!" I took an involuntary step backward. The poor dear was lashed to the stone grinding wheel with inch-thick ropes. His mouth had been taped shut with gray duct tape, but above the tape wild eyes told me all I needed to know. He was still alive.

Johanne motioned me forward. Since he was waving a gun, I complied.

"You tied and gagged the poor man!"

"Of course I have. Come even closer, Miss Yoder. I don't like having to shout over the noise of the stream."

My knees buckled a few times—no doubt I walked like Marjorie—but I did as I was told. I followed orders.

Mercifully, Johanne stopped pointing the gun at me. He did not, however, put it away.

"You have it wrong, Miss Yoder. It's Sam here who's the Nazi, not I."

I tried to read Sam's eyes. "Don't be ridiculous! I've known Sam my entire life."

"I'm sure you have. But I'm also pretty sure your life began well after Sam's career in the Third Reich. How old are you, thirty-five?"

I snorted. "Flattery will get you nowhere, dear! Sam is an honest, God-fearing man, the son-in-law of a former bishop."

Johanne smiled. "I'm sure he is, but he is also known as the Butcher of Tunis."

"You're" — I struggled with my Christian tongue— "full of it! So, then, who are you, the Immigration Service?"

"At your service ma'am. Really, Miss Yoder, I expected you to figure that out too."

"Then why is your name Johanne Burkholder?"

"Why *not*? Is Magdalena Yoder any more American?"

"It's Magdalena *Portulacca* Yoder, dear."

He chuckled. "I suppose Portulacca is as American as apple pie. For your information, our government was keen on recruiting from within the ranks of the German-American community. They needed native speakers."

"But Old Irma says—"

"Old Irma, as you call her, was a German operative, not American."

"That's—"

"Ridiculous? That seems to be your favorite word, Magdalena Portulacca Yoder."

"But she sang in cabarets. And held salons where she entertained Nazis. Now why would a German entertain—okay, but why is she back here in Hernia?"

"Where do you think she'd go? Argentina?"

I pondered ponderously while I prayed some more. I may not be the brightest bulb in the chandelier, but I do have a functioning brain.

"So why didn't you arrest Old Irma this morning?"

"That was my plan until you barged in. But first I needed to get her to tell me where the Butcher was hiding."

"It that case, dear, you can put away your gun. I am not a Nazi. And if Strubbly Sam really is the Butcher of Tunis, you're going to need some help."

Strubbly Sam made a noise not so unlike the ones Aaron used to make when he disappeared into the bathroom with the morning paper.

"He's trying to say something, Johanne. Can't we at least undo the tape?"

"Of course we could, but we won't. You have a lot to learn about his kind, Miss Yoder. First it's removing the tape, then loosening the ropes just a little to keep his circulation going, and then *you* end up with a slit throat."

"But he doesn't have a knife. I mean, didn't you search him?"

"Then it's a crushed skull. What difference does it make?"

Sam grunted again. His eyes were trying to tell me

something, but what? I have never been a good eye reader. Had I been, I would never have misconstrued Aaron's "come-hither" looks as indigestion. I needed a test of some sort.

"You say you want to help me, Miss Yoder? Come here and hold the gun on him while I run up to the house and use his phone."

"Strubbly Sam doesn't have a phone," I said stupidly.

Johanne blinked. "Of course he wouldn't, being Amish. How forgetful of me. We in the Immigration Service refer to it as having a senior moment."

"Then maybe some of you more senior members should retire, dear. It doesn't seem to be the kind of business where one can afford to make mistakes."

"As a matter of fact, I plan to retire as soon as I wrap up this case. Now, if you'll just come on over and give me a hand guarding the prisoner, I'll hike back up the road. I believe the Butcher's neighbors have electric lights. They should have a phone."

The Keeblers did indeed have a phone. They were Presbyterians, after all, and fallen ones at that. They probably even had call waiting.

"Good idea, but I'll do it."

"That won't work," he said patiently. "This isn't a matter for police—this is State Department business. Certain contacts have to be reached—it's all very covert."

"I guess you have a point." I mean, that made sense, didn't it? If I spent my life rounding up Nazis, I'd do it on the q.t. too.

"Look, Miss Yoder, you're not convinced, are you?"

"Well—"

"No, I understand completely. Like you say, you've known this man all your life, right?"

"Right."

"And he wouldn't lie, right?"

"Not if the Good Lord himself commanded it."

Johanne calmly stepped over to his prisoner and ripped the duct tape off Sam's mouth. Fortunately, Strubbly Sam, as an Amish man, is forbidden to wear a mustache and hair on his lower lip. As it was, Sam winced with pain.

"Okay, Samuel Friedrich Burkholder—because that's your real name—are you the Butcher of Tunis?"

Tears rolled down Sam's cheeks, whether from pain or shame. "Yah, that I am."

"This can't be happening," I moaned.

"Yah, Big Magdalena, but—"

The butcher didn't get to finish his sentence, thanks to the butt of Johanne's gun. If it hadn't been for the ropes, Sam would be lying on the floor.

"Why did you do that?" I screamed.

Johanne's eyes were as cold and lifeless as the marbles at the bottom of Susannah's goldfish bowl. "Sorry, Miss Yoder, but I can't stand those Nazi lies. They all claim they're innocent. And even when they don't, well—they're upright citizens *now*, aren't they? Gone straight, they say. Yeah, right. Let me tell you, I've heard it a million times, and it's nothing but lies. They know damn well what they did, and if they had the chance, they'd do it again. That's the scary part, you know. That they're *not* sorry. That doesn't say much for the human race, does it?"

I shook my head.

"Well, it's obvious you're not going to be any help here. So run along, Miss Yoder. He won't be going anywhere for a while, even if I untied him."

"But we can't just leave him like that. Look, he's bleeding!"

"So he is." Johanne pulled a white cotton handkerchief from his left pocket. "Here, see if you can stop the bleeding."

I took a step forward, but something, perhaps my real guardian angel, made me stop. Samuel Friedrich *Burkholder*? Wasn't that too much of a coincidence? What were the chances that Nazi and Nazi-hunter would share the same last name? I looked at Sam, and then back at Johanne. It seemed just barely possible. Fifty years of sedentary living and fifty years of farm life shape a man differently, but the underlying bone structure never changes. There was only one way to find out, so I braced myself to run.

"Why not let the Butcher bleed, dear? Isn't that something the Scorpion would do?"

Johanne stiffened. "*What* did you say?"

I meant to run. But already it was too late. The Scorpion's gun was aimed at the midpoint between my eyes.

Twenty-Five

Singapore SPAM® Salad

✦

Warm Sesame Dressing:

1 cup sugar
⅓ cup rice vinegar
¼ cup olive oil
2 tablespoons sesame oil
¼ teaspoon garlic salt

Salad:

½ head iceburg lettuce, thinly sliced
½ head Romaine lettuce, thinly sliced
1 (12-ounce) can SPAM® Luncheon Meat, cubed
3 carrots, grated
1 cup chopped green onions
1 cup chopped celery
1 green bell pepper, chopped
1 cup thinly sliced radishes
1 (6½-ounce) package sliced almonds, toasted

In saucepan, combine all dressing ingredients. Stir constantly until sugar dissolves. In large bowl, toss together all salad ingredients. Serve warm dressing with salad. Serves 8.

NUTRITIONAL INFORMATION PER SERVING:
Calories 432; Protein 13g; Carbohydrate 36g; Fat 28g; Cholesterol 34mg; Sodium 453 mg.

Twenty-Six

"You *are* the Scorpion!" I hissed.

Johanne smiled broadly. "It is such a more dignified nickname than the Butcher, don't you think?"

"So you two *are* brothers!"

"It's a pity, Miss Yoder, that you weren't around in the war. We could have used a good woman like you on our side."

"In your dreams, dear."

"And full of fire. I like that in a woman. My Samantha is so—well, she lacks passion. Give me a hot woman any day."

"Like Irma Yoder."

He grinned. "Yes, she was hot in her day."

"Well, don't worry, dear. Where you're going there won't be a shortage of hot women."

The grin froze.

I eased back one small baby step. Having played *Mother May I* ad nauseam with Susannah and her little playmates, I was an expert on undetected movement. Or so I thought.

"Come here!"

"Really, you don't want to do this, dear. I mean, you just captured a Nazi war criminal, right? I'm sure you'll get credit for that. Plea bargaining is all the rage these days, I hear. *Or*"—I dangerously took another small step back —"just leave him tied there and you take off. I won't breathe a word of this to anyone. I promise. And there has got to be a home for the Nazi aged somewhere— like Paraguay or Argentina. I'm sure they have a nice schedule of activities. You could take a ceramics class and do a bust of the Fuehrer. Or how about making a stained-glass swastika? You could let your imagination go hog wild and use a color other than black."

"Shut the hell up!"

"Really, dear, there's no need to be rude."

The click of the safety switch was like thunder in my ears. "I said come here."

I should have taken my chances and fled into the night. That's what my brain was telling me to do. It is hard for even the best shot to hit a running target. And even then, unless the bullet entered a vital organ, I might still get away. I knew the woods hereabouts; he didn't. Alas, my legs would not obey. While my brain shouted *no,* my legs wobbled their way over to Johanne, and stood obediently in place while he trussed me up like a Thanksgiving turkey.

The man must have been a Boy Scout in his youth, or the German equivalent of one. He lashed me to a hand-hewn post that was about a foot thick in diameter, and which, along with seven others, supported the upper story of the mill. I must say, his knots were beautifully executed. If ever the Nazi Nursing Home for the Aged needed a macramé teacher, Johanne was it.

"Aren't you going to gag me too?"

"Of course not. I want to hear you scream."

"Well, I'm not going to. You can pump me full of bullets,

but I'm not uttering a sound. I wouldn't give you the satisfaction."

"Oh, you'll scream, all right. I guarantee it."

"Fire away, dear," I croaked. "The Good Lord will stop the pain." I wish I could say I really believed that. God did shut the lions' mouths for Daniel, but Magdalena Portulacca Yoder has never been on the Creator's A-list. And don't tell *me* He doesn't play favorites. Any girl who is five-eight by the time she enters sixth grade, and has her face mistaken for a pepperoni pizza more than once, knows exactly what I mean.

Johanne nodded in Sam's direction. "Ah, but it won't be your pain. It'll be his."

"You're shooting Sam first? Well, that's just plain bad manners. Everyone knows that ladies go first. Or didn't they teach you that in the Fatherland?"

"To the contrary, Miss Yoder, I'm killing Sam first out of consideration for you."

"For *me*?"

"Oh, yes. I want you to have the opportunity to watch him die."

"I'll pass, thank you." I closed my eyes.

"You'll open them," he said confidently, "when his bones start to crunch.

I opened them. "His *bones*?"

"Oh, yes, that's what will happen when I throw this lever" — he patted a thick wooden bar about a yard long — "and engage the grinding wheel."

I gasped. "You wouldn't!"

"Oh, but I would."

"But he's your own flesh and blood."

"He's a traitor to the Third Reich."

"How is hiding among the Amish any more traitorous than teaching history in Pittsburgh?"

"Ah, but Samuel didn't just hide. He became one of them."

"Well, I *thought* he was one. Australia, indeed. I should have known—there are no Amish down under."

Johanne shook his head. "You don't listen, do you? Samuel *is* Amish."

"Nonsense! Amish don't—"

"I mean *now*—in his heart."

"Says who?"

"Tell her, brother," Johanne said.

"Ach!"

"You see, the first word out of his mouth. *Ach.*"

"It's a German expression, dear."

"Ah, but we don't use it nearly as much as the Amish. Now, Samuel, be a brave man and tell her before I make a pancake out of you."

Samuel winced. "It is true."

"Go on!"

"Yes, go on, dear!"

"Ach—well, I did come to Hernia to hide. It was only going to be temporary, you see. Just for a year or two, until I learned enough of the American way to pass as an English."

"Yeah, right! The Amish weren't going to prepare you for corporate America."

"Let him continue!" John barked.

Samuel glanced at me and then looked away. "My first night here, I met my Amanda. It was her father, the bishop, who took me in, you see. I know you won't believe this, Magdalena, but—"

"But it was love at first sight, right?"

"Ach, no! I was going to say I found peace here. Real peace. Something I never knew existed."

"Our father was a monster," Johanne said quietly.

"Remind me to bring violins next time, dear."

"Shut up and let my brother continue."

I looked at Sam. He was weeping again.

"I learned about love here. Not just Amanda's love, but God's love. I learned how to get along with other people. I learned how to love myself."

"So you had a religious experience? Is that what you're trying to tell me?"

"Yah, I think so. My life changed. I learned that I am nothing without God."

"He really believes this crap," Johanne said piteously.

I was flabbergasted. I believe in miracles, but transforming the Butcher of Tunis into a faithful Amish elder— well, that's a tall order even for God.

"He raised six God-fearing children," I finally said, as much to sort things out in my head as to defend Sam. "And they have how many children among them?"

"Forty-nine," Sam said, just a hint of English pride in his voice.

Johanne snickered. "Imagine that. Forty-nine little God-fearing nephews and nieces running around. Our Papa would be sick if he knew."

"Actually, Sam's grandchildren are your grandnephews and nieces. And your papa sounds like he was a very sick man."

"No argument there," Johanne said.

Sam said nothing.

I shook my head. "Wow, this is so hard to believe. I mean, didn't you feel guilty all these years?"

"Yah! Always guilty. But what was I to do? My Amanda—the children—they believed in me."

"You could have confessed your sin. You Amish are big on public confession, that much I know."

"Yah, but—"

"There's always a but," I said sharply. I knew, however, what he was driving at. Once Sam's terrible secret was revealed, his family would never live it down. There would always be whispers and glances to deal with, new rumors to squash. And not because the Amish are particularly virulent gossips—to the contrary, they are not—but because such behavior is human nature.

"Well, that's all water under the bridge now, isn't it?" Johanne chuckled. "Or perhaps I should say, water over the mill wheel."

I glared at the fiend. Now that I'd had a few minutes to think about it, I realized that the mill stone was no threat to Strubbly Sam. The sluice that directed the force of the stream to the mill wheel had been shut off for as long as I remembered.

It was my distinct pleasure to snort in derision. "Don't be ridiculous, dear. This mill hasn't been operating in years. Make that dozens of years. If you pull that lever a six-foot rabbit might appear, but that's about all."

"Ah, that's what you think, Miss Yoder. For your information, I spent the afternoon repairing the wheel and removing the sluice gate. Didn't you see the wheel turning?"

I couldn't recall. I had a memory of water, splashing in the moonlight, but it may have been from another time and place. Not that it mattered, however, because I could definitely hear the water splashing now.

"So you got the wheel turning—big deal. That doesn't

mean the stone will turn. The mill was abandoned, you know."

Sam closed his eyes. "Yah, the mill was abandoned, Big Magdalena, but not because it didn't work. The English grain elevators are much more efficient."

"Still, it's been an awful long time. That wheel isn't going to budge an inch."

"And if the wheel does move," Sam said—and then, although his lips continued to move, he was silent. Frankly, he appeared to be praying.

"Yes, brother? If the wheel does move, then you'll make a nice front doormat for my house in Pittsburgh."

Sam opened his eyes. He seemed strangely calm.

"Yah, but you could kill all of us. You too."

Johanne said an expletive. It was the most vulgar word there is, and one Aaron used repeatedly.

Sam blinked in surprise. "Johanne, I speak the truth. These beams are rotten. There is much termite damage. If there is strong vibration, the upper floor could fall on us."

Johanne used another expletive that was only marginally less offensive. "I don't believe that for a minute. You're just trying to save your—"

"He's right, dear," I said. "Eli Yost over on Sticklegruber Road had his barn collapse on him."

"Is that so? Well, there's only one way to find out if this old building can stand the strain." With that, the diabolical Johanne leaned on the lever.

I closed my eyes and prayed. First I prayed that nothing would happen. Then I prayed that if Strubbly Sam were to be quashed flat as a crepe, it would happen quietly. "No crunching bones, Lord. And no screams. I don't think I could take either, and we sure don't want to give Johanne the satisfaction, do we? And please, Lord, whatever you do, don't let the ceiling cave in and kill us both. Someone has to turn the Nazi in, and besides, I got dressed in a hurry this morning and my underwear is full of holes."

But as I prayed those words the building began to shudder and groan. Even Mama, on her best days, can't produce that amount of vibration by turning over in her grave.

"May the Lord have mercy on our souls!" I shouted.

No one, including myself, heard my benediction. The accompanying crash was heard and felt all the way over at the Stoltzfus farm, where the guests were still playing Rhythm. The cloud of dust, however, was fortunately localized. I nearly choked to death, and couldn't draw a breatheable draught of air for what seemed like hours, although it was probably just minutes. Still, I might do well to consider a career as a pearl diver off the coast of Japan.

At any rate, when I could breathe again, I opened my eyes. I cannot—I mean, I will not—describe in detail the scene I beheld as the dust cleared. Let it be enough to know that a massive ceiling beam had fallen, and whether directed by God, or just by chance, it had landed smack-dab on top of the nasty Nazi. Johanne Burkholder, alias the Scorpion, and recently known as John Burk, was as dead as the flowers I sent Aaron on his birthday. The mill stone, on the other hand, had not budged an inch. Samuel Friedrich Burkholder, now known as Strubbly Sam, was completely unscathed.

"Ach, you're alive, Magdalena."

Thanks to the ropes, I couldn't pinch myself. I wiggled my toes and belched instead.

"Yes, I'm alive."

"It was a miracle, yah, Magdalena?"

"For us. Not for your brother, dear. I'm afraid he's dead."

"Ach!" Still tied to the wheel, Strubbly Sam could not see what I saw.

"I suppose I should say I'm sorry about your brother, Strubbly Sam."

"Yah, I'm sorry too. Not for me, but for him. Johanne did not repent."

"And you have?"

"Ach, a million times."

"That's a start, dear. Now, take a deep breath, because you and I are going to scream for help."

As we waited for help to arrive, I considered my responsibilities. There was one dead Nazi pinned to the floor of the mill—actually, he was halfway through the floor, but I'll spare you the gruesome details—and one live ex-Nazi. The Scorpion may be dead, but the Butcher lived on. But did he *really*? Johanne Burkholder may not have changed much over the years, but clearly Samuel Friedrich Burkholder had. The young sadistic man who had been in charge of the Black Hole was no more. Inhabiting the same body was a loving father and grandfather who had completely turned his life around. To turn Strubbly Sam in to the authorities would result in punishing his family as much, if not more, than it would him.

"Strubbly, dear, what should I do?"

He seemed to read my mind. "Whatever you must do, Magdalena."

"That's Big Magdalena, dear. Now tell me, do you think you've made amends?"

"What is this 'amends'?"

"Do you think you've made up for the pain and suffering you caused?"

"Ach, no! There is no way to make up for that."

"But you've changed?"

"Yah. God changes the heart."

I pondered in dusty silence for several minutes.

"Why did you appear at the PennDutch the day your brother arrived in town? Were you expecting him?"

"Yah."

"He got in touch with you?"

"Ach, no! But I've been expecting him every day since I got to Hernia. The Bible says that our sins will catch up with us, yah?"

"Yah—I mean, yes. But how did you know he had finally caught up with you?"

"Ach, I didn't. Not at first. But I heard from Freni—and then Sam Yoder—that there were American soldiers coming to town, so I kept my eyes open. I had this feeling, yah? And then I saw Johanne. He came to kill me, you know? All these years he wanted to kill me if he found me—to keep his secret safe."

"And were you tempted to kill him?"

"Ach du leiber!" It was a cry of genuine distress, and I knew I had the answer to my underlying question.

"Well, Yoder, you have a lot of explaining to do."

I would have glared at Police Chief Melvin Stoltzfus, but there was still dust in my eyes. My bonds weren't even loose yet, for crying out loud, and he was making *me* accountable for the mill's collapse.

"Look, you two-bit—"

"I must say, I'm really impressed. But don't think I'm going to hire you on a full-time basis. For one thing, you're not properly trained, and, as you well know, we don't have that kind of budget here in Hernia. And then there's the matter of a uniform—we could never come up with one your size!"

"Very funny, Melvin. Sarcasm really becomes you. Now untie me."

"I really don't see what your point is, Yoder, since you'll be going straight to jail."

"Jail! *Me*? What for?"

"Duh—let's see. We have a corpse here, and we have *you*."

"And I'm tied up, you idiot. How can I be responsible for the corpse?"

"I don't know. Why don't you tell me? I ask you to help me look for Old Irma and you find a dead man. A *dead* man! Ask me if I'm surprised."

I blinked the last of the dust out of my eyes and stared at the knot of people standing in the shambles of the mill. Besides Melvin, there was Bob, the cuddly Jimmy Hill, the handsome Scott Montgomery, and the cradle-robber Frank Frost.

"I'm not asking you anything, Melvin. I'm telling you to untie me."

Without further prompting from me, and with no apparent fear of Melvin, the men of the Forty-third tank brigade sprang into action. Within seconds, Strubbly Sam and I were free.

I rubbed my sore wrists gingerly. "Thanks, guys. But what are you doing here?"

"Can it, Yoder. I ask the questions." Melvin focused one eye on Scott Montgomery, the other on Bob Hart. "Okay, so what *are* you doing here?"

"It's a long story," Scott Montgomery said in his charming accent.

"We heard the crash," Bob said.

Frank nodded. "That's right. And someone said there was an old mill down in these woods—"

"Save it, boys." I smiled. "I was pulling your chains. I know what you're really doing here. Besides just keeping track of my whereabouts, that is."

The former warriors looked like a herd of deer caught in my headlights.

"You came to Hernia to find the Butcher of Tunis, didn't you?"

Melvin had the nerve to chortle. "Don't be stupid, Yoder. Hernia doesn't even have a butcher."

"It doesn't anymore." I had yet to look directly at the body of Johanne Burkholder, so I pointed in his general direction. "Well, there he is folks, Samuel Friedrich Burkholder, the Butcher of Tunis."

Strubbly Sam gasped. "But I'm—"

"You're an Amish man with a heart of gold, dear."

"Ach, but—"

"And grandfather of six *happy* children, and forty-nine *happy* grandchildren."

"Yah, but—"

"And how many happy, *innocent* great-grandchildren, dear?"

"Nine," Strubbly Sam said. His eyes were full of tears again. Who knew that men could weep so much?

"What I don't get is," I turned to Bob, "*how* you knew the Butcher was here?"

"Ah, that. Well—"

Scott Montgomery blessed me with one of his glittering smiles. "Mind if I tell that?"

"Go ahead," Bob said, and took a step back.

"It was an interview I did in conjunction with the fiftieth anniversary of D-Day. It was a local interview, but it ended up being carried by several networks on the evening news. Anyway, I mentioned the Butcher of Tunis, and someone wrote to me, in care of my local station, and said that the Butcher was still alive. She— the writer—claimed to have known him. Claimed to have seen him around town sometimes. The woman didn't give her name or address, but the postmark was Bedford."

"Old Irma!"

Both Melvin's orbs swiveled my way. "Irma Yoder?"

"She was the Fuehrer's floozy," I said, "in a manner of speaking. Himmler's harlot, Goering's gal. It's a long story, Melvin, and there will be plenty of time for it after your honeymoon to Aruba. Courtesy of *moi,* of course."

Melvin mellowed.

Scott ran a well-manicured hand through his silver mane. "So we arranged to have our fiftieth reunion here. We thought we'd poke around and see if, through a little detective work of our own, we could find the Butcher, or at least the woman who wrote the letter."

"But why Hernia? Why the PennDutch?"

"That's my fault," Bob said with a grin. "I was in charge of the reservations. I checked on motels in Bedford, but my wife Sandy wanted to stay at an authentic Mennonite bed and breakfast."

"Good choice, dear. The motels in Bedford clean your rooms for you. Think of all the fun you would have missed."

Everyone laughed, except for Melvin. "I'll be holding

you to the long version of your story as soon as Susannah and I get back from Aruba."

I smiled patiently. "Of course, dear."

With any luck, the honeymooners would be hijacked by Middle Eastern terrorists. Everyone but Melvin would be released. Of course no harm would come to Hernia's former chief of police, but he would spend the rest of his days filling hookahs and watering camels in some remote desert outpost.

Twenty-Seven

It may sound crass to you, but Susannah's wedding proceeded as scheduled. The only one who mourned Johanne Burkholder was Samantha, and thanks to Diana Lefcourt's generosity, she was safely ensconced at the Retreat of the Fractured Soul. If only Diana had remained there herself.

"Where's the pastor?" I hissed to Lodema Schrock.

The folding chairs on Elvina's front lawn were filling up fast. There was less than half an hour remaining in my sister's single life, and unless somebody got their behind back from a fishing trip to the West Virginia mountains, my sister was going to be married by Yul Brynner in drag.

Lodema clutched her oversized pocketbook protectively to her chest. "I tried, Magdalena, I really did. I left messages at all the fishing camps along the New River and its tributaries. Apparently one of them got through, because the reverend returned my call late last night. Unfortunately, there's been a lot of rain in those mountains, and a flash flood has left him stranded in a little place called Podunk."

"Bunk," I said.

"I beg your pardon?"

I glanced at the bright blue sky. "When it rains in West Virginia, it generally rains here. Have you ever considered the possibility that your husband's fish stories are—well, fishy?"

"Why, I never!"

"Which may be why he goes *fishing* every now and then. It's none of my business, dear, but you might consider the horizontal mambo now and then. I know it's boring, and a bit messy, but what's three minutes out of your life every month or so?" Imagine! *Me*, Magdalena Portulacca Yoder, giving advice on sex!

Lodema gasped indignantly and strode away.

"No need to thank me, dear," I called to her back. "And don't worry, I won't say a word about Lady Marion and her formula number twelve!"

A familiar cackle prompted me to turn.

"Are you being mean spirited again, Magdalena?"

"Old Irma! You're just the person I wanted to see—well, you and the reverend."

"Oh, what about?"

"The Butcher, dear."

Old Irma's face tightened so dramatically, it was like she had a facelift before my eyes.

"What about him?"

"You knew he was—is—here in Hernia, didn't you?"

"I did not."

"Of course you did. It was you who wrote Mr. Montgomery and ratted on Sam, right?"

"Ach, don't be ridiculous! I don't know what you're talking about."

I steered Old Irma aside. "A secret for a secret, dear."

"I know all your secrets, Magdalena, and there isn't one of them worth repeating."

"Thanks, dear. But yours *are* worth repeating."

"You wouldn't!"

"Not if you fess up to the truth. And if you don't, I might spread the rumor that Melvin is your illegitimate son."

"Don't be ridiculous. If I had a son, he'd have to be far older than that."

I smiled. "Logic seldom interferes with a good rumor."

Old Irma's faded eyes darted in every direction. Still a good spy, she was wisely cautious.

"Okay, so you know more than you should. Yes, I suspected Strubbly Sam. I always have. But I thought he was Johanne—the two boys looked a lot alike in the old days."

"But you know Strubbly Sam very well. You know that he's a changed man. Regardless of which brother he is, he's not the same man he was in 1942."

"Yes, I know. But I always felt guilty keeping my suspicions to myself. When I saw that TV interview with Mr. Montgomery, I looked at it as a chance to turn the problem over to someone else."

"So you washed your hands of Strubbly Sam, just like Pontius Pilate, eh?"

She frowned, and almost a century of wrinkles returned to her face. "Don't be so hard on me, Magdalena. I didn't want to die with a guilty conscience."

"I understand. So, don't die with one now."

"What is that supposed to mean?"

"It means that the Butcher died last night in the old grist mill, and as for the Scorpion, he's off in Paraguay someplace making macramé shopping bags for German tourists."

"I understand." Her eyes flitted to the left and back to me.

I can be slow on the uptake, so I will admit it took me several more flits before I turned.

"Gabriel!"

He looked incredibly handsome in a hand-tailored Italian suit. "I hope you don't mind my being here."

"Mind? Why should I mind?"

"Because I didn't run down to the mill last night after we heard the crash. I figured there were enough people involved. And anyway, those guests of yours seemed to know exactly what they were doing."

"Yeah, well, they were men with a mission. And you were a man busy playing games."

"Am I meant to be offended by that last remark?"

"That's your call, dear. So, who won the game of Rhythm?"

"I did."

"Beginner's luck," I said, not unkindly.

"Excuse me?"

"If I hadn't been so distracted I could have beaten the pants off you."

"That's a laugh."

"What? Look, buster—"

"Children!"

I whirled. "Susannah!"

"Am I interrupting something, Mags? Maybe a little romantic tension between you and this gorgeous hunk of a doctor?"

"Susannah!"

"On that note, I think I'll find myself a seat," Gabriel said.

"So, Mags," Susannah finally said—we'd both been

watching Gabriel's buttocks until he disappeared in the crowd—"what do you think of your baby sister?"

"Huh?"

"How do I look?"

What was there to think? My baby sister looked resplendent in her fifteen yards of royal blue silk, which she had draped behind her in the world's longest train.

"You look gorgeous, dear."

"And?"

I studied her, and finding nothing much to criticize, allowed my gaze to wonder.

"Susannah!"

Standing right beside her—and with remarkable patience, I might add—was that ratty little dog of hers, Shnookums. I hadn't noticed the beast before, because he tended to blend in with the train. He too was swaddled in his own blue silk, and in fact, he had his own little train.

"He's my bridesmaid," Susannah said proudly.

"But he can't be your bridesmaid," I wailed. "He's a dog! And an ugly, spiteful dog at that."

Normally these are fighting words, but Susannah was smiling. Old Irma had begun to warble "O Promise Me," and it was time for the show to begin.

"Ready to give me away?" my baby sister asked.

"And how!" I said.

Twenty-Eight

Ragin' Cajun SPAM® Party Salad

◆

(as served at Susannah's wedding supper)

Salad:

8 ounces wagon wheel shape pasta
1 (6-ounce) jar marinated artichoke hearts
1 (12-ounce) can SPAM® Luncheon Meat, cubed
1 cup diced bell pepper
½ cup chopped red onion
½ cup sliced ripe olives
3 tablespoons finely chopped fresh basil leaves

Dressing:

⅓ cup olive oil
¼ cup creole seasoning mix
1 tablespoon lemon juice
1 tablespoon mayonnaise or salad dressing

1 tablespoon white wine vinegar
½ teaspoon dried oregano
½ teaspoon dry mustard
½ teaspoon sugar
½ teaspoon dried thyme leaves
1 clove garlic, chopped

Cook pasta according to package directions. Drain artichokes, reserving marinade; cut into quarters. In large bowl, combine all salad ingredients. In blender, combine reserved artichoke marinade with dressing ingredients. Process until smooth. Add dressing to salad, tossing well. Cover and chill several hours or overnight. Serves 8 to 10

NUTRITIONAL INFORMATION PER SERVING:
   Calories 325; Protein 11g; Carbohydrate 26g; Fat 20g; Cholesterol 35mg; Sodium 669mg.

PENGUIN PUTNAM

online

Your Internet gateway to a virtual environment with hundreds of entertaining and enlightening books from Penguin Putnam Inc.

While you're there, get the latest buzz on the best authors and books around—

Tom Clancy, Patricia Cornwell, W.E.B. Griffin, Nora Roberts, William Gibson, Robin Cook, Brian Jacques, Catherine Coulter, Stephen King, Jacquelyn Mitchard, and many more!

Penguin Putnam Online is located at
http://www.penguinputnam.com

PENGUIN PUTNAM NEWS

Every month you'll get an inside look at our upcoming books and new features on our site. This is an ongoing effort to provide you with the most interesting and up-to-date information about our books and authors.

Subscribe to Penguin Putnam News at
http://www.penguinputnam.com/ClubPPI